DREAM
WITH
NO
NAME

DREAM
WITH
NO NAME

CONTEMPORARY
FICTION FROM
CUBA

Edited by

Juana Ponce de León and
Esteban Ríos Rivera

SEVEN STORIES PRESS
New York · Toronto · London

A Seven Stories Press First Edition

In Canada:
Hushion House, 36 Northline Road, Toronto, Ontario M4B 3E2,
Canada

In the U.K.:
Turnaround Publisher Services Ltd., Unit 3, Olympia Trading Estate,
Coburg Road, Wood Green, London N22 6TZ U.K.

Library of Congress Cataloging-in-Publication Data

Dream with no name: contemporary fiction from Cuba / edited by
Esteban Ríos Rivera and Juana Ponce de León. —a Seven Stories
Press 1st ed.
     p.   cm.
ISBN: 1-888363-72-X (cloth)
ISBN: 1-888363-73-8 (pbk.)
1. Short stories, Cuban. 2. Cuban fiction—20th century. I. Rivera,
Esteban. II. Ponce de León, Juana.
PQ7386.F5 D7 1998
863'.010897291'09045—dc21   97-50422
                                                   CIP

9 8 7 6 5 4 3 2 1

Seven Stories Press
140 Watts Street
New York, NY 10013
http://www.sevenstories.com

Printed in the U.S.A.

CONTENTS

Acknowledgments *7*

Editors' Prefaces *9*

Introduction
  by Sonia Rivera-Valdés *13*

An Unexpected Interlude Between Two Characters
  Jacqueline Herranz Brooks *19*

13th Parallel South
  Angel Santiesteban Prats *23*

The Waiting Room
  Arturo Arango *33*

Ten Years Later
  Marilyn Bobes *71*

The Hunter
  Leonardo Padura Fuentes *81*

The Tropics
  Miguel Mejides *95*

Small Creatures (*from* La orfandad del esplendor)
  Carlos Olivares Baró *113*

Something Is Happening on the Top Floor
  Reinaldo Arenas *131*

Miosvatis
  Miguel Barnet *139*

A Love Story According to Cyrano Prufrock
  Lourdes Casal *151*

Blind Madness
Miguelina Ponte Landa *163*

Little Poisons
Sonia Rivera Valdés *169*

Curriculum Cubense (*from* From Cuba With a Song)
Severo Sarduy *181*

Skin Deep
Antonio Benítez Rojo *193*

The Charm
Pablo Armando Fernández *201*

Dream with No Name
Ramón Ferreira *225*

The Storyteller
Onelio Jorge Cardoso *243*

The Great Baro
Virgilio Piñera *257*

Journey Back to the Source
Alejo Carpentier *269*

Credits *289*
Authors' and Translators' Biographies *293*
About the Editors *304*

ACKNOWLEDGMENTS

Esteban and I wish to thank the many people who helped make this anthology happen. In Cuba, we are grateful to the friends who helped battle reluctant copy machines, procured copy paper, and made available precious computer time-the seemingly little accomplishments that make or break a project. No words of gratitude are adequate enough for the indispensable go-betweens, Audrey Charlton amongst them, who selflessly carted manuscripts from Esteban's hands to mine, when he seemed to fall away from earth behind a wall of failing phones and faxes to nowhere. Special thanks to Sonia Rivera-Valdés for her invaluable literary suggestions and her willingness to search, retrieve, connect and listen at ungodly hours of the night. To Francisco López Sacha, president of the UNEAC, for a broad perspective of Cuba's literature, and to Alan West-Durán for nuance on the Cuban Diaspora. To Sandra Levinson, director of Center for Cuban Studies, who provided us with beautiful images for our cover. And to the many friends and colleagues whose love of Cuban literature, and of the written word, guided me every step of the way. Michael Greenberg's fine-tuned ear helped shape unyielding passages. James Graham's generous and inspired contribution helped prod this project off square one. To the translators, whose unsung artistry will make of this one of the finest selections of stories rendered into English. I would like to thank Dan Simon, publisher at Seven Stories Press, for his patience and the finesse of his editing. Thanks also to Jon Gilbert, my Rock of Gibraltar at the press, who ensured that all these efforts fell neatly between the covers of a book. And, finally, thanks to Nico and Ana, for deciding to remain my kids through the heat of this experience.

EDITORS' PREFACES

Dream with No Name: Contemporary Fiction from Cuba is an ambitious anthology.

Leaping over years like a guileless deer, condemned to be awkward like the earthbound albatross, its aim is to reflect the many tendencies of the Cuban short story.

In so short an anthology, such intent is limited by the number of pages. Bravely, *Dream* embraces the frustrations and dreams of several generations: those who were awed by a literature that promised a utopia; others who were shaken by a shifting geography and were destined, like Rimbaud's drunken boat, for that place of "infinite possibilities"; those who, like our island itself, were shaped in the eye of the hurricane while reaching for a transitive verb that would be perfectly subtle, amorous, dissolute; and still others who walk to the audacious, libertine, resonant rhythm of their own song.

However we describe ourselves, we are all held under the spell of one passion, subjugated by the ecstasies of a dance, inhabiting, as Ambrosio Fornet has said, "this island, where the desires of the living and the memory of the dead come together."

—Esteban Ríos Rivera
La Habana, August 1998

When the opportunity to help assemble this anthology presented itself, I considered how central to my concerns Cuban literature has always been. Although I reside in New York, Cuba's revolutionary struggle has marked my sense of self, as it has that of Latin Americans everywhere. Where there had been a deep silence, this tiny nation rose up to recapture its own destiny and to speak of new possibilities. The economic embargo was jockeyed into place and a cordon of silence surrounded the island once again. But the effort to stifle Cuba came too late; the Revolution had touched a nerve and renewed inaccessibility only served to make anything and everything Cuban that much more fascinating to those of us outside the cordon. Cultural expression of whatever stripe offered a peek into the minds and hearts of these *isleños*, and literature was no exception.

Once begun, the process of gathering together the work of writers from both before and after the Revolution, those living in Cuba as well as those in exile, has brought with it the pleasure of discovery. Today, many exciting new voices are keeping alive Cuba's great storytelling tradition, already firmly established as world literature in the 1950s and 1960s by the luminous work of Alejo Carpentier and Onelio Jorge Cardoso.

While the well known work of Pablo Armando Fernández, Miguel Barnet, and Arturo Arango displays a rich and complex narrative vein, the unexpected modernity of stories by Jacqueline Herranz Brooks, Miguelina Ponte Landa, and Antonio Olivares Baró were true surprises.

As our work progressed, and word got out, there were coups like being offered the brilliant Reinaldo Arenas's debut story, here translated for the first time into English, and the discovery of our title story, Ramon Ferreira's "Dream with No Name," translated by Paul Blackburn, one of America's great poets.

In an effort to let our readers experience the vitality and immediacy of contemporary Cuban fiction, we have set the stories in reverse chronological order, with our youngest writers up front. Somehow it seems fitting that the established writers should support the up-and-coming, the new, the future.

As Walter Benjamin once observed, it is the truth content in a work of art that allows it to transcend its subject matter and endure. With the present anthology, it is our wish to bring the reader some of the fullness of the Cuban human experience. Somewhere within, mirrored in the narrative, we may find ourselves.

—Juana Ponce de León
New York, August 1998

INTRODUCTION

Sonia Rivera-Valdés

Many of my childhood days in Havana were spent at the movies, perhaps too frequently and at hours too odd given my young age. The films I saw—most of them made in Hollywood—had a clear message. Alan Ladd and John Wayne, the good guys, fought in World War II against the bad guys—Germans and Japanese—whom they had to eliminate. Ann Sheridan spent her time tending to the wounded good guys, and in love with one of them.

That clear-cut world became unfocused during our Sunday lunches, when the family gathered and, invariably, would discuss the Spanish Civil War. Tía Paca—a Spanish refugee from Galicia and a veteran of several battles—had much to say. I listened quietly, astonished that she had survived those years doing more than tending to the wounded and falling in love. The details of the battlefront were horrifying, but more frightening still was to learn that the men didn't know if they had killed friend or foe. That Paca's brothers, Gregorio and Federico, had died fighting on opposing sides was truly incomprehensible.

The events of the last four decades in Cuba and my inevitable relationship to them have made me return, again and again, to my childhood consternation. Yet, if there is anything that can help sort out the complexity of any historical process, it is the stories of the people who have lived through it. As Toni Morrison says, "Since *why* is difficult to handle, one must take refuge in *how*."

That is precisely what the wisely titled anthology, *Dream with No Name*, accomplishes. In gathering stories by Cuban writers on the island and off, it allows us to hear the voices of this difficult history. Truth be told, as Cuban playwright Dolores Prida has observed, Cuba has been a four-letter word for far too long. The tales collected here will not necessarily dispel doubts regarding the whys of events in Cuba. What they will do, however, is help us understand a little better the complexity of the historical process, and the effect that the sociopolitical experimentation has had on the lives of all Cubans, and on the creative expression of their culture.

Stories written on the island reveal an important change that has taken place in Cuban society in the past decade. Sexuality, be it gay, lesbian, or heterosexual, and the use of drugs—aspects of Cuban life that were never mentioned or at most alluded to obliquely in the past—now figure prominently in the Cuban narrative. There has also been a shift from an epic perspective to a more critical and more human treatment of our history and social problems. Ten years ago, even when such stories were written, they were not available to the reader; in

Cuba, censorship would have made certain of this. The unwavering embargo that has managed to keep out Cuban business has also managed to keep the bulk of Cuban cultural expression beyond the reach of American readers.

"Unexpected Interlude Between Two Characters," an award-winning story by the very young Jacqueline Herranz Brooks, illustrates perfectly the newfound frank, unadorned literary approach. It is the tale of a casual sexual encounter between two young women in a movie house in Havana.

> *Asmania, who is called Asmania here because of that* Pailock *novel, amuses me, is completely drugged, and has left her friends. As she moves forward, the sky and everything around her turn leaden. Drugged, at the end of the afternoon, Asmania walks through an alley that leads to a bus stop.*

Through that alley we step into a space encumbered with filth. The manner in which Herranz Brooks lingers on the sordid details of Asmania's surroundings shifts the attention of the story away from the lesbian characters and the drugs to the ambient decrepitude.

The very existence and the critical success of *Strawberry and Chocolate*, a film by Tomás Gutierrez Alea, which deals openly and sympathetically with gays, attests to the importance of gay and lesbian themes in Cuban fiction. It is based on Senel Paz's novella, "El lobo, el bosque, y el hombre nuevo" (The Wolf, the Forest, and the New Man), one of many recent short stories about homosexuality. Included here are Padura's "The Hunter," a gay adventure, and Mejides's "The

Tropics," which deals overtly with issues of heterosexual prostitution and has a subtext rich with lesbian innuendo.

Cuba's participation in the war in Angola is the theme of Angel Santiesteban Prats's story, "13th Parallel South." Told by an adolescent soldier who feels alien and uninvolved, the perspective is personal and critical. Gone is the heroic, internationalist tone of previous narratives:

> Nobody pays attention to orders, not even the captain. We're not in file or spread out: not a platoon or even soldiers. We've torn off our stripes and insignias. We're just a gang of desperate men who barge into a house, take the Portuguese by surprise, push him around and separate him from his shotgun.

This story is considered a classic narrative of the 1990s. Prats received the UNEAC (National Union of Writers and Artists of Cuba) literary award in 1995.

Ramón Ferreira's "Dream with No Name," which lends its title to the anthology, re-creates the Cuban people's disillusionment with the quality of life during the "special time" that followed the collapse of the Soviet Union in 1989. The narrator is a little boy, physically abused by his father, who tries to eke out a living by begging and seeking shelter with prostitutes.

Whereas the personal and the critical points of view are fairly recent characteristics of stories by writers living in Cuba, they are central to expatriate narrative. These stories show the relationship of each author to the island, and make evident the ways in which the adopted cultures have influenced these writers' art.

Although mainstream media here would have us believe that the majority of Cubans at home would give anything to be able to flee the island, three stories penned by writers in Cuba flesh out the ambivalence of their emotions. In Marilyn Bobes's "Ten Years Later," the heroine strolls triumphantly through the streets of sumptuous Florence, yet her heart is tethered to her Cuban lover. "Miosvatis," by Miguel Barnet—author of *The Biography of a Runaway Slave,* and a pioneer in testimony fiction—is the story of a Cuban man who travels through Switzerland marveling at the aesthetic refinement of its cities; yet, throughout his journey, he clutches at a handbag with gifts for home, as if he were holding on to his only reality.

The priority given education during the first few years of the Revolution produced countless writers—an unprecedented event in the Hispanic Caribbean. Along with its many writers came the founding of numerous literary magazines, the establishment of the National Printing House of Cuba, and the Cuban Book Institute. The priority of educating everyone was also seen as a step toward eradicating the old *machista* attitudes by making available work and the possibility of advancement to any Cuban citizen. Despite this concerted effort to equalize the sexes, in the literary world the change has been slow in coming. As recently as 1994 UNEAC published an anthology of Cuban fiction consisting of ninety-five stories; only three were authored by women. As a response to this gross imbalance, in 1996 Mirta Yañez and Marilyn Bobes edited *Estatuas de sal* (Pillars of Salt), the first anthology of Cuban fiction by women, which gathers the work of thirty-three writers from on and off the island.

The strong representation of women authors in the present anthology represents another small step toward correcting this imbalance.

If one is to judge by the many voices found in this anthology, it is clear that the politics of the U.S. embargo has robbed all Cubans alike. The literary struggles and triumphs on the island have had little resonance here in the United States, and Cubans back home are only now beginning to have access to the excellent work of their compatriots abroad. *Dream with No Name* is a beautiful bridge across those ninety miles of separation that some would have us believe is wider than all the oceans combined.

AN UNEXPECTED INTERLUDE BETWEEN TWO CHARACTERS

Jacqueline Herranz Brooks
Translated by Clara Marín

—Thank you, Ezequiel.

Asmania, who is called Asmania here because of that *Pailock* novel, amuses me, is completely drugged, and has left her friends. As she moves forward, the sky and everything around her turn leaden. Drugged, at the end of the afternoon, Asmania walks through an alley that leads to a bus stop. While her friends are still partying, Asmania makes out two meaningful outlines: a dark-skinned girl and a movable food stand. The girl, on her left. The stand, in front. Asmania picks the latter and tries to find change in the bag that hangs, zigzagging, from one of her shoulders. Asmania is drugged and her drugged gaze sways, examining the change. Examining sometimes the change, sometimes the girl. She's not

---

* Editor's Note: *Pailock*, Ezequiel Vieta's novel published in Cuba in 1991, was received with great acclaim. Pailock, a mediocre circus magician, manages the ultimate feat: to make his assistant, Asmania, disappear—permanently. After this outstanding trick, he sinks again into mediocrity.

cold, and the "coolest one" is the girl that says: "Me, I'll go after the man in the shirt with the orange stripes." Asmania has found the change, and now she's counting it; she is thankful, and crosses over to the stand, but not without first looking at the man with the now-drab shirt, since the stripes can hardly be made out in the darkness of the night.

It's night, and the man at the stand is packing up the merchandise: potato-filled potatoes, fried food in bread, and tamales—everything cold and probably dotted with flies, which the owner of the movable food stand doesn't mind shooing. In front of the stand, Asmania again counts her change, and buys one of everything, twice. She pays, crosses the street, and as she crosses, she peels the leaves of one of the tamales and brings it to her mouth, which is open long before the snack reaches it. Back at the bus stop, she looks over at the group of people—which increases in size by the second—and leans her body against the bent metal sign that indicates the bus number she is waiting for. Asmania's hands are disgusting, and the girl doesn't stop watching, and Asmania wonders if she should offer her part of what she bought. Asmania is drugged and smiles a naïve grin, crooked and spotted with yellow flour, and she wonders if the girl wants... Quickly, the girl takes out a napkin from her dark jeans and hands it to her. Here, Asmania thanks her and asks. She asks a bunch of stupid questions that the girl answers, shaken, in her monotonous sequence of "yes," "no," and, now she is elaborating explanations that Asmania is barely listening to, because she's drugged and her perception is slow. They walk a little and at the corner Asmania offers a bit of... and here there's a short and deep silence, and then, talk, cigarettes... but up until then, the bus hasn't arrived, and the girl says that the movie theater is close and empty, and without making any noise, she begins to move.

Asmania—here she is called Asmania because of *Pailock,* and because of the public explosions of her flesh, and because she is drugged like *Pailock*'s Asmania—feels that her fangs are getting long, and enters the movie theater. She looks for a corner where she can press up against the dark skin that is also pressing up against Asmania, as if it were a deep discomfort that is tolerated because it won't be forever. Someone lets out an intense ah, but this doesn't register, because Asmania is drugged and weak, and because of the sound of the nylon shopping bag with the bought rubbish as it slips off the seat and smashes on the floor.

Feeling each other up hasn't been comfortable, because they both have zippers and shoes, and the narrow seats with hard wooden arms hem in their contours. On the screen, bats are screeching and blood is flying in all directions, and the actors, carrying out violent acts, exchange laughter of panic and terror. Asmania moans softly, and the one with the dark skin, as it's called here, also moans, and probably a few other people in the movie theater moan or feel each other up, seeing that two girls—one of them looks drugged—are pressing up against each other in the discomfort of the movie theater seats.

This is a dingy neighborhood theater, and, luckily, Asmania doesn't come to these places often. Being here, now, is because the other one led her. That way, she justifies her tearing apart, her morbid imbalance, and her unexplainable loss of limits. The other one, who was spotted as the evening turned into night, is still holding one of Asmania's breasts, which pulsates, erect, under a careful caress. Asmania smiles and kisses her, with that mouth still filled with bought rubbish. The other straightens up and takes the first step, pulling Asmania by the hand, who is searching for her nylon bag between the seats. All of this is done clumsily, and the knocking against the seat, and the sound of the nylon bag, and the "Come on, come on" of the girl, get the usher's attention—an old lady, grayed by the darkness and, luckily, very slow. Asmania is in the street and everything is spinning, and she puts the things she bought in her bag, and smells her hands, and grins stupidly again, with hypnotic laughter.

The other one has damp eyes, and the line of her jaw reminds Asmania, who is still smiling, of a story about horses; she can't associate it with anything else.

Asmania, who has literary preferences, is indifferent to ethical issues of irreparable mediocrity, just like Pailock could be—seen by those who are unaware of the origin of things, and its inevitable occurrence in time.

13TH PARALLEL SOUTH

Angel Santiesteban Prats
Translated by James Graham

On the horizon behind us only the black smoke coughed out by the trucks was visible. The plane had taken off and we had to go back for a mop-up action. In the middle of our rushing around and the fear, we were able to rescue a man who'd been shot. Trying to fix the radio proved useless; we'd lost touch with headquarters, the operator said. There were eight of us left, and the company captain who'd decided at the last moment to join us on the mission had to be sorry now. So he ordered us to start marching, to try to rejoin our unit.

Medina, who catches up to me dragging his bloody foot, passes me a cigarette; I take a drag and it goes around, mouth to mouth, until the heat burns our lips. Suddenly it hits me that Argüelles, the violinist, has missed his turn; but he doesn't say a word. His only interest is his violin, which he carries under the arm that bleeds where he got shot. I remember we were in front of the trucks when we heard the roar of the plane. We jumped under the bushes without thinking about anything other than saving our skins, leaving behind everything except our firearms. I pressed my AK against my chest. The others put theirs on top of their heads while they chewed on their dog tags. I didn't do that because I'm sure they're not going to send me out of here in a bag; before heading out my old lady gave me this little amulet to hang on my gun; at first I didn't want to carry it on account of the comments and the ridicule, but seeing that it's light and pretty small, I talked myself into it. And I still have it. But Argüelles held on to his violin like a chickenshit, while his AK hung from his back and got in the way. At times I feel bad for him because I think he's screwed up in the head. When he joined our unit, some of the guys weren't happy about it; they thought he was a spoiled brat. Nobody says a word to him and I don't think he cares.

The moon sneaks up on us as we march. We make camp by the thinnest thread of water, sharing the last canned goods that Crespo was able to save in his knapsack. Pretty soon we can smell the food and our mouths are watering. Nobody makes a sound while we read the labels on the cans. Finally, the captain gives the signal and we come for our portions. The violinist does just the opposite. He starts walking and disappears, coughing like a white shadow among the trees. Nobody does anything about him. We stay there, hypnotized by the smell of the food. Then, carried by the breeze, a beautiful and sad music comes from some faraway place; at first it's faint and distant, but it slowly grows more intense. We look at each other without knowing what's going on. We suddenly stop eating, stop moving around, and look up toward the dome of immense darkness that covers us and makes us pray for dawn so we'll know that all this was only a nightmare.

We sit frozen like that for seconds, until Eladio complains that he doesn't understand why they let such a strange guy come along on a mission like this. But everybody calls Eladio the Hardass, and we all generally keep quiet while he's talking. The cook says that the violinist eats only proper food and with a napkin, that's why he doesn't touch this food and why he looks the way he does: jaundiced, and so skinny—just glasses and a violin. Everybody laughs and I say he was the same at camp. I always noticed him, that's just the way he is. Somebody else interrupts because the wounded guy doesn't want to try the food, he's got a fever and he's babbling about how we ought to get ready for the airplanes. All of us are standing around the stretcher when we see the violinist come back, the violin on his shoulder. He sits down in exactly the same spot as before, like always, without saying a word. It seems like he never moved in the first place.

In the morning we decide to keep going without knowing exactly where, to look for a small village. We're not sure what we prefer, where we'll be in less danger, to be right here lost in the forest—keeping an eye out for the cobras so they won't bite through our boots and our pants while we try to sleep—or to chance on the hospitality of some small village full of enemy troops, spying on us with bullets and knives at the ready. We keep marching, using up our last reserves of strength. Exhaustion enters through our pores, in our breathing, in every thought. It's always the same fatigue, which they didn't hand out in Cuba when we left, nor during the whole trip getting here. It hit us, pure and simple, when we disembarked in this land of black magic; it jumped inside of us like a virus, and there's always a little more in every pocket for the tough spots. Our steps are getting shorter and shakier. The trees let go of the last leaves of the season, the broken branches rustle in the wind and we seem like a walking joke. This is a labyrinth where the most cautious of soldiers leaves a trail of crumbs so he can find his way back; and if truth be told, if they gave me half a chance, I wouldn't stop until I threw myself down in bed with the old lady, begging her to ground me like she used to and not let me go out to play war with my pals from the neighborhood, since these aren't kid's games but the mad fantasies of adults. I'm never going to buy pistols or shotguns for my kids. I look back searching for a landmark and all I see are bullet shells and rusty cans with every bit of food scraped away. When all is said and done, it's all the same to me. Them or us, we're nothing more than little fleas trying to kill a monster. We are the ones who've brought about all these disasters.

We go on for several hours without seeing a single human being. No sign of life, not the least whiff of civilization. I catch a nasty smell from Medina's leg, which has already turned blue; he's been dragging it along the road like a madman, tracing a line behind us just like a slug, bringing out all the disgust, grief, and laughter I try to keep to myself. I look back and see a few stragglers. Maybe I turn my head back too violently; I feel nauseous and start to lose my balance; I'm about to fall. Just then the music that before seemed to come out of nowhere springs magically from Argüelles's violin, and I come to a stop. I'm panting and starting to sweat from fatigue. Crespo shoots us a glance—as if this were the time for a little tune! But things are coming unstuck in a weird way, our feet that have marched and marched since who knows when feel light and a little shaky, the hairs on my balls are standing up, my thighs rubbing together excites me, and on top of all that, the rest of my body is getting looser. Once again we pull together. No one has looked at anyone else and no one's said a thing. We keep marching because that's the order: march until we get somewhere...

We all see it, but nobody points to it, afraid it might be an hallucination. We're still unsure as we come close to the window ledge. The wood has been eaten away by termites. On the captain's orders, we surround the place while he moves toward the only door and calls out. A double-barreled shotgun points at his head in response. My first thought is, we're screwed again. I get ready to shoot a few rounds and put my two last cartridges close by. The captain comes back and pulls us together, saying it's a half-mad Portuguese family. They can help us with some food, bread, water, and the hut in the back. They have no medicine to spare, even though one of our men is dying. He will loan us a Negro who can apply compresses of straw and mud. "And may it be as God wishes," I say in a loud voice, but everyone ignores me. I remember that I'm a revolutionary and that revolutionaries don't believe in God. So I spit at the sky and surprise myself by making the sign of the cross. "He'll give us everything on the condition that we leave as soon as possible, because they don't want problems with the UNITA troops," says the captain.

The commander's uniform makes me think of a wrinkled and empty beer can. I want to let someone else in on the joke, but everyone is looking at the violinist, who's moved away from us to watch a flock of white birds heading north. Eladio jabs me with his elbow, saying this is what is unforgivable: he finds any crap more interesting than all of us. And Argüelles stays put, the sharp points of his knees sticking into the ground, his eyes fixed on the spot where the birds disappeared. He's waiting for them. But empty sky is all that's left.

We're standing in the shade under a window, talking about our last words when we left Cuba; guessing at what moment the woman left behind will cheat on each of us, something that will befall most every guy. Jailbirds are always brooding about amnesty. We think about a peace treaty that lets us go home. Argüelles is coughing when he comes back and breaks up our chatter. He squats down on the ground and all of us shift on the wooden boxes, leaving him an empty spot; he's got his eyes closed now just like a cat, which is only so he doesn't have to thank us. Medina whistles a melody, I guess, so he can forget the pain in his leg a little bit. We look over at Argüelles, waiting for his reaction. But he never changes. We're up again, leaving the spot where the boxes are for him. I can see from Eladio's expression that he'd like to spit on Argüelles, whose skin is already as cracked and transparent as the desert.

We throw ourselves down in the barn. Crespo starts cooking outside, doing what he can to make what we'll call lunch. Suddenly we hear music that eats us alive, taking us over slowly, covering everything with a caress we can almost touch. Sweat wets our eyes, a few of us get a bit sentimental because of the music. Nobody moves at all, our eyes are shut tight while we watch the dreams charge by. And why we don't know, but in spite of everything we're smiling.

Now the Portuguese yells for the captain and invites him inside, but he refuses to go in and stands in the doorway talking. They talk until the Portuguese, pissed off, goes back in the house. The captain keeps his eye on us, passes his hand through his mustache. He comes toward us and stands there looking at the violin in Argüelles's arms. He tries to ease off, but seeing the Portuguese's stare bearing down on him from the window stops him. He looks at Medina's blue leg that's no longer a leg and at Luis's bloody bandages. Then the captain tells Argüelles that the Portuguese will exchange the violin for the medicines we need to clean the two men's infections and his arm; five cans of meat; two bottles of homemade brandy; and cigarettes. The entire unit draws up around him, carving every part of his filthy body up with our eyes. The violinist backs off and we stare at him again. The captain says he feels sorry about it because he knows what the violin means to him; but it's a tough situation, and he's got to understand. Silence is the worst response Argüelles can give. The boss keeps pressing at him until he manages to pick him up, dropping him right in front of those of us who are backing up the captain.

"Would you give up your rifle in exchange?" Argüelles asks him. At first, the chief wavers. "No, I couldn't do it, it's the one thing I've got to show for my life, the guarantee I'll get back alive."

The violinist smiles. "I suppose every one of you feels that way," he says, and he shoots us the once-over. "I prefer to give up my rifle." But the chief won't let him. "You're being difficult." The violinist stares at the ground, his eyes brimming with tears behind his glasses, while he squeezes the violin. "No," he says, "No."

Everyone is stock still. We keep staring at him as if he hadn't said a word. He looks at Luis's bandages, with their first layer of bloodstains and a greenish liquid on top of that. He stares at the mosquitoes that appeared on Medina's leg when he began shaking from the fever. He sees the vultures flying in the same spot where the birds from the North were earlier. In a trembling voice he asks, "Is that an order?" and the captain nods. But he can't make up his mind. He drops the violin on the ground, and saying "Shit," turns his back on us and walks away.

He stays away from then on. Four days have passed and he hasn't tried the canned meat or the brandy. He doesn't look at us. If he did we know it would be with hate, and for our part we don't want him with us. The boss has decided to keep going. And so we leave the settlement, dragging our butts through this sterile landscape. Soon enough the house is out of sight, but someone is always looking back, with regret. The violinist follows us like a dog. His being there bothers us. Too bad he doesn't get lost. We wouldn't lose any time looking for him; what's the point of a man being here if he won't talk about where he's from or the people he left behind, if he won't tell a few lies?

We've already covered a few miles and we decide to take a break. Maybe with the violin we'd have walked a little farther. Everybody is quiet. One guy spits and somebody else kicks a rock. He's still standing off, not saying a word. He points the finger at us with his presence, his silence. People are saying that to keep on without provisions is suicide. We give him a look that begs for support, but he keeps ignoring us. We've got three wounded men. There's only one sacred order here: survive. Now he's got his back turned. "War is war," somebody else says. The captain talks about principles, nobody pays attention. In turn, he is reminded that desperation can be measured by degrees. We know that at times, with the bullets flying at us, we forget why we're killing. Because they're wearing a different uniform, who knows? Some guys just want to find a canteen with a shot of rum, others are looking for a skin mag or maybe only a comic book.... The boss asks us if everyone agrees we ought to go back. We're standing with our AKs loaded, waiting for Argüelles, who should be catching up, but he just sits there. He's written "THOU SHALT NOT STEAL" in the mud with the barrel of his gun. Eladio screams at him, "For shit's sake!" and we head back. Nobody pays attention to orders, not even the captain. We're not in file or spread out: not a platoon or even soldiers. We've torn off our stripes and insignias. We're just a gang of desperate men who barge into the house, take the Portuguese by surprise, push him around, and separate him from his shotgun. The Negro tries to stop us, yelling that Angolan comrades are tired of helping out Cuban comrades. A split second after he moves, I give him a poke with the butt of the gun that leaves him sprawled out on the floor. We prowl through the kitchen, the storeroom, the little girl's bedroom, and we find the violin.

When we get back, Argüelles is still making strokes in
the mud with the barrel of the gun. It's a strange picture,
one not from here or from back home. He keeps drawing
without paying any attention to us. So the captain bel-
lows, "Attention!" and gives him a shove, the rifle falling
over into the mud. The captain shouts at him that we're
tired of putting up with his attitude, his lack of consideration, his laziness, and his being pissed off at his mates.
That he could cite him for disobeying the rules and even
shoot him as a deserter. But he'll dismiss all the charges
because he's completely incompetent. The captain says
he's going to confiscate his rifle and Argüelles can go
screw himself; now he'll have to shoot with his shitty
violin. And the boss throws it down in the mud, spits on
it, and leaves. Argüelles gives us a suspicious look, he
crouches there staring at us and he wavers, and then
picks up the violin without taking his eyes off us and
wipes it clean with his shirtsleeve. And he walks away,
leaving us stranded here, hating him.

THE WAITING ROOM

Arturo Arango

Translated by James Graham

—For Senel

It must have been 3:35 in the afternoon when the man in the black sweatshirt walked into the enormous waiting room, which still looked much as he remembered it: the same spiral staircase, its bronze railings worn down to the bone; the same odor of damp clothing and grime; the same mix of voices and far-off engines. The man in the black sweatshirt stared at the ceiling, looking for the signs that indicated the position of the waiting lines, but they had disappeared. The line for Manzanillo ought to be in back, to the left, in front of the Bayamo line, in a sequence that mimicked the silhouette of the island. The waiting room was crowded with perhaps even more people than he ran into twenty years ago, although not so many as he had feared. He figured, if there were less than thirty in the line, he had a good shot at leaving in the next twenty-four hours. "That's if they don't put on an extra bus before."

The man in the black sweatshirt followed the labyrinth of benches, legs, suitcases, kids sitting on the floor, sacks and cardboard boxes. The last person on the Manzanillo line seemed to be a mulatta well-along-in-years, who was sitting in the last spot of a long row of seats. He spoke to her quietly. The mulatta looked him up and down, as did the six or seven people sitting next to her. "I'm behind a couple who got on line and left immediately," she said. "And they are behind him." She pointed out a bald man who never stopped moving his jaws. The man in the black sweatshirt leaned against the wall, with his nearly empty knapsack hanging from his shoulder, and the mulatta well-along-in-years advised him to find a place to sit. "It's going to be like this for a long time, my boy," she said. The bald man, who seemed very preoccupied, assured him that since the night before, when they had sold two tickets, the line hadn't moved at all. "It seems that a lot of buses are broken down," he added, and turned back to concentrate on moving his jaws.

The man in the black sweatshirt looked around him: the only place to sit was on the floor, and it's being so close to the men's room, it was unthinkable even to sit on top of the knapsack. "You're not getting in line for Bayamo, too?" asked the mulatta well-along-in-years, trying to read the words on the front of his sweatshirt. He made a vague gesture. "If you're going to get in that line, I'm the last one there too. You've got to get on all of them...." In the Bayamo line there were more or less the same number of people as on the one for Manzanillo: just a little over forty. A long wooden bench filled from one end to the other, and several more people stood or crouched nearby.

The blazing heat and humidity of the August afternoon was brutal, and the guy in the black sweatshirt had been sweating for some time. If not tonight, then by dawn his clothes and skin would be a disaster, and along with his fatigue he would have the bad mood that comes with being filthy. The benches made from strips of wood were a rotten place to sleep, or even to sit for a few hours, and he thought that he would do as he used to do: as soon as the sun fell, he would look for a spot on the terrace where he could spend the night. Twenty years ago, the evening chill, a stiff neck, and sticky hands hardly got to him at all. But now, only fifteen minutes after arriving, he was having a hard time containing his impatience. "If only they would put on an extra bus tonight." But he had yet to hear the loudspeaker, even once, announce the departure of a bus.

The man in the black sweatshirt was the last on line until 5:45. During those two hours, he stood almost immobile, leaning against the wall, searching the faces before him, trying to decipher the movements of the employees, who at times came into the waiting room, talked among themselves, made notes on cards, looked at their pocket watches, and left. It occurred to him that his legs weren't bothering him yet, and that he had eaten a big lunch late, in order to last throughout the night without falling prey to hunger and weakness. He imagined: the moment when he would be going down the stairs with his ticket in hand; being lulled to sleep by the bus engine; looking out the side window at girls and buildings, which always looked different when he left the city for a few days.

The sun was coming straight through the high windows, when a skinny young guy arrived, wearing dark glasses and hitting the floor with a white cane. The guy stumbled on a cardboard box, and the bald man got up to show him the way. He was looking for the last spot on the Manzanillo line, but before, he wanted to speak with whoever was in charge of people with disabilities. At the back of the waiting room, very close to where the lines began, a bunch of employees were killing time around a small portable radio. The bald man brought the guy in the dark glasses up to them. The employees pointed to a woman with dyed-blond hair, who was talking on the telephone.

The guy waited for her to finish so he could explain his problem. Without saying a word, the woman extended her hand. The guy didn't respond. "Show me your physical-impairment identification card," the woman said. "My card?" "If you don't have the card from the National Association for the Blind, I can't put you at the head of the line." The guy rolled his head like Stevie Wonder. "This always happens to me. I lost the card and all my papers when my wallet was stolen." He took out a tiny piece of paper from the back pocket of his jeans. "This is my claim notice," and his hand went back to resting on the bald man's shoulder, who didn't know what to do. The blond looked at the small piece of paper. "This doesn't say anything about the blind card. If you want to explain your case to the people on line, you can see if they'll let you go first. I can't."

The bald man led the guy to the head of the line and stood there, silently enduring the hostility of the people staring at both of them. "Who's first?" the guy asked, as if he were addressing a big crowd. His voice was very mellow. A heavily made-up woman told him to forget it.

"Everybody's here because they have to be." The man with the moving jaws was looking at the rest of the line, one by one. A wrinkled old lady, who looked like she was part of the bench, volunteered that she didn't have any problems helping, as long as they sold her two tickets. If they sold her only one, she would feel bad, but at 6:30 it would be two days that she had been on line, without ingesting anything other than coffee. She took an empty jar out of her purse. "You should have gotten here yesterday, like me." The fourth on line was a recruit with a one-week pass, who hadn't seen his mother since the beginning of the year. The boys in the fifth place, dressed in colorful T-shirts and Bermuda shorts, were staring at the ceiling, with the whites of their eyes showing. The woman, half of a young married couple that took up the eighth and ninth places, commented, "It's outrageous, the things that go on in this country."

The man with the moving jaws had shrunk under the blind guy's hand. "It's the survival of the fittest," said the guy, and he asked the man to take him to the end of the line. The man with the moving jaws gave the blind guy his seat, and stood next to the man in the black sweatshirt.

Between 7:30 and 8:00, a young woman with very nice manners and a guy wearing a baseball cap joined the line. The man in the black sweatshirt took out bread and cake from his knapsack and offered it to the young woman who'd just arrived. She was carrying a bottle of water, another with tea, and a small pot with white rice and oca fritters that both the man in the black sweatshirt and the guy in the baseball cap shared. The guy in the baseball cap, in turn, offered a nasty-looking guayaba pie,

which both turned down, because they said it gave them
indigestion. The mulatta well-along-in-years shared a
peanut bar and a handful of hard candy with the man
with the moving jaws, who only had a small piece of
garlic bread left, and the blind guy, who hadn't brought
any food with him. "I bought them by the station
entrance. They're pricey." She explained that the lady
who sold them came every morning after 10:00.

In the middle section of the line, there were only
bottles of water making the rounds, a bit of leftover
coffee that belonged to a heavy man with the air of a
peasant, who was resting his feet on top of an enormous
cardboard box, and a few peanut bars that almost
everyone had bought the night before. Apart from the
child sitting with the woman in the third spot, the only
minors in the group were a pair of twins about eight
years old, traveling with their grandmother. "I feel badly
for them," said the mulatta well-along-in-years, "but I've
got nothing to give them." The man with the moving
jaws was afraid he might break his dentures on the
peanut bar, and offered it to the little girls. The woman
with the nice manners offered them a little rice and half
a fritter, but the twins' grandmother insisted that they
weren't hungry, and that since morning, a rumor had
been making the rounds that there was going to be an
extra bus. "Not one bus has left this week, and here we
are in August."

One of the boys in the bright-colored Bermudas
knelt down in front of the young woman, his hands in
front of him in the shape of a bowl. She covered the
small pot and handed it over to the woman in the third
spot. "Thank you so much, my dear girl. It really isn't

easy to stand in line with a young child. If circumstances were different, I wouldn't dream of being here." The young woman kissed the boy's head, and assured the mother that the fritters were fresh and the oca batter—which can be so treacherous—had been well cooked. "I had to take him to the doctor," the mother explained while she sniffed the fritters with a pleased look. "To make a long story short, they didn't find a single thing wrong with him." Meanwhile, the recruit had become very pale, and stared at the small pot with the intensity of an autistic child.

After eating, the children and the old people started to get sleepy. The blind guy went to the bathroom accompanied by the man with the moving jaws, and when he returned, asked the man in the black sweatshirt for a cigarette. The man in the black sweatshirt didn't smoke. The guy in the baseball cap took out a pack he'd hidden in his socks, and offered one to the blind guy. The blind guy suggested that they go out to the terrace, but the guy in the baseball cap, who was still the last on line, didn't want to give up his spot.

The night air was as hot as ever and there was a flash of lightning to the south. The girl with good manners was also outside, and she made a sign for them to come over. Standing in the terminal's lanes were three buses with their lights on. "Let one of them be for Manzanillo," she prayed. Seeing a baggage man pushing a cart crammed with suitcases, the man in the black sweatshirt came to the conclusion that at least one of the buses was going long-distance. The two boys in the Bermudas were close by, and the one who had knelt down volunteered to take a look.

In spite of the heat, the young woman looked as if she had just showered. The man in the black sweatshirt looked around: on every terrace wall where he remembered sitting there were clusters of shadows talking or sleeping. "The worst thing is to spend the whole night wide awake," he said. "And we don't even have a place to sit on a bench," the girl added. While they waited for the kid in the colorful Bermudas to return, the man in the black sweatshirt and the blind guy learned that the young woman had been born in Manzanillo, had moved to Havana when she was very young—"to El Vedado," she stated definitively—and after fifteen years had returned to search for some missing papers she needed in order to get married. She'd made a deal with her boyfriend that while she was on line, he had to come at least three times a day with food and boiled water. "Those water fountains are for pigs; I won't put my lips on them." "With a boyfriend like that," the blind guy threw in, "I'd get married without papers." The young woman took the joke in stride. "And you, you're a musician?" she asked, while she stared at the inscription on the black sweatshirt: Ronnie Scott Salutes. "A *jazz* musician," offered the blind guy.

The kid in the Bermudas came running back, euphoric. He had heard the static of the loudspeakers being turned on. Everyone ran inside. The voice of the woman announcing the bus departures was lost inside its own echo, and only the last vowels could be heard clearly: *oa*. People in the different lines stood up, and a few went up to the ticket counters. "Baracoa, Ciego de Avila, and Manzanillo," the kid in the colorful Bermudas said breathlessly, and his friends jumped for joy. "All that's left for them to do is to lose the reservations," said the mulatta well-along-in-years, who had woken up and was making use of the uproar to stretch her legs. The crowd in the waiting room carried on in high spirits, expecting the call for the waiting list. "Down below they say that gasoline is not the problem. They don't have enough drivers," explained the kid in the Bermudas. He added that they were visiting the drivers at home, and it was hoped that by tomorrow things would be back to normal. He also told how he was able to enter the area designated solely for passengers with reservations. "I said to the guard that I was Fernández's nephew, and that did it."

"We've almost made it," said the man with the moving jaws. The blare of the loudspeaker silenced the room, and a woman's voice announced that two tickets for Baracoa would go on sale, one for Manzanillo, and none for Ciego de Avila. The heavily made-up woman let out a shout for joy, lifted her bags, and ran to the ticket counters. The wrinkled old lady sat on the edge of the bench, and the mother kissed her son on the head. "They're shameless," said the good-looking woman. "There are always at least four seats available. My father worked with the buses for a long time, and I know all about this stuff. They must be getting more than a hundred pesos for each ticket."

The man in the black sweatshirt hurried back out to the terrace and found a wide stretch of wall with just a small amount of light from the waiting room. He gave himself a good brushing off and lay down, using the knapsack as a pillow. At 10:00 it was just as hot as before and the lightning to the south had ended. He wasn't sleepy and his belt or a strap on his pants was digging into his waist. He tried to sleep on his side, facing the terrace, in order to wake up if the line moved. Leaning against the wall that faced the avenue, the blind guy and the young woman shared a cigarette, and seemed to be in an intense conversation. The guy in the baseball cap came over to the man in the black sweatshirt. "I always sleep in this spot," he put in. Although he was still the last, it was unlikely that anyone was going to arrive at this time of night. The man in the black sweatshirt drew up his legs a little and made space for the other man, who lay down with his back to the terrace.

Inside, most of the people on the bench had managed to squeeze their bodies onto the cruel wooden slats. The wrinkled old lady seemed imperturbable, her head leaning slightly to one side, her eyes closed in a deathlike calm. The small boy in the second place tired early, and his mother tried to stay awake, fanning him from time to time with a strip of cardboard. The twins had made use of the space left by the recruit—who also preferred the terrace, along with the young boys in the Bermudas— and curled into balls sitting opposite each other, intertwined like the sign of Gemini. The young married couple slept in a similar position, the woman stretched out inside the man's legs, while he lay along her back; they seemed to be enacting a complicated sexual game. The heavy man with the peasant air had rounded his body even further, and made a single bed out of the bench and the box on which he rested his legs. Once again, the man with the moving jaws had taken his place and rested his head on the back of the seat, the Adam's apple moving to the rhythm of his snores that wouldn't let the mulatta well-along-in-years get any sleep.

At 11:00 the lights in the waiting room were turned
off. Only a single bulb, which was hanging over two
guards, was still burning. The man in the black sweatshirt slept badly, bothered by his sweat, by the gravel in
the wall that poked at his arms and his ears, and every
time the guy in the baseball cap kicked him, he was sure
someone was trying to steal his shoes. The young woman
and the blind guy kept talking until very late. The man
in the black sweatshirt felt as if the night stood still, that
his fatigue wasn't enough to keep him sleeping until
dawn, that a conversation was better than the hardness
of the wall, and the cramp in his hands which he was
using as a pillow. But from time to time, sleep was
stronger than his will.

In spite of the news brought by the kid in the
Bermudas, the day began like the others. When he woke
up, the man in the black sweatshirt looked toward the
lower level: a lone sweeper stirred up the dust on the
walkways. The young woman and the blind guy were still
sleeping, lying one against the other, close to where they
had been talking. The man in the black sweatshirt had to
get in line to go to the bathroom, and inside he ran into
the man with the moving jaws, who'd woken up with a
bad migraine. The toilets were flooded, and men came in
with their pants legs rolled up, hopping like acrobats. "If
they don't clean this up soon, we're going to have to pee
in the doorway," said the man with the moving jaws. "Or
on the terrace," the man in the sweatshirt shot back.
Fortunately, there was running water and he could wash
his face and scrub his hands, and trick himself into
thinking he had gotten rid of the dirt and grease that was
driving him crazy.

When he came out, the boys in the Bermudas were reselling the peanut bars and hard candy that they'd bought on the lower level. Those from the third spot had gone out to explore the surroundings—a reckless move, according to the mulatta well-along-in-years—"If suddenly there's an extra bus for them, they'll have lost two days on line." "Two and a half days, auntie," responded the sharper one in the third spot, "but forget about that extra bus." The latest rumors said that at noon they were going to set up regular departures, and make more frequent announcements in order to cut down on the black market. "What happened yesterday was the limit," declared the mulatta.

The young woman's boyfriend arrived just after 8:00. She looked a little beat up from a hard night, but she had changed clothes and greeted the man in the black sweatshirt with a beautiful smile. "We have to speak later," she said. Her boyfriend, who also looked like he had just bathed, kissed her on the forehead, passed a finger along the circles under her eyes, then took her out to the terrace. The people on line couldn't take their eyes off the thermos that the boyfriend took out of his nylon bag. "That's got to be coffee," said the mulatta well-along-in-years, "if only she'll remember us." The man with the moving jaws complained, "The hard candy is giving me indigestion." He seemed to be withering away by the minute.

Moments after her boyfriend had taken off, the young woman called the man in the black sweatshirt out to the terrace. Indeed, the small thermos did contain coffee, and it pained her to carry it past the line because there wasn't enough for everyone. They agreed that they ought to give preference to the wrinkled old lady, the mother of the child, and the man with the moving jaws. If there was any left, they would give some to the recruit, who seemed the most out of sorts of everyone, and who endured the bad conditions without complaint. She pointed out to the man in the black sweatshirt that she wasn't including the blind guy. "I'm punishing him." She added, "I'll fill you in later."

Midmorning, a few employees had come in to throw buckets of water into the toilets. In the steamy heat, several people tried to pull themselves together still sitting on the bench, having gotten only snatches of sleep at night. They shook their heads like rag dolls. By noon, the waiting room was a furnace and there wasn't an inch of shade on the terrace. The blind guy had passed the morning alone on the terrace. On line, it was noted how well he had learned to move among the benches without stumbling and the men testified they had seen him move about as easily as anyone in the flooded bathroom. "He looks for the toilet with his knees, like this," explained the guy wearing the baseball cap as he leaned on the bench, "and he never shoots outside the rim."

It was past 1:00 when the strident blare of the loudspeakers once again shook up the waiting room. "Santiago de Cuba and Camagüey," guessed the kid in the bright-colored Bermudas, who once again was passing himself off as Fernández's nephew. "Manzanillo is the asshole of the world," said the man with the moving jawbones, his gaze fixed on a point in the air, a vein on his forehead beating without pause. "No, the paper to wipe it with," corrected the mulatta well-along-in-years, who was losing her patience by the minute. She was the cook in a pizzeria and should have been back on the job the day before. "Aside from my wages, I'm fined two hundred pesos every day I miss work."

This time the quota of tickets for the waiting room was generous: twelve tickets for Las Tunas, fifteen for Jiguaní, and seven for Santiago de Cuba. The young woman's boyfriend got to the station after 2:00, explaining that he had to walk more than twenty blocks. The man in the black sweatshirt was treated to bread with guayaba preserves, a cup of tea, and the promise of a cup of coffee later in the afternoon. The young woman put part of her rice and beans aside to share with the twins and the young boy, and a bit of tea for the blind guy. "It hurts me to do it, but this has to be a harsh punishment," she said to the man in the black sweatshirt. Then she repeated, "I'll tell you about it later."

The others only ate tidbits that some daring souls had gone down to buy: peanut bars, toasted peanuts, sliced coconut in syrup, and a fish sandwich that the young married man had bought for eight pesos. "It's amazing to see how people abuse this situation," the mulatta said. The man with the moving jaws started to complain about a sharp pain in his stomach, and the young woman commented to the blind guy how pale the man was getting. Nevertheless, the frugality was lightened by the hope that in late afternoon there would be other departures, and the young boys in the Bermudas commented to their captive audience that they were sure at least seven seats would be on sale on the first bus leaving for Manzanillo.

The loudspeakers blared again and again throughout the afternoon. Several buses departed for nearby towns:

Matanzas, Varadero, San Juan y Martínez, San José de las Lajas, Unión de Reyes. In every case there were generous ticket quotas for the waiting area. Around 5:00 the couple sitting behind the man with the moving jaws showed up. They were almost adolescents, very small and thin, and the mulatta well-along-in-years greeted them with her meanest look: It wasn't fair that they came to reclaim their place on line a day after taking it. "Anybody will get on board that way," she summed up. The guy in the baseball cap, who didn't even know about the existence of the couple, said they should get in line behind him if they were really serious about having to travel. Otherwise, let them keep walking around. The couple chose to stay standing in front of the man moving his jaws, refusing to give up the space they were so poorly defending. The young wife wanted to take off, but the boy insisted that his family, who awaited them for Carnival, had already bought their return tickets. What's more, they had heard that between that night and the next everyone who had spent several days in the waiting area would get a bus out. The girl with the nice manners asked him to clarify. The young couple had been informed by a man in a bus driver's uniform—he was angry because it was his turn to drive during the day to Sagua de Tánamo. "Even more reason," said the guy in the cap, "for them to stand behind me."

Evening fell and lightning again illuminated the south. It seemed to the man in the black sweatshirt that it had rained somewhere nearby and he hoped it would be cooler at night. Over the last several hours he had invented a cycle that helped him forget time: some ten minutes standing in his place on line in silence; later, talking the situation over with the mulatta or the man with the moving jaws—more or less the same words, the same phrases of hope or improvement; then out to the terrace to gaze at the city or the sky from the three walls that enclosed the space; leaning against a wall to rest his back, searching for a place to sit; looking at the young woman who had spent the afternoon inventing games to entertain the twins and the boy who was second in line; then back inside, walking through the lines for the towns far from his—Cruces, Cifuentes, Mayajigua, Santa Rita, Maffo—hoping to meet some old friend with whom he could dissipate his loneliness and fatigue; then into the bathroom once more on the tip of his toes, to pee, wet his face, scour his hands again; and finally returning to his place on line. These thirty or forty minutes summed up his second day of waiting. "I'd give anything to get out of here tonight."

He was outside on the terrace, keeping an eye on his patch of wall where he had slept so that it stay unoccupied, when the young woman came up to him. She brought him his cup of coffee, the third that day, and a secret: She had discovered that the blind guy wasn't blind. The man in the black sweatshirt was hardly surprised. "He's shameless!" The young woman assured him that the guy really wasn't a bad person; a bender the day before was to blame. "As he's already been deprived of special consideration, he's very torn up, panicking that he'll be found out. Just think of the bald man getting wind of it. Last night I called him all sorts of terrible things, but we've got to help him."

One and a half days of hunger and fatigue began to get the best of him. When the young woman said that she didn't know how she was going to sleep, he went back to dust off his strip of wall, making the spot ready for her, turning his knapsack into her pillow. He lay down where the guy in the baseball cap had been, also with his back to the terrace, convinced that while he slept, the loudspeakers would not make any announcements.

At 11:00 they turned the lights out in the waiting room. Inside, a kid could be heard crying; maybe it was the son of the woman in the second spot. "He has to be dying of hunger," said the young woman while she arranged her stuff on the wall as if she had been there all her life. The man in the black sweatshirt went to sleep, aided by exhaustion. His legs grazed the young woman's, and at times wrapped around them, entrapping them. When a cold breeze started to disturb them in the morning, he sensed that she was reaching for him.

It was already daytime when he woke up, certain he was by himself. The place where the girl had been was empty, and he didn't see the blind guy, the guy in the baseball cap, the recruit, or the boys in the colorful Bermudas on the terrace. Inside the waiting room the Manzanillo line had formed a circle around a huge fellow who kept shouting, "Let me explain!" The young woman drew close to the man in the black sweatshirt: "I didn't want to wake you"; she brushed his back, handed him a little nylon bag with a tiny piece of herbal soap and a tube of toothpaste. According to the mulatta, she explained, the man had offered the guy in the baseball cap a ticket to Manzanillo for two hundred pesos. Even though the man made it clear that he was simply asking what hour the next bus was leaving, the boy in the

Bermudas testified that he'd seen him around the walkways the times he had gone down and passed himself off
as Fernández's nephew. The mulatta well-along-in-years
demanded that he hand over the ticket, in exchange for
not calling the police. The man raised his arms, taking
on the look of a victim. "Frisk me, if you like." The boys
in the Bermudas stepped toward him. The man lowered
his arms and took a step back. The woman with the
young boy blocked his retreat. The man took a ticket
out of his pocket, handed it over to the mulatta, and
took off at a clip. The mulatta read the ticket. "It's for
this very afternoon."

The man with the moving jaws assured everyone that
the ticket had to be fake. The man with the cardboard
box suggested that someone take it down to the adminis-
tration because it could be stolen. "This is so unfair," said
the wrinkled old lady. The grandmother of the twins suggested that they give it to the blind guy. The blind guy
lowered his head. The man in the black sweatshirt
thought it would be better if they gave it to the woman
with the two kids. The old lady complained out loud that
old people always get the worst treatment. The boys in
the Bermudas said it's true, that children are the hope of
the world.

The young woman asked to speak: There were a
number of things that could be done. First, take a vote to
decide who deserves the ticket. Second, form a committee
to speak to the manager of the station. The man in the
black sweatshirt and the grandmother of the twins agreed
with her. The committee would have to register a complaint that the management was allowing marketeering
and also make certain that the person they selected would

not be prevented from using the ticket. The young woman added that the committee would have to bring up the cleanliness of the waiting area and bathrooms. "We're not accustomed to living in shit." The recruit said something about the roving vendors, that they had to be prohibited from coming up to the waiting area.

After counting the votes, the mulatta noticed that the adolescent couple one place ahead of her had once again disappeared. "Now they've really lost their rights, you're all witnesses," said the guy in the cap. One of the boys in the Bermudas had lifted both his hands, and the man in the black sweatshirt asked everyone to pay attention before counting the votes. The woman in the second spot got fifteen votes, thirteen for the old lady, and four for the blind guy. The young woman consoled the old lady, promising her that as long as her boyfriend was faithful, she wouldn't lack for food. The guy in the baseball cap proposed that the man in the black sweatshirt be the head of the committee, and no one objected. The young woman and the recruit would go along with him, "because," according to the mulatta, "a uniform is always impressive." She, in turn, was put forward by the mother in the second spot, but the mulatta complained that her legs hurt far too much to be going up and down stairs.

Before setting out on their mission, the man in the black sweatshirt came up with the idea that it would be useful to hold talks with the nearby lines, in order to present a united front to the manager. Already, in Bayamo, Las Tunas, and Jiguaní natural leaders were stepping forward, but nothing had happened in Santiago de Cuba or Holguín, who were sure that they would be lucky and get on the next outgoing buses.

In order to find the manager—he was in fact named
Fernández—they had to get through a labyrinth of gate-
keepers, stairways, and secretaries. They found him in
the repair shop next to the terminal, where several men
were trying to push a bus whose engine had blown out
with a snort like a sick animal. The manager asked them
to come with him to his office, and as they walked, he
placed a hand on the man in the black sweatshirt's
shoulder. "Nobody can imagine what a hell this is," he
said, and he handed him a cigarette that the man in the
black sweatshirt gave to the recruit. His office looked
like the army tent of a soldier in retreat. The writing
desk was buried beneath papers and a dozen dirty cups of
coffee or tea. There were crankshafts and a large rack for
motors set up on the floor. The shirt and tie from his
uniform were hanging on a hat rack, and a floor fan in
the corner pushed the heat around the room.

The man in the black sweatshirt was energetic in
laying out the charges. The manager agreed. It was
impossible to control the speculators when the day
started with 70 percent of the buses out of service and
the level of absenteeism of the drivers, not to mention
the other employees, was growing all the time. While
they were talking, he asked an assistant to get the name
of the man who had sold the ticket. The cleanup of the
waiting area would be taken care of that same afternoon,
with voluntary labor from the terminal's workers, and
the concierges would clean the bathrooms twice a day.
"Three times," the young woman demanded. "We'll do
what we can," the manager assured her. "And the buses,
what about them?" asked the delegate from Bayamo, a
competent man wearing glasses. "Between today and

tomorrow we will get at least one bus out to each destination. Think about it: that's one hundred and sixty-eight departures in two days. But definitely, I'm sure we're going to do it." As for the strolling vendors, explained the man with the black sweatshirt, the issue was to stop them from taking advantage of hardships in the waiting area with price gouging. "We've got nothing left to eat, " said the young woman. The manager promised that the cafeteria's employees were going to come up to sell beverages and suggested the possibility of a quota for cigarettes, ten packs for each line. The committee demanded the vendors come up no farther than the stairway, and it was agreed that two representatives from each town would make the purchases so that desperation wouldn't push the prices up.

The assistant came back with the news that the ticket was a fake. "Nobody takes into account the hell we've got going down here," the manager repeated as he threw the worthless paper into the trash. He begged them to come whenever they had a complaint, promised to visit them in the waiting room when time permitted, and said good-bye.

The mother in the second spot cried when she learned that the ticket was fake. "It's going on three days this poor kid has gone without milk." Every one of the representatives met with their group. The Manzanillo group chose the mulatta as treasurer, and the young married man and the man with the air of a peasant and the cardboard box to take care of the purchases. The man with the cardboard box refused: he had a bad head for numbers. His place was taken by one of the boys in Bermudas, who got a sharp look from the man with the moving jaws: "That little nut could go play down there and leave us to die of hunger." The young woman made a count of the smokers, who totaled nine, so they would have an extra pack as a reward for good behavior.

The man in the black sweatshirt suggested that everyone take out their ticket money, and the remainder be handed over to the mulatta. It was agreed that those who were only going to Manzanillo for a visit—the young woman, the boys in the Bermudas, the guy in the baseball cap, and the man in the black sweatshirt— would keep what was needed for the expenses of the stay. "In short," the man with the moving jaws complained, "I'm in the dark as to how they're going to spend the money." The young married man calculated that they ought to have reserves for fifteen days. The young woman and the mother in the second spot thought that was an exaggeration. "Let's hope so," said the man in the black sweatshirt, "but our duty is to prepare for the worst." They also agreed that new arrivals would have to contribute to the survival fund, as the young woman called it, as soon as they got on line. What's more, she took all the money her boyfriend had on him when he arrived with her lunch.

At noon, the boys in the Bermudas took a tent out of their knapsacks, set it up on the terrace, and gave it to the kids to play in. It was big enough for twelve, so when it was ready, they brought together the children from Bayamo, Jiguaní, and Holguín. The mothers got together with a retired teacher from Half-Moon to watch over the school-age children. The man in the black sweatshirt asked those who brought suitcases to store them in the tent—they could be used as seats—and he thought to himself that they had to get milk soon. "Forget about those vendors," said the boy in the Bermudas. "Now they're trying to charge me seven pesos for a peanut bar."

Busy with the duties that went with his position, the man in the black sweatshirt was surprised how quickly the afternoon had passed. He and the young woman— she had been made his deputy—were both tired and pleased. There were already ten kids playing in the tent, the purchase committee had collected more than enough funds and had managed to get a pair of vendors to lower their prices on the fish sandwiches and the guayaba cookies after promising to make daily wholesale purchases. Along with the regular departures for the nearby towns, in the afternoon buses had left for Nuevitas, Sagua de Tánamo, and Chambas. For every bus, five tickets had been sold to the waiting list. The young married man remembered the manager's promise: "At this rate he won't be able to keep his promise, not even in a week." Now he feared that he had been too optimistic in his fifteen-day estimate. The man in the black sweatshirt asked him to be discreet: "Panic can do just as much harm as hunger."

The mothers made the tent into a dormitory for the children, and so that the women could get some rest, the man in the black sweatshirt organized the men into a watch that changed every two hours (he himself began at midnight). The sky was clear, the children slept like angels, and from time to time the breeze cooled off the night. The man with the moving jaws, who was on from 2:00 to 4:00, showed up early—he found it impossible to sleep on the bench and he had taken his last sleeping pill the night before. His wife, who suffered from Saint Vitus' dance, had spent almost a week alone waiting for him. "Imagine the torment she's going through." The man in the black sweatshirt promised him that he would be reunited with her in two days at most. The man with the moving jaws dismissed it with a wave of his hand: "I'm losing all hope now of getting back to see her."

His watch finished, the man in the black sweatshirt looked for his spot on the wall. The young woman was huddled in her space, and even while she slept, she wore the look of a satisfied woman. He moved a large lock of hair that had fallen onto her lips and she took hold of his hand. "You're done already?" She moved closer. "I'm cold." The man in the black sweatshirt sat down next to her and the young woman put her arm around him, sheltering him. "You're cute," she said, and gave him a kiss on the tip of his nose.

It was barely dawn when the blind guy came to call on the girl. He had just found an empty can of Russian meat thrown into a corner of the bathroom, and he was sure it belonged to the guy in the baseball cap. "He was the only one to go in before me, and he stayed in there a long time before coming out," the blind guy explained to the man in the black sweatshirt. The young woman advocated confiscating his suitcase immediately, where they were sure to find more food: "He's got the face of a speculator." The blind guy remembered that he couldn't have seen anything. "I left the can in the same place, it's important that he be the one to find it," and he pointed to the man in the black sweatshirt. The wisest thing to do, thought the man in the black sweatshirt, was to hold a meeting as soon as possible, explain what had happened without stirring up false accusations, appeal to civic conscience, and promise that items used for the public good would be paid for. If the guilty person didn't hand the food over, they would take action to inspect the baggage. When the man in the black sweatshirt checked out the bathrooms, he saw white drops that could be milk near the washbasins.

The assembly met on the terrace so as not to wake those still sleeping inside. The guy in the baseball cap's shock and indignation seemed as authentic as that of the mother in the second spot and the grandmother of the twins, who cried when they heard the word *milk*. The appeal went without success. It was decided that the man in the black sweatshirt, the young woman, and the young married man—who were already called the Executive Committee—would set up in the tent and go through the baggage, piece by piece.

The boys in the Bermudas helped a few women carry their suitcases. The small bag belonging to the man with the moving jaws had only a few pieces of underwear, a pair of plastic slippers, and two Ocean Atlantic sweatshirts. In the rest of the baggage they found only medicine— mipramine, novatropin, levamisol, bicarbonate that the wrinkled old lady and the man with the moving jaws were taking to their families—some soap, and tubes of toothpaste. They took inventory of everything, in case of an emergency. "So the one holding out has to be from another town," said the young married man. "But he's close by," the young woman insisted. It was unlikely that anyone would dare to walk through the waiting room with a can of meat, even early in the morning.

They went off to talk to the representatives of Bayamo and Las Tunas, when one of the boys in the

Bermudas caught up with them. The enormous cardboard box hadn't been checked. They had tried to take it, but its owner assured them that it was full of clothes from an uncle who had just died, showing them through an opening the pleats of a linen guayabera.

He greeted them with a surprised and friendly gesture. Of course the box didn't have anything improper, he'd simply wanted to spare them the trouble, and he lowered his feet from the top of the box and opened the flaps, which had been folded inside each other. The young woman picked up the guayabera, which was on top. The collar was destroyed and there was a large spot of mold covering the back. There were also strips of sheets made of flannel, cashmere pants in the same bad shape as the shirt, and pieces of lace from what was once a tablecloth. The young married man moved his hands past the clothes. He smiled.

The box held ninety-seven cans of Russian meat (the less fatty kind from China) and eighty bags of powdered milk (the yellow kind distributed to diabetics). "None of it's mine," the box's owner pleaded. "I'm just doing someone a favor. There's thousands of pesos' worth here I can't touch." The booty was hauled over to the tent, and the Executive Committee decided to share it with children from the other towns already in the tent, and with any others who could be found. Also, they must include any older people who seemed unwell. The young woman was of the opinion that the owner of the box was amoral and should not be paid for the goods. The young married man believed that confiscation was excessive: "Let's put a price of fifty pesos on every bag of milk and thirty for the cans of meat. That's more than seven thousand pesos." The man in the black sweatshirt made the decision that everything would be paid for, but at the official price. The mulatta counted out 196 pesos, 40 centavos. The owner of the box wouldn't accept it. "I'd rather get slapped with a fine, or be put in jail."

At 6:00 sharp that afternoon the manager came up to visit them. He was wearing the dirty uniform they'd seen in his office, but his hair was slicked back and newly combed. "I have good news for you," and he led the Executive Committee out to the terrace. Five buses were standing near the platforms, ready to leave. "That one, number one-thirty-three, is going to Manzanillo. With it we've carried out thirty-eight percent of the schedule." The young woman clapped twice for joy. The manager nodded his head: "The bad news is that with so many breakdowns we've accumulated a lot of people with tickets." The young married man argued that nothing be said to the people on line, so as not to raise false hopes. The manager wanted to walk around and check on the cleanup of the bathrooms and the waiting room. While he was at it, he picked up papers and cigarette butts from the floor, spoke briefly with the employees killing time at the ticket counters.

When the beverages went on sale, he drank tea with the Executive Committee. "You have to get the people to understand and work together with us." Later they took him to see the tent, where the children were eating their first ration of Russian meat. The retired teacher said she was surprised by the natural intelligence of children these days, "who learn things in a flash." "That's the attitude we need from you," the manager said as he was leaving. "You already know that you can count on me unconditionally."

The woman on the loudspeaker announced that one
ticket for Manzanillo would go on sale. The mother in the
second spot tearfully embraced the wrinkled old lady, who
was shaking in disbelief of her good luck. "Until I'm
riding in that bus I won't believe it," she was saying. The
manager accompanied her through the business of
buying the ticket, and nearly everyone from the line said
good-bye to her on the stairway. Before starting down the
stairs, the wrinkled old lady took the nylon bag that held
the medicines out of her purse and handed it to the man
in the black sweatshirt. "Let's hope they won't be necessary." The boys in the Bermudas, who carried her suitcase, went along with her. The others saw her step up
into the bus from the terrace, and a few waved as the bus
exited the roofed area of the terminal. "She was a good
woman," said the mulatta well-along-in-years when she
got back to her seat. The mother of the boy had run for
her spot on the bench, her eyes still moist. "The old lady
got here ten minutes before me," said the recruit, sitting
next to her.

When night fell, the Bayamo representative came
over to talk with the Manzanillo Executive Committee:
how to deal with couples had yet to be resolved. Several
mothers had complained that during the night moans
had been heard on the terrace, and a child had been
playing with a condom he found next to the tent. "We've
got to set up a free zone." The perfect place was the tent,
if they managed to convince the mothers that the children should return to the waiting room to sleep. "We
could even rent it," suggested the representative from
Bayamo. The young woman thought this was pointless.
The man in the black sweatshirt found a rope to cordon

off the section of the terrace farthest from the tent. The boys in the Bermudas were put in charge of distributing flyers and of spreading information to the other lines. Sanctions with stiff fines were set up for the couples who indulged in amorous entanglements outside the liberated zone, or during the day.

Before lying down, the man in the black sweatshirt stuck his head in the tent. The recruit finished his watch and, except for a young girl who had a bad cough, everyone else was sleeping quietly. The young woman, wide awake, was waiting for him. "Tomorrow I'm going to wash that sweatshirt," she said while she passed the back of her hand through the stubble of his beard. He came closer to give her a kiss. "Not here." The man in the black sweatshirt looked toward the darkness of the liberated zone. "Let's go." "Wait up. Come here." The young woman lay against the wall. "I'm too tired. Are you hungry?" The man in the black sweatshirt sat down next to her. The faint smell of a popular perfume lingered on her skin. "Are you happy?" "Very." He kissed her on the ear.

The fifth and sixth days on the waiting line went by smoothly for the man in the black sweatshirt. Rumor had it that the other towns were setting up Executive Committees similar to theirs but larger, with as many as seven members each, responsible, among other things, for the watch, for internal order, for the management of money and services, and for care of the children. Three people had joined the Manzanillo line, but left when they found out what was happening. The young woman washed the black sweatshirt, which he changed for another of the same color but without the logo. She also asked for his dirty underwear, but he made it a habit to rinse them out daily, when he brushed his teeth in the morning. During the day, lines were hung on the terrace to dry clothes; at sunset, when the shade from the waiting room had grown longer, there were games of checkers, Parcheesi, and dominoes which the manager joined a little before beverages went on sale.

In the tent everything went exactly as desired. The little girl who was coughing no longer had fluid in her lungs, and the Russian meat, although raw, hadn't caused any stomach problems. The watches were rigorously carried out, and at least for the moment, the couples were using the liberated zone to their advantage. One remaining concern was food for the elderly. The man who sold fish sandwiches had a habit of disappearing, and they were having trouble with the hard candy, peanut bars, and the various herb teas.

The fifth day, at breakfast time, the young woman's boyfriend arrived empty-handed. After the customary kiss, he headed with her over to the stairway. From a distance, those on the Manzanillo line saw the two of them in heated conversation, their hands punching the air. The boyfriend gave the woman a hard shove. The man in the black sweatshirt was just about to go over to them when the young woman came back crying. An hour went by before the man in the black sweatshirt could get a word out of her. "He's so arrogant, he's insisting that I go, that I give up everything. What a jerk."

At night they lay down as usual along their part of the wall, the man in the black sweatshirt embraced her, sniffed a faint trace of the popular perfume, and fell asleep. A short time after they put the lights out in the waiting room, the young woman woke him up by biting his ear. "Let's go," she said, and for the first time they crossed over into the liberated zone.

On the seventh day the man with the moving jaws woke up with a high fever and a sharp pain in his stomach. The mulatta well-along-in-years suggested he take novatropin, and the young woman went over to the other towns in search of duralgina or a light sedative for the digestive tract. Seated in his usual place, his hands crossed over his belly, the man with the moving jaws was unnaturally pale and the vein on his forehead was an intense blue. "Get a doctor over here," said the man in the black sweatshirt, but in the whole waiting room there was only a young woman from Caribarién who said she had been a nurse. The mother in the first spot brought over a half glass of milk, but it was impossible to make him drink it. He couldn't get any of the teas down either. By 10:00 that morning the fever had not abated and he went into his first convulsions. Someone suggested that his dentures be taken out. The man in the black sweatshirt ordered the recruit to hurry over to the manager and ask that he bring a doctor.

Fernández arrived at a run and said the words everyone feared: "We've got to get him to a hospital as soon as possible." "It's not fair," the twins' grandmother complained. "We can't do this to him." Fernández ignored her protest and tried to get the sick man up on his feet. His body was rigid and the look on his face was so intense that Fernández did nothing more than pass his hand over the man's damp forehead. Ten minutes later the man with the moving jaws was delirious, and the mulatta well-advanced-in-years placed a handkerchief soaked in alcohol on his forehead. The doctor arrived even sooner than the manager expected, but it was useless. At 11:00 in the morning, the man with the moving jaws was dead.

Now came the formalities. As far as anyone could tell, he didn't have family in Havana, and the few belongings he carried in his pasteboard suitcase didn't reveal any facts about his life apart from an address in Manzanillo, the number of his identity card, and a name so out of the ordinary that it was used only on the most essential documents. "The day after tomorrow he would have been seventy-seven years old," the mulatta announced. The man in the black sweatshirt tried to put together a simple telegram for his widow, but he couldn't find the words to communicate with the woman whose loneliness had caused the man with the moving jaws so much suffering. In a meeting with the manager and the doctor, the Executive Committee decided that the corpse would be embalmed, stored in the manager's office along with his suitcase, and sent on the first bus out.

The wake was held on the terrace, and to avoid frightening the children, the retired teacher took the kids on a tour of the repair shops in the terminal. When the corpse was ready, the mulatta well-along-in-years busied herself giving him a shave, putting back his dentures, and dressing him in the best clothes to be found in his suitcase. The boys in the Bermuda shorts carried the casket, and the funeral cortege—people going to other towns and a few workers—walked in silence to the manager's office. With the casket resting on the motor block, the man in the black sweatshirt took two steps toward the front, dried a tear, and gave the mournful send-off: he had little to say, but the sadness everyone shared was sincere. The man with the moving jaws had been a good man, without doubt a model husband, a hard worker and honest. He deserved to rest in peace. The blind man took off his dark glasses, and the mulatta well-along-in-years lamented that she didn't have a flower to place on the casket.

The emotional outpouring caused by the death of the man with the moving jaws did not stop life in the waiting line. After the funeral service, the children returned to the tent, the venders from the cafeteria came up to sell their beverages, the man with the fish sandwiches made a slight discount due to the circumstances, and night had not yet fallen when several couples spread throughout the liberated zone.

In the following days the boy in the first spot learned how to identify geometric figures and the twins to divide two-digit numbers. The young married man proposed—and people agreed—to distribute only five of the ten daily packs of cigarettes (there was talk that some people smoked less and were beginning to barter for money of their own) and to use the rest in exchange for food. The plan was a great success, and coffee started to turn up (two liters for a pack), ham sandwiches (two packs for one), cheese pies (two for three packs), and hard-boiled eggs (one for one). There was also ham, toothpaste, cans of deodorant, razor blades, and some detergent that was sent back because it hardly made any suds. The manager was distressed by the size of the black market, but he agreed that the best thing was to take the long view.

By now those with the longest tenure had completed nearly two months on line when, at the behest of the delegate from Santiago de Cuba, the first Assembly of

Municipal Representatives was convened to create a
Directorate. In principle, the idea was to bring together all
the Executive Committees; however, the idea of a unified
body—presented by Santiago and Guantánamo, and supported by Manzanillo, Bayamo, and Sancti Spiritus—was
opposed to the thesis of a President with full powers, and
an Advisory of Delegates, brought forth by Camagüey and
Ciego de Avila, with supporters in Holguín, Cienfuegos,
and some towns in Matanzas. These were days full of running around for the man in the black sweatshirt, who in
the end found himself among those who felt that it was
preferable to postpone the decision before dividing the
country with pointless arguments.

The Assembly was held in the center of the waiting
room, with the benches placed in a horseshoe around
the ticket counters, where the leadership sat. There were
166 delegates present—Varadero and Matanzas had
insignificant lines—and the manager, who was extended
a special invitation, came with his uniform freshly
ironed, a new cap and tie. The most debated issues were
the permissibility of the black market, the cleanliness of
the bathrooms, an entry fee for the liberated zone, the
establishment of medical services, and the need to find
another person to help the teacher with the care and
instruction of the children. At the end, proposals such as
the creation of a police force to maintain order inside, or
a permanent brigade of volunteer workers to assist in the
repair of the buses and the maintenance of the terminal
were not approved. On the other hand, it was agreed that
the next Assembly had to meet within two months, with
the hope that by that date there would be consensus
about what governmental structure to adopt. As a means

of getting there, a Provisional Presidency made up of leaders of both viewpoints was chosen, which pleased the partisans of the unified body above all. The closing speech was delivered by the manager, who said that never in the history of the Bus Terminal had he come across a group so organized and efficient, and he praised the judgment of those who knew how to put the interests of the country above personal ambitions.

The Assembly came to a close with a party on the terrace. A group of women had spent the afternoon washing down the terrace with buckets of water, decorated it by hanging taro and palms that they rescued from a few offices in the terminal, and converted the tent into a kiosk. With the help of the manager, there was a tape deck and a stand with ice cream floats, and, except for a few people who hid out in the waiting room in order to get some early sleep, everyone was dancing until very late. The young woman was happy, and as the man in the black sweatshirt turned out to be a clumsy dancer, she was in great demand by the boys in the Bermuda shorts, by the representative from Bayamo, who proved to be graceful in the spins around the social club, and by the blind man. The children had an extra portion of hard candy, and their mothers let them stay up with the grown-ups until the very end of the party.

The political activities had died down and now it was the flu that danced from the tent to the villages closest to the stairway, when the young woman had the first inkling that she could be pregnant. The flu didn't present major complications except for the little girl with the cough; her lungs were blocked up again and she went through several sleepless nights, terribly sick and coughing like a barking dog. The representative from Bayamo was able to get his hand on tubes of penicillin, the workers in the cafeteria agreed to boil a needle and syringe (later they were given a pack of cigarettes as a gift), and with an injection from the steady hand of the twins' grandmother, the little girl was back on her feet in a few weeks.

The man in the black sweatshirt didn't want to go public with the news that he was going to be a father until there was solid proof. Meantime, they quit going to the liberated zone. Now she lay by his side and he slept with his hand caressing the smooth skin of her belly, imagining he could feel the tiny and still unformed creature inside grow. Two weeks later, it was impossible for the young woman to button her pants. The Manzanillo women were delighted with the possibility of a new member; the grandmother of the twins lamented she didn't have a needle and thread to sew some baby socks; the mulatta well-along-in-years made it her job to go about getting the necessary material for a crib; and the young married woman, giving her husband a reproachful look, said that the young woman was very brave.

The first rumors started to come from below when the young woman had to exchange almost all her clothing for baggier outfits. There were extremely vague statements from sources no one could identify, and people listened to them with the bitter expression that comes from hearing a joke in bad taste. In the next two days the rumors took on a threatening life of their own. When the time for dominoes rolled around, the man in the black sweatshirt went to see the manager by himself. Fernández looked at him with an ambiguous expression and lowered his head to respond: "Don't worry, everything's in order." But that night they didn't talk of anything else in the waiting area. The man in the black sweatshirt, taking the manager at his word, tried to convince his subordinates that it was nothing more than a ruse, perhaps something prompted by the supporters of Presidentialism, in order to stir up anarchy and undermine the authority of the Provisional Presidency. Bayamo's representative was the most skeptical. He had it from good sources that the repair shops were working twelve-hour shifts and that an important shipment of spare parts had arrived.

The young woman refused to believe it. "They can't do this to us." The man in the black sweatshirt went out looking for a member of the Presidency. Holguín's representative had also spoken with the manager and, like the man in the black sweatshirt, he had faith. Camagüey's representative said he didn't have the authority to call a special session of the Presidency, much less of the Assembly, and the representative from Santiago didn't turn up. "He must be over there," someone said, gesturing toward the liberated zone. There was nothing else to do but wait.

They all slept badly. Throughout the night there was a buzz at the guard box in the tent and the lights on the terminal's patio were on while workers carried bundles from one side to the other. The young woman lay down with her back to the terrace. When the man in the black sweatshirt tried to run his hands over her belly, she gave him a brusque shove. He felt that he was responsible: "Forgive me. It's true. There's nothing to be done." She sobbed and wanted to be left alone. Dawn found them both wide awake.

As soon as he had rinsed out his mouth, the man in the black sweatshirt went down to see the manager. He wasn't around, but the hustle and bustle everywhere in the terminal left no doubt. A group of drivers in brand-new uniforms were hanging around the entrance to the cafeteria talking, the pharmacy and the post office were open, and the cleaning staff were back with steel wool on the stone steps. When he got back to the waiting area, the man in the black sweatshirt met with the young married man and the representatives from Bayamo and Las Tunas. The young woman stayed on the terrace, alone, her back turned to everyone. The boys in the colorful Bermudas were taking the tent down and the blind man had starting wearing his dark glasses again. "We've been betrayed," said the man in the black sweatshirt, making his case. "The only honorable thing to do is quit."

It was hopeless trying to get a response from the young woman. She was sitting motionless, crying in silence, far from the world collapsing treacherously all around her. It must have been 11:35 when the man in the black sweatshirt went down the stairs for the last time. He hadn't said good-bye to anyone and his two-month-old beard accentuated the sad expression on his face.

TEN YEARS LATER

Marilyn Bobes
Translated by Chris Brandt

There it is again, Piazza del Duomo and Santa Maria del Fiore, with its black and white marble stripes insistently beckoning, offering the chance for sweet intimacy. Yes, Florence with its round arches and its columns, reaches across the plain toward Perétola, Sesto Fiorentino, and the sea. Here you can find the most beautiful dresses and shoes in the world, the most fabulous jewels and ceramics. It's the city where she'd imagined her dreams of happiness would be fulfilled. Still, so many things had changed in her since then.... She no longer even thought to leaf through one of Dr. Schnabl's books; first, she'd lost her patience, then her confidence.

Walking along the street by the Palazzo Strozzi, she paid no attention to the East Portal of the Baptistery with its Old Testament scenes and its figures of prophets and sibyls, or to the North Portal with its representations of the evangelists and the doctors of the Latin Church;

she didn't know which of the two Michelangelo had
deemed more worthy to be the entrance to Paradise, and
Jacques was not here with his historical comments and
archeological accuracies to tell her. And this was not the
night when, after a bottle of rosé, they had made love in
a cheap hotel by the Arno—she with her thoughts fixed
on the Apollonian torso of the David, which they'd contemplated some hours earlier in the Galleria dell'
Accademia. Those narrow hips and muscled legs of a
dancer were so unlike Donatello's sad little shepherd—a
bit of a lad in bronze, sickly and effeminate, resting the
sword's immovable weight against the ground.

She'd returned to Florence with no desire for anything that was not Michelangelo's impetuous David,
whose replica was now enticing her in front of the Piazza
della Signoria. Suddenly, she was Bathsheba, whose husband, Uriah, would be sent to battle and certain death by
the King of the Hebrews—himself the victim of a devastating love. She was beckoned by the true David, who
was wrestled by Buonarotti from that imposing block of
marble, with which Agostino d'Antonio, and even
Leonardo da Vinci had already struggled; seduced by *The
Giant*, as he was baptized by the great Florentines—so
vigorous and astute in the arts of war.

No one had ever reminded her so much of Bebo as
that particular sculpture, with its protruding testicles—
of a piece beneath the patch of curly hair—making the
penis appear ever smaller and more manageable; how
different it was from Jacques's member, magnificent in
its dimensions, rigid and hypersensitive between the two
hanging sacs. She'd even thought then that it was
Jacques's penis—for its marblelike hardness and its

engorged veins at the moment of greatest erection—that really belonged on the David. (Although, thinking it over again, David's penis has just the right proportions for the state in which the hero is presented: a few moments before his confrontation with Goliath, the stone ready in its sling.)

That night in the hotel, she'd hardly had time to fantasize herself entwined around the statue's narrow pelvis (Bebo's agile, snaky, playful hips), when Jacques came, as always, only a few seconds after he'd begun to penetrate her. It was useless to hint to him the possibility of a therapy recommended by Dr. Schnabl for such cases. It was even more useless to ask him to keep on stroking her clitoris with his mouth or fingers. Her lack of assertiveness in such matters was due not only to a sort of false shame nourished by a conservative and timid education but to this reflection: she had learned to let the man's excitement provoke her own. Thinking of her husband, already satisfied, coldly executing such an operation just to relieve her, was possibly even more disillusioning than the way they usually concluded the act. Jacques compensated for the brevity of their encounters by holding her close for a long time after. He stroked her hair tenderly and purred phrases full of poetry and gratitude, but he'd never thought to ask her how she felt, nor gave signs that he had the vigor necessary for a second act. Out of delicacy or timidity, she never spoke. She told herself that perhaps with a little patience, she could learn to speed up her own pleasure until she caught up with him. It was all a matter of a little patience, she assured herself, of not losing confidence.

Decidedly, Michelangelo's David was the spitting image of Bebo, a mix of pride and defiance hurled out at the infinity of space. Something in the expression reminded her of the look her ex-fiancé had given her that day on the Malecón in Havana when she announced she was marrying Jacques. After a few days at the Hotel Messidor on the rue Vaugirard, in Paris, they'd be leaving for a honeymoon in Italy. Bebo had looked at her with that arrogance so typical of a poor man who knows himself owner of the world by right of his ability to adapt to any circumstance. Out of the blue, he proposed they celebrate an amicable farewell in the San Lázaro Street room, where they had often met in the months before that fateful night, when, inexplicably, he had gone off alone to the dance they'd had a date for in the gardens of the Tropical. It was the same fateful night in which she would first meet Jacques.

Her ex-fiancé had asked her to undress for him, and later joked about how thin she'd gotten. With Jacques's health-food diet—undertaken with a determination to convert her into a European *honoris causa*—she had succeeded in reducing perceptibly the fat that had timidly lodged itself around her abdomen. Beneath the wide skirt of her silk dress, however, her massive hips, and her high-swelling buttocks remained the same; but Bebo didn't notice, he was so busy seducing her. He murmured a thousand sweet vulgarities, words that stimulated glands Jacques knew nothing of, and produced the miracle of an abundant, uncontainable lubrication, the like of which would never dampen the sheets of the many hotels and boarding houses, on the long and tortuous road from Paris to Padua, on to

Venice and Urbino, finally passing through Florence to reach Naples.

After the incident, she began to research obsessively this business of the words. It didn't seem to be dealt with in the books she consulted by sexologists like Masters and Johnson and Siegfried Schnabl, not even in those chapters dedicated to frigidity and the lack of orgasm, nor in *Is the Sexual Act Too Short?* which the German doctor seemed to have written just for them. Too bad. She'd never have guessed that such words could have become so indispensable to achieve an orgasm. She even got a little scared when she read an article, signed by several Danish doctors, describing the pathology known as coprolalia: the unhealthy inclination to utter vulgar words. Maybe Bebo suffered from that strange aberration. Though she continued her research, she could find nothing to tell whether the sickness also included those like her, who liked to hear the words rather than speak them. What did David whisper to Bathsheba during the long nights of Uriah's absence, when Solomon was conceived? *"Mami, qué rica estás"*? or *"Amore mio, ti voglio bene"*?

She knew that in every language there are vernacular words for the genitals and the sexual act; but in French, when Jacques said *baiser,* which definitely signified nothing else but kiss, or when he called her vulva *la châte* and his penis *la queue,* these words became too innocuous, even slightly musical. She felt not the least bit excited. It all seemed like a kid's game that turned the act of love into an innocent masquerade along zoological lines, and robbed it of any sinful connotation.

On the way to the Galleria della Accademia, just as she was passing the smooth walls and little windows of the

Convento San Marco, she remembered the Chilean who loved Fra Angelico's paintings. They had met in Toulouse, in 1995; she'd been staying alone in the country during one of Jacques's business trips. Already she had completely lost patience, and also confidence. From Havana, her godmother Clarita had made the pronouncement: Jacques would never be Schnabl's famous *special man*, he was not the man to lead her to pleasure. But he gives you everything. *"I'm telling it to you straight: don't you dare trade what you have in hand for castles in the air."*

Nevertheless, Clarita had been tolerant when she'd told her that every so often she'd take someone, *never Bebo*, to really pleasure her. With a transnational executive's briefcase and his gentlemanly and responsible air, forty-three-year-old Gonzalo had appeared like a promise of plenty in the desert of those fleeting and ever-less-frequent encounters with Jacques, which took place under the duvet, beneath a print of *The Last Supper*. She'd been languishing for some time in her mother-in-law Adele's house, dying of boredom and nostalgia.

Inventing all kinds of stories to dispel the distrust of her meddling mother-in-law, who missed nothing, she and Gonzalo were able to travel to titillating Amsterdam and visit the Van Gogh Museum, and, afterward, make love in some Chileans' apartment—aficionados of songs by the Cedrón Quartet. And in spite of her fear that the recurrent David fantasies and the constant auditory hallucinations of Bebo's words would be repeated yet again, she managed to feel moderately good in the arms of this experienced man. He knew how to control his excitement and with slow, calm foreplay, full of subtle caresses and delicate games, wait for her and induce her pleasure.

Still, it lacked the laughs, the joyous vitality she'd always felt with Bebo. Gonzalo hadn't the gift of expressing his sensuality in words, even though they both spoke the same language. He remained serious and quiet, like someone putting beautiful finishing touches on a fine piece of work, attentive to his companion's reactions but invariably distant. Like Jacques, he had a way of holding her to him once their lovemaking was over. Completely nude, they drank rosé and talked. Talked about Florence, about the Ponte Vecchio. Above all, they spoke about Fra Angelico's frescoes—where he'd first discovered realism (the realism of the fifteenth century)—and the way the painter introduces himself into the world of the saints and confers on them nobility and class. Fra Angelico himself, asked to be the archbishop of the city by Pope Eugene IV, refused so that he could go on tending to the sick and continue painting.

Gonzalo, who liked the David fine, preferred the Moses, a mature work that graces the sepulcher of Pope Julius II in Rome. Through her lover, she learned that Michelangelo suffered panic attacks and was convinced that he was clairvoyant. The sculptor did not shape the marble a little at a time. Rather, he entered into the stone, tearing off layers of the material, making the brow first so that the extremities appeared to be born of the block of stone itself. Sometimes, suddenly, he would throw down his hammer and chisel and whisper: *If I remain here one more minute, something awful will happen.* At such times, he'd buy a horse and go to Bologna or to Rome. The first time this happened to him, in 1492, it was after the death of Lorenzo de Medici, the Mæcenas under whose influence he had learned to prefer Plato to Saint Augustine or to Saint Paul. Sculpted around 1501, the David was chiseled by the violent blows of that tortured, insatiable sensibility—what Spengler called *the terrible* in the forms made by Michelangelo.

Her meetings with Gonzalo had all the allure of a forbidden adventure (he was married to a Belgian violinist who spent long periods of time on tour around the Continent) and she sensed that these escapades were a sort of substitute for the transgressive power that Bebo's words had bestowed on lovemaking. But even so, something rang false with the Chilean, perhaps that resolution to integrate himself into a culture of which they could never really be a part. She did like his odor, the gentle curvature of his upper back, accustomed to responding with authority, and the French tinge he added when pronouncing her name. Still, Gonzalo never awakened in her the viscous luxury, the wild shudders, the multiple orgasms her body experienced with the ungrateful Bebo— just that year he'd completed a sentence in Havana penitentiary for stealing cotton from the hospital where he'd been working.

She was thinking of all this as she walked toward the Galleria della Accademia, passing the Annunziata, listening to the discussions and the emphatic judgments of the Florentines, already able to make out the imposing marble statue at the end of the passage. *To free the image within the stone, ridding it of all that is superfluous, of the slag that imprisons it inside the raw material.* That was what Michelangelo had wanted before he completely lost his patience, when his sensibility was still directed toward that sense of eternity, of distance, and not yet to the eroticism of the fleeting moment. He, too, had allowed the slag to penetrate the form and become the mannerist of the Rondanini Pietá. And there before her, at last, was the David, the embodiment of all this patience, with his powerful neck, curly hair, and enormous hands so wise and experienced in the art of caressing Bathsheba. And still, she could not determine whether this David was also the recently liberated Bebo: the one who ten years ago had refused to accompany her to the dance at the Tropical; the one with the voice like a waterfall, who had never ceased to whisper in her ear his tender filth and irrevocable decisions; and, above all, the Bebo of a few months back on Havana's everlasting Malecón, when she—desperate and sure that he was her *special man*, refusing to listen to Clarita's advice—had spoken to him of her possible divorce, of leaving Jacques for good so that she could have him, so that she could rescue him from this inferno of poverty and take him with her, show him the Piazza San Firenze, Botticelli's *Spring*, teach him to drink rosé and speak Italian.

And yet again Bebo disguised as David—with his face slightly tilted, slingshot slung back over his shoulder, his body ready for a life-and-death battle before the enemies of his people, humming a song about a faithless woman and the torments her betrayal have cost him—refused to take her once more to the little room in San Lázaro Street, now shored up to keep it from falling down, the wooden window frames eaten away by termites. He preferred enduring the continual police interrogation, the snooping around the exit doors of the Tropical, the certainty of the elemental truths sung by the latest salsero—"You left and lost it all/I stayed, and now I'm king"—at peace with an incomprehensible, one could almost say maniacal, determination.

THE HUNTER

Leonardo Padura Fuentes
Translated by Harry Morales

Compact powder is a mild comfort on the cheeks. Creamy and reliable, its scent dominates the sense of smell and for an instant he almost forgets to dab the powder puff gently on this shadow under the eyes to blot out the bad night and the persistent traces of juvenile acne from a childhood already gone by. Something somewhat ghostly remains on his face when he looks at his reflection in the mirror. The eyebrow pencil, barely a little stub, is difficult to handle, it's so small. He moistens the rough, black charcoal pencil with saliva and only then starts to draw it across the left eyelid, which becomes taut outlining the roundness of the eye, giving it a graceful Chinese shape. And then the right eyelid. Now he darkens his eyebrows, the pencil passing back and forth, creating a slight yet provocative angle pointing upward, forming a sustained wink. Faint music arrives from the living room while he paints his face and mentally sings every song from that fabulous Simon and Garfunkel concert in Central Park. The Chinese-made air conditioner is running on high, stirring his robe, but nothing bothers him more than an unexpected, furtive drop of sweat unpityingly marking the makeup that he takes great pain in perfecting. Sky-blue shadow now covers the eyelids—he adores blue, it's always been his color—which move rapidly, dazzling the eyes that look at the image of those same eyes in the oval of the mirror. With rouge he starts to outline his lips in a burning scarlet, but stops. Delicately, he also shades the highest region of his cheekbones and it's as if he had blushed. Then he returns to his mouth, painstakingly works on it, and puts the charcoal pencil into its case. With a natural and precise gesture he brings his lips together, presses one against the other, and when he returns them to their original position, the mouth is a red rose, open, perfumed, warm. With his thin and spatulate fingers, he musses his just-washed hair, which falls softly, as if carelessly, across his forehead. Now is when he stops singing "Mrs. Robinson" in his head; now, he only has the eyes and the mind to admire himself in the mirror: the eyelids delineated and covered by a blue cloud; the smooth and lightly flushed cheeks; the reddened, mature lips. He feels, rejoices in, and enjoys the beauty of his face, the tangible reality of his conquered loveliness, the desire to please men and feel love, masculine heat and rugged lips like Anselmo's that from the first kiss swallow the makeup.

Before he starts to cry, he dips a ball of cotton into the cream and starts to rub away the work in which he invested twenty minutes of learned skills and repressed desires, and while he recovers his original eyes, lips, and cheeks, he asks himself why life gave him what he didn't want.

Outside, the night is full of promises. He adores these clear and fresh April nights, so good for walking around in La Habana. While he puts on his pants, adjusts his belt, places his keys and money in his pockets, he thinks about where he'll go. Deciding is always difficult and he doesn't know why it's even more so now. He has a presentiment that this could be a special night and he fears that a wrong choice perhaps will thwart an encounter that is already written in the stars. In reality, every night that he doesn't feel depressed he thinks that something is going to happen, and afterward, when nothing has happened, it's worse in the solitude of his unshared bed. He finishes dressing, likes how his shirt looks tucked inside his pants, and goes into the kitchen of his apartment. He takes out a quart of milk and pours a small amount in his cat's dish, asking himself, "Where is that bandit hiding?" He takes a piece of cloth, wipes away the wet imprint left by the quart on the table and once again the kitchen is immaculate, the way he likes it.

"El Vedado or La Habana?" he asks himself. If it's destiny, then destiny already knows. Before going out, he looks at himself in the mirror for the last time and places a few drops of perfume on his neck. On the street he walks slowly toward the bus stop without stepping on the lines in the sidewalk. Now he starts to get nervous, as his future depends on the first bus that destiny sends, bound for Vedado or old Havana. Were it his choice, he would prefer the surroundings of Vedado, even though, truthfully, the street has changed tremendously and it's now difficult to meet someone classy among all the crazy, bitchy men. In La Habana Vieja, he's annoyed by those depressed people who hang around El Capitolio and La Fraternidad, with their aggressive desperation and insulting vulgarity. Six minutes later, destiny sends him an almost empty bus—given the state of transportion this has to be destiny—which travels along a route that ends at El Prado, the major hunting grounds of Havana.

Night was made for hunting, and prey roams through the city jungle. Anyone can be attacked, but not everyone falls into the traps. One has to have a sense of smell and know what to make of the shots, avoid scandalous failures and possible misunderstandings that don't help anyone. He learned these lessons from Ever, the friend who initiated him in the most sophisticated pleasures of love and the mysteries of the hunt. But Ever had a special grace that he lacked, and that he was sure he would never attain.

The yellowish lights of El Prado, the intense traffic noise, and the unrestrained persecution of tricks in search of a stranger and a dollar, have taken away all the charm this area once had; now it's worked only by desperate men who accept anything and risk suffering the worst consequences at the hands of professional hustlers. Nevertheless, he walks slowly toward Parque Central, appraising every look, weighing every gesture, studying every possibility. He's still euphoric; the nine o'clock cannon shot has barely sounded and there are many hours ahead; the good couplings occur around eleven. As he walks, he takes in his surroundings; he imagines how things could be. He's tired of short-lived relationships, often so traumatic, which end in premature disillusionment or abandonment. His regular friends, with their cups of sweet-smelling tea, selections of classical music, familiar gossip, and usual sentimentality, have never been able to satisfy him completely. He needs to find a man like Anselmo again, a male from head to toe, who is also capable of understanding why one could fall in love with him and capable, for that same reason, of returning love. Those never-to-be-repeated months he lived with Anselmo have marked him forever; three years later, his heart still beats wildly and his skin becomes cold when he sees the dark face, the full mustache, and the pair of eyes that evoke the person he has loved the most in his life. He would like never again to remember the terrible days that followed their breakup; Anselmo told him he had met a woman and thought he was in love with her. It was then that he knew loneliness had crawled into his bed again, that their nights of clean and unbridled love were ending, their unforgettable afternoons in the most discreet reaches of the beach, when they played naked in the ocean, when he felt Anselmo's lukewarm fluid falling on his hands despite the cold water, dissolving into a wave, infertile just like him. Damn, how he had loved him! Depressed, what foolish things he'd done to stun himself with the crazy whores from Coppelia, those unstable, wandering, unrestrained pleasure-seekers who give it all up according to the hazard of a public bathroom, the risk of a dark stairway, the uncertainty of shelter in some park bush, forgoing the plenitude of a clean, well-tended bed and, in the morning before work, a shared breakfast and a deep kiss with the taste of a man.

But it's much too early for El Prado, he thinks when he arrives at the end of the avenue. He'll return later and maybe lady luck will favor him; after all he's a Capricorn, he tells himself. He crosses Neptuno and enters Parque Central trying to find an empty bench. In front of him there are two lines of people on the sidewalk: one is for the pizzeria and the other is for taxis for the tourists. He doesn't see anyone who could interest him, though. There is an empty bench along the main path of the park, and he rushes to claim it. The truth is, it's a beautiful night, and he's prepared to wait, watch, and scrutinize.

In one corner of the park there is a group of more than twenty men, who are discussing baseball. They're all talking at the same time and even he barely hears a few shouts that dominate the solid chatter. On the other side of the street the lobby of the theater is now empty. The ballet began at 8:30 and he imagines the euphoria of the aficionados—I can't stand them—who have come to see Josefina and Aurora, and are so eager to feel like them: slender, languid, praised. Surely, they've put on their best garb, and totally moved by each formidable gesture their dance goddesses make, they grab at each other's sweaty hands so that they can then scream, "Dyke," with an irreverent and unbearable unfurling of feathers thrust in the air. My God, he can't stand them.

If only he wasn't so shy. He's going to be thirty-eight and he can count the meaningful relationships he's had on the fingers of both hands. In reality, he can count them on ten fingers because he has never wanted to include the crazy flings he had after Anselmo left him. What would really be incalculable is the number of pla-tonic loves he's had and which his timidity impeded him from developing into full romance. At his job, he has loved three co-workers to tears, but for sure this never crossed their minds. The worst of his infatuations was with Wilfredo, chief of propaganda. He'll never know what he saw in that skinny, pale, obsessive man who still possessed that peasant look and clothes so outdated that they went out of style in 1970. Maybe Wilfredo's helplessness and listlessness were indications of a love never solidified because of his own unredeemable timidity. He could have ensnared Wilfredo with a couple of invitations to dine on his spaghetti carbonara and go to the theater, but for some reason he couldn't pursue him at work. Neither deep down nor on the surface did he want the rest of his co-workers to know the truth—although a few of them must know already. The fear of possible reprisals had turned him into a clandestine hunter and street rambler who only went out into the city at night thinking that the man of his dreams—who looked so much like Anselmo—would appear in some park, movie theater, or maybe even on a bus.

He knew that if only he weren't so timid, one day he would go out into the street with his best makeup on and scream out what he wanted to feel; he would be prettier and crazier than the craziest crazy woman. But he just can't stand them.

Couples, unaccompanied men and women, and the most daring tricks—who are willing to do anything for those magic, yearned-for dollars that are capable of turning into shiny Adidas sneakers, Levi's, Ocean Pacific T-shirts in a thousand garish colors, and even bottles of whiskey for those with more exotic taste—are walking on the main path in the park. Old people, policemen, newspaper vendors, and students still in their school uniforms are also walking there. Any one of them could be the one he has been waiting for, so he eyes discreetly each potential candidate and sometimes, when the presentiment grows stronger, gives a subtle nod.

Nothing happens, but there is no reason to become impatient either. He decides to go by the Payret movie theater, because—as Ever always says—like everything in life, one has to hunt down the prey. At the movie theater, the lit marquee announces that the present film will also be shown at midnight. It is more than ten o'clock and there are a few night owls waiting for the midnight show line to form. He eliminates everyone who is accompanied by a woman, appraises the rest one by one, and then as if absentminded, walks among them while they wait on line. He looks at them, asks one of them for matches, another one about the movie, and one more for the time, because his watch is slow.

"Mine is too," says the young man regretfully.

He is eighteen and dressed discreetly and carries a briefcase underneath his arm. His eyes are green, and a distinctive forehead predicts premature baldness.

He feels his heart beat faster, but tells himself no, things never repeat themselves. That young man looks too much like Juan Carlos, he met him in the same place he had encountered Juan Carlos, and he asked him the same questions he had asked Juan Carlos. He knows he can't be so lucky twice. Before Anselmo, Juan Carlos had been his most intense and important relationship. Juan Carlos was barely twenty-one when they met and he became Juan Carlos's teacher in the ways of love, just as he himself had once been Ever's student. But Juan

Carlos turned out to be a disappointment: he became a raging, crazy bitch, like the kind who go around in gangs; the original purity of their relationship became lost forever.

He looks at the young man's briefcase and asks him if he has just gotten out of school.

"The School for Languages," the young man replies, "on Manzana de Gomez."

"English?" he asks.

"No, German," the young man says, smiling. "I'm a biochemist, and a great deal of the reading material is in German."

"But do you like that language?" he asks.

"I don't know about liking it, but I still have to learn it to get it, and you know what that's like," says the young man.

"And why are you going to the movies so late?" he asks.

"There's no alternative," says the young man. "I work during the day, go to school at night, and my weekends are always busy."

"My God, how boring!" he exclaims, and offers the young man a cigarette.

"Thanks, but I don't smoke," says the young man.

His heart is beating uncontrollably. Juan Carlos didn't smoke either, and going to the movies was what he liked to do most in the world. Like the Juan Carlos he once knew, this is a handsome, normal, shy young man whose green eyes can weaken one's knees with one look. He imagines him in his apartment, asking to hear a certain cassette, approving of the taste of the fritters, letting himself drop, tired, onto the sofa, and then talking and talking; asking him to stay the night, his hand on his thigh, remarking how late it is and the buses.... Will he go to bed with him? Will he kiss that young man with those green eyes, visibly shy, caress and embrace him to asphyxiation and then finally mount him, let him enjoy a stranger's hardness driven into his innards?

"Excuse me," says the young man, "but I have to make a phone call. My wife should have been here at ten o'clock."

"Don't worry about it," he says, and almost feels like hitting him.

He returns to the Parque Central where nothing has changed, although the discussion about baseball has ended and car noise filters through the air. It is now past eleven and there are more empty benches, but he doesn't want to sit down. He is furious and weary and refuses to spend another night alone. No sooner is he in El Prado than he comes across the persistent tricks who are pursuing some Italians and a few couples kissing indiscreetly, just to make them jealous.

The last time he saw Anselmo he was with his wife and he was carrying a child who was a year and several months old. They were walking along number 23 when he spotted and recognized them from more than a block away. He didn't feel the usual wild beating of his heart, nor his skin turning cold: this time it really was Anselmo, and his presence was so forceful he thought that he would faint on the spot. He couldn't talk, let alone have the strength to move. Anselmo had shaved off his mustache, and his wife was blonder than he had imagined, with wide hips and a face that was becoming more beautiful the closer she approached. His mind was a cyclone of jealousies, romances, memories, nostalgia, and the renewed hatred of an abandoned person. Eventually, he managed to make a half turn and left before Anselmo could see him.

He returns along Louvre Street. The pizzeria is closed, but the line of taxis is still there ready for service. No sooner has the theater let out than a small group of crazy balletomaniacs in the lobby begins to comment on the performance, coloring the dialogue with a few little screams, short pauses, and a pitiful *fouetté*. They're such queers! Once again he feels the urge to hit somebody, to hurt and humiliate them. He crosses the street and heads toward Parque Central.

He doesn't stop to look toward the benches. He crosses Zulueta Street and goes through the No Admittance doors of the Centro Asturiano. The stench of dry urine accumulated over the years assaults him, but he endures the sudden onslaught until he comes out on Floridita, which is closed for repairs. He turns right, jumps over puddles of more recent urine, and finds himself in the dark, where an enormous black man, leaning against a pillar, his legs flexed attempting to penetrate a young woman who is repressing her wails of pleasure— or pain?

He doesn't want to go by the Payret movie theater again. He feels empty, yet full of hatred, lust, and desperation. He can no longer endure the loneliness that gnaws at the weeks and months. It hurts him to know that there are happy people, and he almost wants to be like the crazy, bitchy men and scream that he needs a man, a man, a man.

He doesn't want to do it, but he walks to the end of Capitolio and positions himself on a short staircase, prepared to wait, to hunt. It is now past midnight and there's always prey at that hour, although it isn't hunting down an Anselmo, a Juan Carlos, an Ever, nor even a fickle egocentric like Niño Antonio. Two couples, a soldier, and three women who look like cheap whores pass by, looking at him, soliciting. Two young men, one white and one black, also pass by and go into the corner of an old building to smoke very quickly a tiny cigarette that has a foul smell, like wet grass. Then he sees him approaching. He is the one: he is eighteen, clean-shaven, and caresses his chest while he walks. There are many like him, although it is strange that he is alone. Perhaps he's been abandoned, like me, he thought. No, he doesn't want to call out to him, he tells himself, he doesn't want to go back to the staircases, the half-demolished buildings, and the fear. He isn't interested in that perverted and arrogant kid who exhibits his precocious homosexuality like a coat of arms.

Nor can he continue being alone, hunting unsuccessfully every night, smelling like masturbation, waiting for the miracle of love. He needs to give himself over to someone or have someone give himself over to him.

"Listen, kid, do me a favor," he tells him.

He closes the door and slides the bolts. He places his shirt on the sofa and takes off his shoes without untying his shoelaces. He goes to the bathroom and looks at himself in the mirror before he washes his injured hands. The usual dark circles under his eyes have grown into enormous bulbs that are about to come loose. He tries to spit out the bitter taste that tortures his mouth, and the vomit surprises him. It is a deep retch coming from the pit of his stomach that pushes open his lips. When it is over, the dark circles have gotten bigger. He hates his reflection in the mirror and hates his hands that, unexpectedly, had begun to hit that young man who had quite shamelessly offered himself to him. It was an unforeseen yet logical impulse, like the retching, something that had occurred in a simple manner and that he couldn't stop. The young man, without screaming and barely protecting his face, ended up looking like an aborted fetus underneath that staircase where they had made love.

He undresses and sits on the toilet bowl. While he is urinating, he starts to cry, almost without tears, but with a few deep, sorrowful snorts. He doesn't recognize himself, nor does he know who he is or what he did. He also doesn't want to go into the bedroom and see the empty bed where he will sleep alone again, again, and again. And then he thinks he should end it all.

He had been beset by suicidal impulses for a long time: they come when he feels ill and is afraid to suffer alone; when he feels good and wants to share his euphoria and doesn't have anyone to share it with; and when he goes out to hunt and returns home alone. He knows that because he wants to do it so badly, one day he will, and thinks that this morning must be that day.

Naked, he walks into the kitchen. He looks for the sharpest knife in one of the drawers and notices that the cat's milk dish is still full. "Where is that cat hiding?" he wonders, and looks out the window, trying to find some trace of his cat, considering how much it likes milk.

"That one is roaming around nearby, in love, hunting."
He looks at the knife with which he is going to cut his
wrists. It's going to be a complete relief: the memory of
Anselmo will end, the shyness, the successful and unsuc-
cessful hunts, and above all, the loneliness and the
double life that deplete his energy, and even his happiness. Sitting on the edge of the bed—empty, empty—he
studies his arms. He clenches his fists and sees the
blue—his favorite color—of his veins rise slightly. He
thinks that perhaps Anselmo will never know about his
death, that his father will be happy to be rid of him, that
he doesn't have anyone he can write a good-bye letter to,
and while his weeping comforts him and the snorts are
ending, he thinks that it was all the work of destiny. He
looks at his blue veins again, opens his right hand, and
then the knife clanks to the floor like a bell out of tune.

"Oh, Anselmo," he says, and he lays himself to rest
upon the mattress.

THE TROPICS

Miguel Mejides

Translated by Clara Marín

Humboldt held Mrs. NG's pinkie and placed a kiss on it. Mrs. NG woke up startled and said smack!—imitating the sound of the kiss—and smiled. Then she realized that she had wet herself and ran to the bathroom, and for the first time she mentioned the word *flee*.

This happened just two days ago, and now she is in the tropics, floating like a dolphin in the ocean and looking at the scenery of the hotel where she has rented a room loaded with Caribbean paraphernalia. "What's better, fish or dreams?" she thinks, and at the same time remembers.

After Humboldt's kiss on the pinkie—which had been preceded by a violent love scene—Mrs. NG decided to give herself a vacation. She paid a quick visit to her friend the Hungarian and handed over her son to be taken care of for two weeks. She didn't mind, but inquired about the reason for such an insane decision. Mrs. NG brought up the word *flee* again and walked away on the boring Frankfurt avenues, and at noon she entered the Morocco Salsa and demanded child support from her ex-husband. The latter, screaming like a true Venezuelan, went from accusing her of sleeping with one of her students from the Conservatory to practically begging her to give their marriage another try, and finally handed her the money.

Mrs. NG paid no attention to him, and just as the travel agency downtown near the train station was about to close, she reserved a ticket to Cuba for the next day. Toward the end of the afternoon she went to her parents' house, knocked on the door, and nobody answered. She mumbled something about fear, trips, and the lack of love, and headed home. Once there, after having something to eat, she put on the record player and lay down on her bed. All she could think about was that at seven in the morning she would be getting on a plane to Cuba.

Now, yes right now, she is on the beach and is still looking at the scenery. Occasionally she gets upset with her fellow countrymen who, sheltered by the coconut palms, curse the nights of orgies and question themselves for not using condoms, which are practically impossible to find on the island.

Upon her return to the hotel—and only here does this story begin—she watches the beach men. With the last traces of light, between the cove grape shrubs that make up a path to the doors of the hotel, boys appear with their flies open. Mrs. NG, who has paid to see men undress in a club in Frankfurt, is horrified. She thinks that her friend the Hungarian would be pleased to see such different and attractive penises. In the early evening, Mrs. NG misses her friend's perfumes, her aromas. However, she stares at the young man walking toward her smiling, with his hair parted in the middle and a book of poetry by Lord Byron under his arm.

—It's snowing now in Frankfurt, says Mrs. NG in Spanish with an east Venezuelan accent, lying next to the bathtub. Snow is very white this time of year. Have you ever seen snow?
—In movies, says Tito.

Mrs. NG can't fathom that a human being could live without ever having seen snow. She thinks that something should happen so that the freezing weather could reach the tropics. After such thoughts, she lets herself fall into the bathtub water and becomes a transparent woman. Tito watches the scorpions, the ants, the dragonflies traveling through the rivers of Mrs. NG's life. Tito soon gets bored. He paces back and forth in the room, fishes in the icebox for a beer, notices the labels on the piled-up cans, sniffs the case with razors, lipsticks, makeup that Mrs. NG keeps cold so that they don't rot in the treacherous heat. He goes toward the closet and examines a dress, black as a butterfly for a dance, the wool pajamas, the brassieres that engird Mrs. NG's entire body. He says something like here you would fry with those fucking clothes. Mrs. NG doesn't listen to him because she is floating in a sea of salts. She is traveling through a storm of southern scents. She dreams again of Humboldt, of his drum-taut stomach, of mulattas spying on him to then lay him in a state of ecstasy so similar to

sudden death. Tito looks at Mrs. NG's wallet. First the
driver's license, then the picture that must be of her
son—the same boy in the silver picture frame on the
bureau. Then the money: the marks, the adorned Queens
Elizabeth, and most abundantly the dollars, with their
inscription of deep faith in God.

Outside, in the hallway, whispering is heard, an
almost inaudible dialogue. Tito realizes that it is the discussion of someone trying to convince a chambermaid to
knock on the door to the room he is enjoying with Mrs.
NG. The maid refuses and the man insists. It's almost
three in the morning and the hotel is still vibrating with
its crazy timeless life. Mrs. NG has started to sing a
German folk song. Tito has finished his beer and now he
pours himself half a glass of whiskey. To accompany Mrs.
NG, he starts clapping, and dances to the beat of the
strange melody.

Morning has sneaked up on Tito and now he won't
be able to leave the room until nightfall. The guards'
stern watchfulness won't allow it. Mrs. NG can't seem to
grasp that natives are forbidden to share a room with a
foreigner. Tito reacts to the word *native*. He opens Lord
Byron's tome and reads the poem in which a British man
makes fun of imperial German pride. Mrs. NG laughs
with such irreverence that it obliterates the nationalistic
implications, and she says that for her, the Germans are
children who can only be still while going from
preparing for one war to the next. Then, with cautious
sobriety, she takes out the hashish and in it finds an
escape from the seclusion that she is just beginning to
experience. Her Hungarian friend had stocked her up
generously, with the excuse that there is no better place

than the tropics to revive the senses. It is true that, on other occasions, Mrs. NG has smoked hashish, marijuana. But that was in her first youth, at group-sex parties, during her student years at the Conservatory.

—If my mother could see me, she'd kill me, says Mrs. NG.

—Why?

—She always told me that I could sleep with anyone I wanted, but not with a black man.

—It's always sad, those people who don't like blacks.

Now Mrs. NG remembers the baths during those harsh winters in Dusseldorf. She still hadn't managed to flee to Frankfurt; they lived in a little attic, and every Saturday her mother would move the furniture out of the way to make room for a bathtub. The family would strip and throw buckets of water on each other. Her mother would shamelessly lather up her wrinkled old stomach. Her father, who worked in a steel mill, filled the entire house with a metallic smell. The girl NG saw with wonderment that hanging thing below the father's waist. On one occasion—now she didn't know exactly at what age—as she was getting out of the tub, she grabbed onto her father's member. She had used it like a handle, with an innocent jerk, and with that momentum had gotten out of the water. Father and mother cracked up, and in time there wasn't a party or family gathering at which they didn't bring it up.

—You have a nice one, Mrs. NG tells Tito. I wish you had my name there, she says in a flattering tone, that you

would walk naked through the streets of Frankfurt and
everyone would read my name.

Mrs. NG can no longer stand the seclusion and decides to
go to the pool. As she exits the room, she notices next to
the door a man sitting on a canvas chair. The man
smokes a cigar and is wearing white pants, white shoes, a
guayabera, and on his head a Panama hat. The man is
holding a frond fan, which he passes from one hand to
the other. When he sees Mrs. NG, he starts babbling
about something. She tries to meet his gaze and notices
that he has very small eyes. At the pool, Mrs. NG realizes
that the waiter is staring at her like a monkey caught
doing something obscene. She has taken off her top and
is warming her breasts in the sun. The waiter is a sad
young man, who works every day at the hotel pool. From
nine in the morning until well into the night, the waiter
serves the tourists, going back and forth, not laughing
much, watching. With the tips of her fingers, Mrs. NG
puts on suntan lotion. By turns she lifts each of her
breasts from underneath, stretches them to release them
from the constriction that clothes have imposed on them
for so many years. The waiter stares and stares, comes
and goes. The waiter doesn't know whether to look at the
faraway beach, or at Mrs. NG's breasts. Just to get her
kicks, she orders a piña colada. As the waiter brings it, he
loses his balance and spills the piña colada. Mrs. NG
tastes the piña colada and spins around and dives into the
pool. Feeling the warm water, she remembers her son. In
Frankfurt there are those filthy indoor pools, protected
from winter. Sometimes she takes her son, and he swims
like a boy fish. What are you doing now? she thinks.

When she returns to her piña colada, she sees that next to the bar they are setting up a platform. A sign announces something she can't make out. Mrs. NG puts on the top to her bathing suit and calls the waiter, and asks him why there is so much commotion.

—"The great magician's show," he answers.

Mrs. NG thinks again about her friend the Hungarian, her smell, her small body. Then she imagines a winter with that sun that is now in the middle of the sky and that soon will overtake noon. She stays like that for a good hour, until she decides to go back to her room. A big sign announces the Great Cipolla, magician, illusionist, and necromancer.

Moving on, she realizes that the man from the night before has disappeared from the hallway. She stops on the tiles where the canvas chair had been. She feels hatred, and can't explain the sudden nausea that in a flash has reminded her of all the people that she has wanted dead.

—"The man? The chair?" she asks the chambermaid who walks by her.

The woman gestures that she doesn't know and keeps walking. The woman is young, black. Mrs. NG has the feeling that she has seen her somewhere, perhaps in a dream, but she can't place her.

Mrs. NG finds a tremendous mess in her room. Her clothes have disappeared, so has the suitcase, and the wallet with her money. Even the picture of her son in the silver frame is gone. And not even the smell of Tito remains. Mrs. NG feels like crying. It's such a deep rage that she begins to tear up the pillows. The room turns into one of those crystal weights in which it snows beautifully. The only thing Tito has left is the Byron poetry, the credit cards, and the winter dress. She reproaches herself for ever having looked at that contemptible black boy. Furiously, in German, she curses all the generations that came before him, shamelessly proclaims the supremacy of the white race, and promises to persecute every black person on earth.

She lies down and can't hold back the tears. She cries like when she was a child. She cries, in a heap, bent like an *s*, sucking on her thumb. She remains that way until she falls asleep. When she awakes, it's dark, and she feels free of her circumstances. It's always that way with her. During the first moments, her impulsive reaction leads her to plan her revenge and she even manages to think about a possible murder. Then sleep takes care of her hatred and, once again, she becomes the ingenuous Mrs. NG.

At exactly nine o'clock, the group of tourists is seated facing the stage. The waiter bustles about serving beers and crispy french fries. The night is beautiful, lovely, cool. A breeze blows from the ocean and everything seems enchanted. Mrs. NG has turned the night into a slogan. The day before the trip, she read so many tourist pamphlets that now her mind reacts with stereotypes. While meditating on this, the stage lights are turned on and a beardless man appears.

The little man speaks in terrible English, then in just-as-awful German, and finally in side-show Spanish.

He presents the Great Cipolla from the Egyptian cata-
combs, resuscitated in Jerusalem, who has chosen the
tropics to end his millennarian existence.

A loud band plays a guaracha, and the Great Cipolla
appears onstage. He is wearing the same white shoes that
Mrs. NG saw in the morning, although he has changed
the rest of his attire. A pair of latex pants outlines his
mousy testicles, and he has covered himself with a long
cape of lace, which gives the performance a vernacular
flair.

Onstage the Great Cipolla seems younger than he is.
Without the hat, the necromancer's extreme black hair
gleams with hair tonic. Without uttering a word, the
Great Cipolla takes a magic wand and waves it a few
times around a magician's box. He takes off the cover to
show it's empty. He closes it again, and with three waves
of the wand he breaks the ties and two macaws fly out, to
perch on the rings on one side of the stage.

The applause livens up the tourists. However, Mrs.
NG has not been won over by this enthusiasm. In Torre
di Venere, the other Cipolla—or perhaps this one—had
managed the same thing. Perhaps now will come the
hypnotism, the changing of personalities that agitates
the human soul to the point of pain.

Mrs. NG swallows dryly, clenches her fists, and says
to herself, You will not be dominated by this perverse
mind. Even if they all follow him, she will resist. At that
precise moment, the Great Cipolla comes up to her and
says very softly: "Lady, in the Tropic of Cancer, everything changes!"

Agile, followed by an unknown shadow, he returns to
the stage and the music fires up the people again. Cipolla

begins juggling, then he reads the cards which he hands out to the audience; he laughs freely as he turns his wand into a handkerchief, and cries openly when the macaws fly off into the night.

That is when the shrill clamor stops completely. Cipolla announces the much-awaited transmutation, boasts about his power to change a woman into a man or vice versa. He travels all the way to the end of the stage and drags back a trunk. He takes the chains off and shows that it, too, is empty. Then he closes it and with shaking typical of African rituals, saying the magic words, everything comes alive, begins to reverberate, to fill with smoke. The Great Cipolla, with one arrogant movement, uncovers the trunk, and a black girl—the maid that Mrs. NG had intercepted in the hall at noon—appears like a ghost.

The girl steps out of the trunk. She is wearing a simple stewardess dress, white blouse and blue skirt with an apron, and shoes with graceful heels. The girl reminds Mrs. NG of her friend the Hungarian. Observing her carefully, she recognizes the same shape around the hips as the Hungarian, the same sense of self, and maybe the girl is made more sensual by the dark shadow above her lips.

Cipolla begins to speak of feminine selves that men, with their games, keep hidden beneath the pillow. He says that he has witnessed medieval metamorphoses— women dressed as priests, men who wore nuns' habits.

—"Nothing in the world is new, everything repeats itself," he declares in a listless voice. Then, without further ado, he returns the girl to the trunk, locks her in.

Again, the music stops. All that is heard is the Great Cipolla's uneven breath.

—"They are changing skins, feelings, memories, biographies, dreams!" he says. He gives an order and the band is heard again. He opens the trunk and out comes Tito, Tito who had escaped a few hours before, the same Tito with his hair parted down the middle, wrapped in a sheet, his eyes so bewildered that they look as though they're going to pop out. Mrs. NG has stood up. Cipolla looks at her sarcastically. Mrs. NG waits for Cipolla's order to make her the laughingstock of the colony of tourists. She waits for him to make her bark, meow, throw herself on the floor. But Cipolla wants none of that. His patience, his enjoyment, lies in the moment of dominance. Ridicule never gives him the same pleasure as surprise.

—"That's all, ladies and gentlemen!" he says. The lights go out, the music slowly dies out, the applause dissipates.

As Mrs. NG places her key in the lock, tired from the creamy midnight heat, she doesn't expect to go back in time. She yearns for a demiurge to appear and end Cipolla's harm. Nevertheless, she finds in her room all of the belongings that had disappeared at noon: the suitcases on the bureau, her son's picture intact in its silver frame, the wallet with money, the closet doors open and the dresses hanging. In the bathroom, the makeup, the creams, the hair conditioners, all the supplies of a traveling woman. And best of all, she finds Tito wrapped in the sheets.

—Forgive me, NG, he begs.

She says nothing. She is about to tell him to leave, but feels pity. At that very moment Cipolla is surely about to place his canvas chair in the hallway and begin his lurking vigilance for the rest of the night. Because of that, Mrs. NG doesn't want to find an explanation for Tito's return, doesn't want to find an explanation for the return of each of her belongings. A diabolical or heavenly justice has returned them. She believes that justice has the right to condemn appropriation, but not to punish it with the pretext of necromancies. She vows never to return to the tropics, that in the morning she will reserve a seat on the first flight to Frankfurt.

Mrs. NG has also been punished. The Great Cipolla punished her in front of everyone. Now she has Tito by her side again, and her soul is empty, nothing keeps her from, nor brings her close to, love. She could no longer sleep next to him, stand the touch of his long legs. Always concerned with taking the untraveled roads, seeking adventures, she has never loved anyone. Perhaps her friend the Hungarian is the only person with whom she has felt transported into a communion of the souls. But Mrs. NG's heart cannot belong to another woman; perhaps, in a moment of lust, she can share a sublime caress, but intimately she needs a man.

Tito insists that she lie down. She refuses and grabs a pillow and goes to the bathtub. Lying there, on water-proof tiles, she thinks about the stupid discussion she had many years ago with a friend at boarding school where she had slept in a bathtub for the first time. Now, a mature woman, once again she's on the cold tiles. She ponders how pleasant it would have been to have traveled with her violin; when she was young, she dreamed of being a great concert violinist. With time she realized that she would never be successful. She taught, she had a lover who was still a boy and would only bite her nipples. How crazy had her life been? Why did life put her through such tests and conceal the future? She entertained these thoughts until dawn. Then she fell asleep and saw Humboldt dressed up in a silk suit. Humboldt was putting on and taking off a three-cornered hat.

The early-morning rain is strangely enchanting in the tropics; a captivating dewy light comes off the ocean while the waves take over the beach. Then, it rains with sudden fury, the sun shows itself, and a wet-greenness gets a clean day on its way.

—It has stopped raining, says Mrs. NG.

—"Toast and coffee?" asks the lunch waiter.

Mrs. NG gives a barely audible *yes*. Her bad mood reached its peak a little while ago, even with the sifting of the recent rain. Once again, Mrs. NG found the Great Cipolla in the hallway. As she walked past him, she tried to ascertain if he was sleeping in his canvas chair. Under the Panama hat, she was able to make out the necromancer's shiny red complexion. Cipolla, without becoming agitated, made a movement that seemed completely intentional, and Mrs. NG was able to see, on his lap, a tricolor rooster. Mrs. NG was about to say something insulting, but instead she chose to walk away and go reserve a seat on Saturday's flight to Frankfurt.

—"Did you see the movie they showed on TV last night, ma'am?" asked the lunch waiter.

Mrs. NG doesn't answer. She's now debating how to kill Cipolla.

—"I never get sick of seeing it," continued the waiter in that tireless monotonous tone so characteristic of people in his line of work.

A god cannot offer prayers to himself, nor can the devil exorcise himself. Cipolla won't be able to defend himself; he'll never believe a woman capable of killing him. With what weapons? How to plan the crime? wonders Mrs. NG.

—"The best scene is when Al Pacino takes his brother by the cheeks and slaps him a little, and then gives him the kiss of death. That was in Havana, you know. It was around New Year's that Al Pacino was in Havana."

The sand is pliant and will cover up a murder. A few shovels full and Cipolla will be forever concealed on a beach. But has he several lives? Mario, that boy from Torre de Venere, didn't he kill him?

—In these hotels there are no adventures like in the movies. It's the same thing day after day. Toast, coffee, the same thing. Nothing happens in a hotel.
—No, I want no part in a killing, says Tito.
—But nonetheless you are in Cipolla's hands, answers Mrs. NG.

—Maybe he wants you and not me.
—Why me?
—I was his prisoner and he let me go.
—He's in the hallway, waiting for you to come out.
—No, I'm just an excuse for him to get what he wants.
—Then get out! Go on, leave!
—Impossible. Then I cease to be an excuse and I become
a victim.

Mrs. NG thinks about not having hemlock in her posses-
sion, or that horrible substitute, a dried hummingbird's
heart. She doesn't have a simple rope to twist around
Cipolla's neck. There is just the bathtub in which to try
to drown him. He will never let himself be killed. He
threatens Tito with alerting the hotel management that
he is there, threats to expose the strategy of not wanting
the maids to make up the bed, the strategy of not
allowing them to clean the room or change the towels,
the strategy that has won her the reputation of a dirty
neurotic German. Tito brags about her not being able to
turn him in, saying he'll tell about the hashish, he'll
accuse her of kidnapping.

Mrs. NG insults him in German. For the second time
Mrs. NG doesn't order the succulent room-service dinners. She goes to the restaurant, and upon her return
talks about the dishes that were served, she praises the
prawns, the French sauces, the red snapper broiled with
salt. Tito has kept up his precarious pride. To alleviate his
hunger, he drank the muscatel wines and heavy cognacs.

The nights are never ending, endless nights with a
drunken Tito beating a tune on the armchairs, the doors,
the table. And the hotel, without waking up, without a

complaint, without any inclination to abort such malice. It's Cipolla's fault, thinks Mrs. NG lying in the tub, wanting to do away with the noises, with the night. It's his fault because the bickering is confined to these four walls, imprisoned with this percussion that doesn't penetrate any other part of the hotel. Cipolla has the power to control the agony of those blows; however, he does nothing. Mrs. NG thinks that she has come to the end of her rope. She misses her son, her house in Frankfurt, winter, her friend the Hungarian, and chestnuts.

In a few hours I'll be in the air, among the clouds. Who knows if Providence will be the one to condemn Cipolla. However, he seems eternal, indivisible, and he goes on with his shows, repeating the ostentatious and crude dirty tricks with cards, and at the end the tragicomedy with the trunk, now without Tito, just with the dark maid who has ended up like an offering for the night.

To leave, to liberate oneself and to forget the punishments, to go back to being a trustworthy German professor at the Conservatory, lover of classical music.

—"Who cares about the tropics? Snow! Snow!" she screams, floating in the enameled tub, naked like a fish caught in a net.

It's early, time to go, and Mrs. NG finds the tricolor rooster looking at itself in the bathroom mirror. The rooster's presence indicates Cipolla's inability to prevent her from leaving. The rooster shakes its Napoleonic crest and insists on looking at itself in the mirror. The rooster sets its jet-black eyes on the concave surface, takes short steps, steps of a lovestruck rooster. For an instant, Mrs. NG considers grabbing it, but she fears that the contact with its saffron-colored feathers will lead her into another event. Could this rooster be a bridge between humanity's repressive foulness and Cipolla's necromantic sophistry? No, let it stay there, looking at itself in the mirror.

Tito doesn't hear her leave the room. He sleeps like an angel, with measured breathing. Mrs. NG looks at him for a second, seemingly wanting to impress his image like a print on an old daguerreotype plate. She doesn't see Cipolla, either, just the forgotten canvas chair in the hallway.

She enters the lobby and is mortified by the haggard Germans drinking orange juice to cure their hangover. She pays her bills and calls a taxi. As she waits, she sees a rare night butterfly who has been surprised by dawn. The butterfly flies, bumps itself, threatens a quick getaway from the hotel lobby, and at the last minute lingers.

—"Witches," says Mrs. NG.

Once in the taxi, Mrs. NG watches the slow disappearance of that hotel built on a small peninsula surrounded by mango trees and coconut palms. She feels like she's coming out of a dream, waking up from the uncertainty of dreams. Her son and her friend the Hungarian are waiting for her, and she is comforted by that. Surely, while she's been gone, they've built a new skyscraper in Frankfurt. One of those crystal needles that appear in the autumn skies of Frankfurt. She still can't say good-bye to the ocean, because the car winds around the narrow channels. At this hour, Mrs. NG thinks, the beach police are beginning their job of scaring up the boys with their flies open. She doesn't care, she is leaving, going back to her world. The tropics, she tells herself, are a fetish. So much magic only lasts until the sun warms the ground with its unbearable heat.

—"How many kilometers to the airport?" she asks.
—"Thirty, ma'am," says the driver.

The ocean just reappeared. Now the car is driving next to it, next to this ocean that the incipient sun severs like a fakir split at the waist. It's an ocean that is half dark, half joyful, half sunny, half in shadow. In the distance all you can see are three figures running against the waves. Having them there, next to the window, Mrs. NG realizes that evil always accompanies those who leave. The Great Cipolla trots along the beach, and in front of him are the dark maid and Tito. They both search the sand and sniff around and bark. The Great Cipolla laughs, showing the rack of his dangerous, sharp teeth.

—"Do you see them?" says Mrs. NG.
—"The sea, just the sea, ma'am," answers the taxi driver concisely, refusing to look, his eyes fixed on the asphalt strip.

Mrs. NG thinks that she is forever condemned to the impossibility of seeing a white sailboat among the jungles of an island. She curses Humboldt. That night she will be in Frankfurt with her son and her friend the Hungarian.

SMALL CREATURES

(from *La orfandad del esplendor*)

Carlos Olivares Baró
Translated by Mark Schafer

THE FLIES

the houseflies are happy and they're always flying around and landing on my sisters' mouths and spinning around in the bathroom and flying out to the gutter on the corner and returning with other flies and getting into the bedrooms and having conversations with my grandma and perching above my Mother's spools of thread and twirling on the pedal of my Mother's Singer sewing machine and they gobble the chunks of old bread in the kitchen and drown in the orange root casserole and swim in the white milk for my uncle Faustino's breakfast and follow Scout and gobble the green snot from his eyes and get into my grandma's ears and sing and play on the dining room table and when my aunt Amparo buys fish they gang together and carry off the scales and in the afternoon when it's time for the siesta my Mother gives me a piece of cardboard to shoo away the flies while she sleeps see I always get really hungry I kill like twenty of them and eat them with salt and old bread /

when my *Mother* tells me to dance with her I get real happy and I jump and run and yell and stick out my tongue at my sisters and do somersaults when my *Mother* grabs me by the waist and dances with me with the radio turned up real loud on the ten o'clock program of *los compadres* and then my sisters make faces at me and I dance and dance with my *Mother* until the show is over when the announcer says farewell from radio see-em-kew which is the station my aunt Amparo listens to but dancing with my *Mother* is the best 'cause my *Mother* kisses me and laughs with me shows me how to do twirls and says when I grow up I'm going to be a fine dancer at the fairs and then I start feeling happy and go on dancing and don't want to miss a single tune by *los compadres* and my aunt Amparo says now this is what I call music and just like that while we're dancing my *Mother* is not my *Mother* anymore and she turns into my girlfriend who dances with me softly to the beat of *los compadres I don't cut the cane the wind will cut it quick so will Lola when she gives her hip a flick* and my *Mother* takes a sip of my uncle Faustino's cross-eyed rum and my grandma watches her and laughs and I'm as happy as I get and my tattletale sisters are fit to be tied and me dancing with my *Mother* who's my girlfriend from the fair when I grow up and now I don't want to let go of her waist and we dance and dance into the night and my sisters have died of jealousy and Puchita brought the big bum to dance and my grandma is dancing with my grandfather Hilario and my uncle Faustino with my aunt Amparo and we dance on top of my sisters who are completely dead from jealousy and we dance and dance and my uncle Faustino goes to the three black men's store and buys another bottle of cross-eyed and we dance and my *Mother* says how well her son dances and my sisters dead of jealousy fidget around out of spite and pinch each other and my *Mother* gives Puchita a kiss and another one to the big bum and my uncle feels up my aunt Amparo and I'm in another house that isn't my house 'cause now we're all happy now we're all dancing with *los compadres* now my *Mother* isn't shouting and the beat of *los compadres* fills the room /

I think my *Mother* dreams of the garden 'cause when I get close to her when she's sleeping I see in her shrieking *Mother's* face bunches of all kinds of leaves of sweet basil wormseed tomatoes parsley cilantro mint if she could see while she's sleeping the way the ants over there are dragging the cat by the paws and crawling up the teeth of the poor cat killed by my sisters if my *Mother* could see that her garden of bushes and bunches of leaves and flowers was crawling with worms coming from underground 'cause of the stink of the dead cat with its mouth half open and its tongue green and blood red and my sisters choking and laughing and my *Mother* asking for water you son-of-a-bitch and the shovel damn you and plant more still and my *Mother* says how pretty her garden is no one should walk here 'cause she's going to put up a fence to make sure the cat doesn't walk here and the sun the summer the heat of this town so you always sweat day or night you're sweating and and she doesn't know when it's going to stop and me plugging the holes the damn rats make 'cause the house is full of their little black turds and they shit their turds and they fall on top of you and they breed wherever they feel like and my *Mother* says if things go on this way she's going to tell black

Manuel to find her another house the rats that get into
the boxes that prowl around in the wardrobes that sleep
in the drawers that eat your feet and blow on you that run
in the darkness that walk back and forth across the beams
the rats that dance the rats that laugh at my *Mother* the
rats that carry back to their caves what little food there is
in this house /

my *Mother's* gotten up today like a wild animal like a
she-wolf like a she-dog like a cyclone like a bolt of lightning it's my *Mother* shouting it's my *Mother* who's like a
snake who slithers who writhes my *Mother* who has
gotten up today with the buns in her hair all twisted
around on her head and the first thing she does is slap
me and call me a faggot and say to me damn you look at
this mattress you son-of-a-bitch it's my wild animal
Mother who goes over to Puchita and insults her and
shouts at her that what hour of the night did she get
home and says to her damn you and you whore I don't
want any whores in my house it's my *Mother* who sends
me to the three black men's store to buy three kilos of
coffee and two kilos of sugar it's my *Mother* who damns
god to hell and all his angels and curses herself it's my
Mother this morning it's my *Mother* she-wolf nursing
her children while we eat the chunk of old bread with
thin coffee it's my *Mother* burning herself on the stove at
my godfather Luis's candy store it's my *Mother* unsewing
the morning with her constant rage with her daily spite
it's my *Mother* kicking Puchita out of the house again it's
my *Mother* who got up today like a demon like my
Mother /

my brother you and I will sing in the afternoons / we will run through the ravines / in the leafy mud of our mother's loathings / we will be ornamental trees in this house / you will plug the holes / you will walk among the cockroaches / you will be the target of our sisters / our mouths will silence them all / our lives are not these lives where agony reigns / at any moment / I will fly through your dreams / you will protect my absence /

—Puchita

the afternoon Puchita left the house was filled with giant moths and there were also butterflies of every color black red green yellow white and the green meat fly came from the bathroom and my uncle Agrepo's pigeons came and Scout came barking and the cockroaches were dancing in the kitchen in spite of the daylight and the rats were chasing one another across the roof despite the heat coming off the zinc sheets and the hens of the old gossips got all agitated and the turkey my aunt Amparo was raising went into the living room just like that and the scabby buzzards were flying black over the house and the waterworms from the well at my grandma's house climbed out in the pail of water wriggling their tails and the horses of the neighborhood cart drivers whinnied like never before and the burros that were heading for the sierra barely wanted to carry their packs and the *macho* who killed the drunk friends of my uncle Faustino couldn't be killed so easily and they stabbed him five times in the same place but the *macho* didn't even seem to notice until my uncle Faustino said his mother was shit and then the *macho* began spurting

blood all over the patio and my grandma crossed her fingers in the shape of a cross and pulled out her rosary and
cursed my uncle Faustino and then repented and shooed
the animals out of the living room of the house when
night had fallen she took me with her to the patio and
showed me the enormous white moon and told me that
that was where Puchita was I shouldn't tell a soul that
she and god were the only ones who know

**Look how beautiful
Libertad Lamarque is
on the road to glory/
—MY MOTHER**

red flower yellow if you feel bad tell another fellow is
what I said to my sisters when I managed to get through
the roof after they locked the door to the living room
and the front entrance and I had to climb onto the zinc
roof that was melting and falling into my *Mother's* eyes
and my grandma was suffocating from all the heat and
my sisters were taking a bath in the cistern full of my
Mother's sweat and I was burning up my feet on the zinc
sheets and the rats were running 'cause of the heat and
some were roasted and I ate the little tail of a rat roasted
over the zinc fire and then a back section of the room
melted over the kitchen and I jumped through the hole
and fell on top of the coal stove where my grandma's pot
of soup was cooking and she said careful with my soup
sonny don't go sticking your feet into it and come over
here and drink your Carnation water 'cause it's already
1:00 in the afternoon and you're still perched up there

on the roof that's why your *Mother* scolds you that's why
I have to defend you 'cause your head's always in the
clouds you're always mule-headed you're a moron come
over here and drink your glass of water and put out the
fire under the soup and get the bread and two kilos of
butter and tell your *Mother* to give that sewing machine
a rest and have a bowl of soup and put her feet up for a
while and lie down and that your sisters should get out
of the water and wash up and come eat their soup and
don't you pay no mind to what they say and behave
yourself for you're coming with me at seven o'clock
your *Mother* treats you very badly here and Puchita isn't
here and that's all your *Mother* thinks about and when
she finds her with you she hits you in the head and it
affects your studies that's why you're so dazed and
yellow sometimes and why you hang out with Grau
singing mexican *ranchera* songs and go off to sell
coconut nougat and spend the whole afternoon on the
platform of the train to caimanera that is why you're
coming with me at seven o'clock until your sister
Puchita shows up /

*I'm a pitiful woman that's what I am a woman
plagued with bad luck what does life have in store for
me with a little shit of a son who only knows how to
wet his bed let himself be pushed around by the boys
at school and a whore of a daughter who goes out
every night with the big bum that guy from the
corner who doesn't even have a piece of ground to fall
dead on one of these days I'm going to light myself
on fire one of these days I'm going to throw myself
off the black bridge one of these days I'm going to
disappear one of these days I'm going to take off for*

havana and never come back one of these days I'm
going to throw myself on the caimanera train tracks
one of these days I'm going to kill them all one of
these days /

—*My Mother*

my *Mother* picks up a Butterfly flower sniffs it strokes it
with her hands the same hands that just a little while
ago gave Puchita a hard slap picks up the Butterfly
flower strokes it again looks at me asks me for more dirt
and plants a white Butterfly flower in her garden with
the same hands that just a little while ago hit Puchita
now my *Mother* picks up a Liana sniffs it adjusts one of
its green leaves and plants it just behind the Butterfly
flower and then she asks me for a yellow Buttercup
almost like a tiny sun with its tiny green leaves and she
strokes the Buttercup gently that I gave her and plants
it between the Butterfly flower and the Liana and she
leaves and brings back a wicker basket full of Gall Oaks
and Periwinkles and she says something to me about the
vivid red of the Gall Oaks and other things about the
lilac color of the Periwinkles and first she plants the
Gall Oaks and a little while later the Periwinkles and
then I bring her an Hibiscus and it smiles between the
brilliance of its redness and the eyes of my screeching
Mother who's now planting in her garden and looks like
a girl my *Mother* playing with the Gall Oaks and talking
to the Periwinkles and who tells me that not the
Creeping Ivy they're too limp that instead I should bring
her a branch of Orange Blossoms that instead I should
bring her the Bougainvilleas and that finally in the
center she's going to plant the only Sunflower she could

get her hands on and then my *Mother* spins around twirls rises into the sky my *Mother* brings more flowers and her hands are not the hands that hit Puchita and her eyes are not the eyes that looked at me in the morning full of rage and her lips whisper sing in the afternoon of the Sunflower and the Periwinkles that afternoon when Puchita took off and my *Mother* planted the yellow Buttercups the white Lianas and the soft Butterfly bush with the same hands she used to hit Puchita /

poor Saint James you who are always standing
on the bank of the river provide me with what I've lost
and if my son ran off to where you stand protect him
from death and whirlpools /
—MY MOTHER

and everything was melting and the houses and the balconies and the walls and my grandma and the old gossips and my aunt Amparo and Scout the dog with the green snot in his eyes and my *Mother* and the trees in the Martí Park and the kitchen where my aunt Amparo is running thin coffee through a sieve and my cousins are melting and running down the path along one side of the river but the heat catches up with them and they melt faster than we do my cousins evaporate my cousins on the path by the river and Puchita lost doesn't melt thank god says my grandma who's slowly melting away and the smoke that rises and rises and the hot steam from my uncle Faustino's hot water which my aunt Amparo pours into the bathtub when he comes from the base in the afternoon and we go to meet him almost at the street of drowned sailors and we snatch his lunchpails from his hands and we eat the leftovers my uncle Faustino brings from the base smelling like an old closet just like my grandma /

MY GODFATHER LUIS: (smelling of cross-eyed rum) Come here, godson (and he takes me into his office at the back of the candy store) is it true that your momma sleeps with a black man called Manuel? /

ME: (a bit embarrassed) I don't know all I saw once was my Mother crying and that man on top of her /

MY GODFATHER LUIS: (smiling) that's what I'm talking about that's sleeping with someone (he takes my hand and fondles my little butt) come over here closer close the door don't be afraid afterward I'll give you all the candy you want (you can see my godfather Luis has a bulge under his white apron and his hands are sweating and he smells of cream and guava marmalade and smiling again he begins to softly fondle my butt) /

> **I didn't like it there were no more women after Rosita Fornés /**
> **—MY MOTHER**

what a shame you have such a daughter with her head on backward so disobedient and unmindful you who made so many sacrifices for all your children you who sew like a madwoman you who are such a

*good mother you who does nothing but suffer for
them what a shame a mother like you doesn't deserve
that kind of punishment /*
The old gossips

and the old gossips arrived and tell my *Mother* that
Puchita is in boquerón at the bayou where the marine
captains go who pay more that look that to have raised
such a well-bred daughter for her to be walking around
boquerón on some shady bayou and the old gossips say
Puchita is hanging out with Ernestica in the bars on los
maceos street by the plaza where lots of helmet heads go
on the weekends after Friday which is when the marines
from the base are there and the old gossips say Puchita
drowned in the guaso river in the current that flows down
from the top of the sierra where the rebels are taking
everything they can lay their hands on and the old gossips
say Puchita is in caimanera with the old bum they saw
them on the three o'clock train when they caught it at the
soledad station and the old gossips say Puchita left for santiago on a santiago-havana bus with air-conditioning with
a man dressed in white and the old gossips say Puchita is a
bad daughter just think of doing that to my *Mother* who's
such a decent and self-sacrificing woman with her children and the old gossips say they should keep me under
lock and key 'cause I'm heading down the wrong path and
the old gossips say children don't understand the sacrifices mothers make and the old gossips say they saw
Puchita with the old bum in the dark passageway at the
train tracks and the old gossips say god help us and may
god protect my poor *Mother* and give her the strength to
raise her children and the old gossips say I spend the

whole day in the patio talking with the bees like a dimwit
and the old gossips say all I know how to do is to plague
my *Mother* and the old gossips say I always come back
pale and grainy from the river along with my nut of a
cousin Grau and the old gossips say Puchita should be
given a cleansing when she shows up and the old gossips
say my sisters behave themselves quite nicely and the old
gossips say black Manuel is a good man and the old gossips say I spend the livelong day looking between the bars
on their windows and the old gossips say /

I left an oven and returned a refrigerator /
—PUCHITA

ME: (a little afraid) mommy what's a loose-living woman /

MY MOTHER: (looking angry and not wanting to answer)
that's what your beloved older sister is doing with that
hooker Ernestica /

ME: (more afraid than before) and what's a hooker /

MY MOTHER: (looking indignant) look boy you'd be best
off letting me sew in peace and going to the plaza to buy
the pork lard and *malanga* roots /

now we're in the country in the big house of my uncle
Germán right near san luis right near where the soledad
river passes by and the santiago train on the gigantic
farm of my uncle Germán full of animals and chickens
and cows and wheelbarrows on my uncle Germán's

gigantic farm that has a grocery store and you should see
how my uncle Germán sells things out here in the
country and the pool table and the drunks and the drunks
shouting and my aunt Germinia my uncle Germán's wife
alright get inside boy and me looking through the
window with my cousins Venancio and Saladriga at the
drunks who are drinking methuselah rum and hot polar
beers 'cause my uncle Germán's cooler doesn't work and
the way these country people drink more than my uncle
Faustino after having worked the whole week at the base
and my uncle Germán who's selling rum and they're
playing pool and we're in the house and my sisters
playing jacks and me watching the drunks a little frightened and one drunk falls to the floor with a thud and
begins frothing at the mouth just like my *Mother* when
Puchita was lost and the drunk turns red as a tomato and
continues frothing at the mouth and the pool room is as
if nothing were happening and that man in my eyes spitting up green and yellow things and white froth coming
from his mouth rolling around on the ground and Terry
my uncle Germán's dog sniffs the drunk and eats up
those things and sticks his tongue in the drunk's mouth
and the pool room with its sounds of white and blue and
red balls clicking and falling in the holes of the green
pool table and the men suddenly taking gulps and aiming
their sticks at the balls and the drunk on the floor and
Terry eating him up and all of this in my eyes while my
sisters play jacks and my cousins Venancio and Saladriga
sleeping like babies and I'm practically crying but I don't
'cause my aunt Germinia might wake up and then she'll
scold us and that's worse and all of this was when my
grandma was dying over there on seventh street between

fifth and sixth south and she couldn't hold on any longer
until she grabbed Puchita with one arm and hugged her
so hard that I got scared and ran out of the house and all
along seventh street up to drowned sailors street and I
passed by the luisa movie theater that looked like I don't
know what until I made it to san lino and I told my
Mother that my grandma was red with Puchita in her
body and the drunk foaming at the mouth and my
grandma hugging Puchita and the eyes of my grandma
that say something strange that we feel in our soul and
Puchita and me telling my *Mother* what's happening to
my grandma then they sent us to the country with my
uncle Germán until my grandma died and the drunk kept
on foaming at the mouth and my uncle selling rum and
my aunt Germinia saying don't leave the house and it's
Sunday and the drunks from the country with their big
horses and people closing their doors and locking them
and the drunks who stumble around on their big horses
and leave attempting tricks on their big mottled horses
and my aunt Germinia my uncle Germán must be crazy
he should close that goddamn store of his and the drunks
who are drinking and playing and walking over the drunk
on the floor who's in my eyes and is in my hands and
Puchita takes this opportunity to go with Chichí to the
empty room and not even knowing they're cousins says
Germinia the wife of my uncle Germán that she'll not
allow that kind of fooling around in her house that she
didn't bring up children to have them fighting with the
children of other parents and me watching the drunks /

how indulgently my uncle Germán sells rum /

how calamitously my eyes hold the drunk on the floor and Terry the dog devouring him little by little /

how compassionately my hands carry a glass /

how passionately I think about my sick grandma /

how desirously Puchita goes to the empty room with Chichí /

how shamefully I cry and try not to let Venancio and Saladrigo see /

how joyfully I pee in my bed /

ever since they killed the drunk right there in the hallway of my uncle Germán's store Venancio says a man appears right there dressed in black yelling for someone to sell him a bottle of cross-eyed rum /

ever since they killed the drunk right there in the hallway of my uncle Germán's store aunt Germinia says watch out at midday for the spirit bless him amen /

ever since they killed the drunk right there in the hallway of my uncle Germán's store Saladrigo says the spirit of Terry the dead dog of my uncle Germán appears right there carrying one of the drunk's hands in his mouth /

ever since they killed the drunk right there in the hallway of my uncle Germán's store the neighbors say

that my own uncle Germán's mansion is inhabited by
strange and mysterious affairs of the devil /

they say it and say it and they call me and call me bedwetter again and say I should go to guantánamo and boy
do I stink of piss and my cousins and my sisters calling
me a bedwetter and Puchita throwing stones at them but
my uncle Germán says it's true I'm a bedwetter and takes
the stones away from Puchita who goes with Chichí into
the empty room and Sico who came from guantánamo
says my grandma is better now and that my *Mother* says
we should behave ourselves and be sure not to let me go
to the river and to be careful of the mountains that
they're full of Fidel's armed rebels and to be careful sundays with the drunks who go play pool at my uncle
Germán's who's telling Sico I'm unmanageable that I'm a
bedwetter this boy grabs everything he sees and steals the
change from the store cash register that he's sorry but to
send him back to guantánamo with my *Mother* and
Puchita who was in the empty room with Chichí came
running out her hair all disheveled and said that if I was
going so was she /

THE ANTS

*the ants form lines on the columns in the house
emerge from the floor emerge from the cracks come
from the patio and steal the brown sugar from the
kitchen along with crumbs of old bread and carry
them off climb up the legs of my aunt Amparo when
she's in the kitchen ramble over the table are in the
bathroom as if it was nothing drag away the scraps
from fabric my Mother is sewing walk around the bottles of fermented orange root and my grandma's*

*gallon jugs of honey some ants are black and my
grandma says they're crazy ants for they're always
rushing around carrying whatever they can and the
others are red and bite and my grandma says they're
fierce ants and when I climb into a genip tree at my
aunt Esperanza's house I come down red as a tomato
from the ant bites and Puchita brushes them off my
neck and my cousin Nicolaza puts alibur lotion on me
and the bites stop hurting and when I get home my
grandma puts alibur lotion on the bites again which
are all over my neck and my Mother slaps me hard
and then through my tears I see that the ants are
crawling down every column in the house heading for
the kitchen and I see in the glass of tears my aunt
Amparo is scaring them with hot water but the ants
keep crawling down and they cover my aunt Amparo
and they take out one of her eyes and they eat one of
her ears and they carry off the paper bag full of brown
sugar and my grandma's gallons of honey and the
bottles of fermented orange root and the chunks of
old bread and they leave my aunt Amparo with only
one eye and one ear /*

*O blessed virgen mary who have filled me with hope/
you who took the sweet name of perpetual help / I
pray for you to consider assisting my wayward grand-
daughter / and that your help might reach her with
all haste / in her temptations following her falls / in
her hardships and in all the distresses of her young
life / and may god forgive her especially at the hour of
death / make it her habit merciful mother of always
turning to you / reach her with your grace and virtue
/ and provide her with your perpetual help / benevo-
lent mother bless her / and pray constantly for that
unfortunate creature and amen / (blow out the candle
and go to bed and may the unbeliever of your grandfather not find out about these prayers for your sister)*

—My grandma

Guantánamo is pretty /
with lovely women /
who fill our souls with fervent dreams /
they let men taste /
of the sweetest pleasures /
and when they swear their love /
they offer their hearts.
—BOLERO-SON / MATAMOROS TRIO

SOMETHING IS HAPPENING ON THE TOP FLOOR

Reinaldo Arenas
Translated by Dolores Koch

A bird is singing,
perched on
the high electric wires.
If I could, I would also sing,
until my voice gave out

Now the man looked down on the street, which appeared
to be trapped in a thick network of wires of all sorts. And
he started thinking. On the top floor, no city blare
reached him to interrupt his thoughts. There were voices
rising from the street, and the drone of motors, unintel-
ligible conversations, vituperations, shrieks, music that
was not music but clatter adding to total disharmony,
fragmented echoes of marches and demonstrations, gib-
berish, and whistles.... But all that cacophony gradually
faded as it passed the lower floors, so that on the top terrace, where he was, only the reverberations from a truly

extraordinary noise could reach him, which never happened.... A bird was singing, perched on the telegraph or
telephone wires or electrical cables. The bird seemed to
be glued to the wires, and the man stuck out his tongue
and made a threatening gesture, but the bird did not
leave and kept on singing. "It doesn't matter, it will be
dark soon, and you'll have to go away," the man said
aloud. The bird raised the pitch of its singsong, and the
man then had to make a great effort to put his thoughts
in order within the set time. But the afternoon, *except
for that stupid bird*, was a good one for reflection.
Standing next to the void, the man felt his ideas come
and go; sometimes they stayed for a while playing in
front of him, and he saw them coming at him like tiny
sunbursts. Once again it was time to start the story.

A chorus of fixed ideas surrounded the man and left
him naked. One of them, very wrinkled and heavy-set,
jumped at his head from the roof of the building, and the
man shrank, turning into a boy. Looking down, he saw
himself in the street, running, hawking newspapers from
his battered bicycle, and trying to escape from his
mother, who was chasing after him with a long mop. He
laughed uncontrollably and dreamed he was falling.... Up
high, ideas would appear and disappear, changing their
garb and instruments, sobbing or letting out strange
bursts of laughter, dragging themselves on the floor or
soaring up in the sky, singing or playing trumpets,
shaking their buttocks or making undefinable gestures. It
all resulted in a struggle among unusual furies which, in
their wild commotion, kept falling into the street and,
though invisible, crowding the sidewalks.... It was noon,
and his mother was sitting on the couch, in the middle of

the living room. "Your father is dead," she said when the boy came in. "Your father died," she said. The boy walked to the washstand to wash his hands, but there was no water, the bowl was empty. He stood on tiptoe to see if there were any drops left at the bottom, and the bowl went crashing to the floor, its enamel cracking and chipping off. "Whose father?" the boy asked. The mother walked over to him and hit him on the head with the bowl, chipping it even more. It looked totally ruined. So much so that its screams were heard as the chips were flying away. "You broke the bowl," said the mother. "You broke it..." It was that particular time of day when it's neither day nor night, the time when things change shape, growing bigger or smaller; the time when all the shadows lying at the bottom of things, which had been in hiding during the day, can now escape and stretch until they touch each other and form one single shadow. From his lookout the man could see the sun gasping as it sank into the sea in a cloud of vapor. Below, the boy managed to get across the street without being run over by the heavy traffic. He slid between two tractor-trailers, caused several cars to collide, and knocked down an old man who, upon reaching the corner, dropped dead in a rage; but the boy was not hurt.

He got home, ran to the bathroom, and to his horror verified that he was turning into a monster: he was growing a lot of hair in some unimaginable places. With arms raised, he walked to the places. To a mirror, then ran to the sewing machine, picked up the scissors, and did away even with his eyebrows and eyelashes. More at peace, he got out onto the patio. But it was the same the next day, and though he couldn't tell anybody, he felt an enormous urge to start screaming.... The screams, which never left his throat, reached up to the man who was struggling with his thoughts on the top floor, since they were extraordinary sounds. The man, outraged, threw a cluster of thoughts into the void, and the boy was transformed. That's how he flashed back to the distressing period of his adolescence when, without even a dime to go to the movies, he was smoking in secret and masturbating while looking at a girl with a shaved head. " You have to work," said the mother. "With the English that you know, you could find a job." "Young man," his ad read, "fluent in English, seeks position..." The man above had started pacing. He was walking fast from one corner of the terrace to the other, occasionally leaning over the railing. The city lights were beginning to appear... The following day he received a response from a distillery where cheap rum was made, aguardiente or firewater, people call it. And though while on his way there he told himself, "Damn it, you are not really going to do that to me and start sweating now," by the time he arrived, his hands were already dripping wet. He walked between the columns of bottles that obstructed his path, leaving little puddles behind him. But the job did not work out. Yes, it was true he was fluent in English, but that was not the issue. His knowledge of the language was fine, but just broken English would have been enough; what's more, it was not useful to know it too well, and especially not with a Shakespearean accent. Of what use was that Elizabethan thespian diction coming from the throat of a youth whose job was to persuade ("no matter how") tourists from cruise ships to go with him to the firewater distillery, and once there, to get them drunk? "That's

what your job is. To convince them, lure them, drag them
here so that they drink our rum. It pays twenty pesos a
month..." The terrace clouded over for a moment with
hundreds of ideas of all sizes, their membranous wings
grazing the man, lifting and shaking him, raising him up
to the ceiling and dropping him again to the floor. The
man finally got hold of himself and continued walking.
Breathing heavily, he cleared the way with his hands, and
lit a cigarette... The first day he managed to drag along an
American tourist, an old teetotaler who thought the boy
was taking him to a museum; the next day he carted away
two young men who didn't drink but were eager to get to
a brothel; on the third day he took with him two very
leggy, lanky women who did get drunk, didn't pay, and
wanted to have sex with him. On the fourth day he was
fired, though he got paid for his three days of work. "He's
no good for this kind of work," he heard people say while
he hid behind the rows of bottles. "The boy has no drive...
We need someone lively who can bring people here, no
matter how, and doesn't shy away from anything." And
doesn't shy away from anything. And doesn't shy away...
Now it all became a dizzying return to the same point
where his storytelling had started, or rather, to the point
where he would end it... He saw himself going in and
coming out of one restaurant after another, one drug-
store after another, one cafeteria after another. In short, a
whole parade of useless and implacable jobs that would
only atrophy the beautiful images of the future that he
had envisioned for himself in times past. During the
whole review of his life, the most peaceful moment was
that of the death of his mother. As soon as he found out,
he went out onto the patio (the place where he used to let

off steam when something important happened). "She died," he said. "She is dead," he said. He went back inside and saw her face, so serene: a look that he never had been able to see at all while she was alive. He carried the coffin himself, and paid for the funeral. All his aunts gathered around her tomb, all in black. The scene made him think of a vulture devouring a rotten carcass. "Come here, kid," the vultures said, in tears. And he ran away, in between the crosses, and disappeared into the last bustle of the day. Something was telling him that he had been saved. Someone inside him was shouting at him that he had been liberated, that he would no longer need to become an obscure man who bites his lip, and who often gets phone calls saying that everything is fine. And he ran into the crowd. And he wanted to start screaming, "Mother died at last." And he did. And he felt as if an enormous carapace that had been crushing him since the moment of his birth had been lifted... He got married, changed jobs, had children, left the country. He kept on moving from one place to another, trying to escape relentless hunger, and eliminating the possibility of any relief, of any chance of doing a genuine act. Always tied to the damned routine that ruled his time, but waiting... And old age was creeping up even into the most minute corners of his body. The press was reporting exciting stories about the latest events in his country. A revolution, what could that be...? So he returned with all his relatives. Up there, the battle against those membranous beings was coming to an end; the majority of them had fled; others had accepted defeat and were vanishing in the air. Only the very largest ones remained, unforgiving, their beaks threatening. Sounds of children yelling were coming from the living room, and of the mother closing the door to the hallway. "They are back," said the man. And with a gesture, he made all the vermin disappear. But the most powerful ones quickly climbed up the walls, up the drain pipes, and quite intent on staying, they positioned themselves between the man and the door. The clamor of children's voices was no longer audible. Now only the woman was speaking, but he didn't hear her either. "I am sure," he said. "I am fine," he said. "I am at peace."

And he shooed away the ideas that, adopting mosquito shapes, were buzzing around his ears, and biting him on the neck. With great effort, he delved into the retelling. All his life he had been in the grip of those vermin, and now he found himself at peace, with the triumph (was that the word?) that alleviates the horrors of getting old. Again he could hear the children's yells. I am doing fine. Here is home, my home, and behind the door, are my wife and kids. I have a decent pension. Here is home. And his hands caressed the walls, as if the house were a domestic animal... The voice of the woman could be heard, calling him. "I'm coming," he said. I'm coming, I'm coming. And he groped in the dark trying to find the door. This is peace: a home, a pension, and the kind of weather that always remains the same. Always remains the same, he repeated as if trying to accelerate his steps by means of words. And the kind of weather that always remains the same, he said once more, and stopped. Then he leaned over the railing again. Way down there, past the metallic network, the streetlights were swarming at their peak... There were voices that the man did not hear. Moving like a performer, he passed his feet over the railing and, once on the other side, he held on to it with only one hand. Then he let himself go, without haste, like someone at the edge of a swimming pool, and sliding into it. "Aren't you coming in?" the woman asked from the dining room. And she came out on the terrace. "Oh," the woman said, raising one hand, not to any part of her face but to her neck. Like that she went into the dining room, and in a reassuring manner, began to serve dinner... The man, bursting through wires, flagpoles, and neon signs, was coming down with an impish smile. Shattering the last light bulbs, he fell headfirst on a car top, and bounced three times... The boy, standing on the sidewalk, saw him hit the ground and smash into pieces. Then he took his battered bicycle, and continued hawking his newspapers, but with a little more verve. He was glad to have watched that spectacle, which he had only seen in an occasional movie when he had money (rarely) for the ticket.

The bird, frightened by the thud, flew away circling the deep red sky, already fading slowly into the horizon. The bird finally landed, perching on the telephone wires of a neighborhood street. Its song was heard for a while in the dark of night.

La Habana, 1963

MIOSVATIS

Miguel Barnet
Translated by Chris Brandt

—For Wolfgang Eitel

The Zurich museum is square. And cold. But it's got the best collection of Giacometti I've ever seen. They're pretty sad, these sculptures by the Swiss master: old patinaed bronze figures—attenuated, contrite, their arms fused to their bodies—recall Baulé or Senufo carvings, I couldn't say which for sure anymore. Restricted, those arms rob the body of freedom, turn the figures into prisoners chained to the artist's fancy. Of all the pieces in that museum the saddest is a skinny but enormous dog mounted on a base which could be wood or marble, I don't remember that anymore either. It's the famous Giacometti dog reproduced on postcards that have been sent all over the planet. I didn't look at it for long because I like my animals alive, especially dogs. But Wolfgang did. Wolfgang looked at it carefully and then said, "Let's go downstairs and have a drink. I'm going to buy the postcard of Giacometti's dog."

In the cafeteria, I opened a diet Coca Cola and watched as Wolfgang hurried off to find it. "This postcard," he told me when he returned, "you're going to take it back to Cuba and deliver it to Miosvatis, my black love, who lives in Trocadero Street. She's a very beautiful and tender black woman. Do you mind? "

"Of course not, Wolfgang, I know your sweethearts always expect to get something from you."

Zurich is a gray city, an untouched cardboard stage set with a river and bridges like the ones in Leningrad, with ice-cream and peanut vendors and violet-breasted pigeons that light on your shoulder and eat from the palm of your hand, just like in a Vittorio de Sica movie. In the summertime, Zurich opens up like a music box, but in winter it's as sad as a cenotaph.

Wolfgang and I walked over the bridges, through the city, along the narrow medieval streets. We visited cafés where Tristan Tzára, Lenin, and Thomas Mann sat to contemplate those same steel skies.

In one of those cafés, Wolfgang wrote up the card I was to take to Havana. "I'm called Juanito over there," he said, "because my real name is so strange." Then sitting beside me, he wrote:

> *Dear Miosvatis - this skinny sad dog is what I'm like here in Switzerland without you. Soon we'll meet in Cuba and I'll be a happy dog again. I'll be your puppy. All my love, Juanito.*

The black-currant ice cream I was eating spilled on my trousers, making a harsh-colored stain contrasted to the pale amber of the Heineken Wolfgang was drinking, as we sat on a bench facing the river. An overcast summer sky made our conversation the more intimate. We talked about Cuba as always, about the future, about the city of Dada; we saw a black barge loaded with Japanese tourists, and we were glad to be together again, my friend Wolfgang—what am I saying, Juanito—and I... setting the world to rights while the Japanese tourists photographed the bridge and the pigeons; maybe we even appeared in the photograph.

"We're going to buy some shoes for your mama, tell her the German sends them. And then we're going to buy some perfume for Miosvatis, and a blue Swatch; blue will go well with her skin."

Zurich is elegant. It's not a city where the crowded rush of consumer culture presses up against you. You shop in peace, and nobody comes along to shove merchandise in your face. We bought the shoes, the perfume by Giorgio, and the watch with a blue wristband and a kaleidoscopic face.

Wolfgang and I said our good-byes until we'd meet again in Havana.

The next morning I took the train for Paris. I crossed the most beautiful lakes in Europe with the postcard, the Giorgio, and the Swatch in my leather briefcase. My mother's shoes traveled in my luggage.

Juanito came along to say farewell at the station, but first we had mint tea in one of Zurich's most elegant pastry shops.

During the following month, I trotted all over Paris with Miosvatis's watch and the Giorgio in my bag for fear that someone would steal them or I'd lose them in one of the houses where I slept. In Paris the whole story seemed unreal. Paris is not made of cardboard, it's a gray elephant that breathes with exuberance. The watch was a little more expensive in the Paris stores than in Zurich, but not the perfume; that we could have bought cheaper at any counter in the Galleries Lafayette or La Samaritaine. I sent Wolfgang a card—a lovely photo by Man Ray of a sleeping Marcel Proust—and I assured him that the perfume, like the watch and his postcard, were safely stowed in the leather bag that never left my side.

Miosvatis became an obsession, rather a talisman protected by a demiurge. When I opened my bag and saw the card, the watch, and the perfume, I got an odd feeling: I wanted to be in Havana immediately and meet the object of Wolfgang's passion. I didn't want to take the things out of my bag. It was as if my city, the barrio Colón, and idyllic Miosvatis were all very close to me. Sometimes I felt this was the only real thing I possessed, my strongest affective tie to the world.

Flying back in the Iberia DC-10, I wondered whether the customs officer at Jose Martí would ask me to account for the blue watch. No! Anything but give up the watch that Juanito had bought for his beloved. And so it was. Since my suitcase was small and I was carrying all the books and chocolates in my shoulder bag, no one asked me to account for anything. And the little watch entered Cuba duty-free, pretty and glowing with its wristband of a translucent turquoise blue, shining just as it had in that Swiss showcase—the chimerical faraway dream of Miosvatis.

As I got off the plane, even before I'd set foot on the tarmac, the humidity steamed up my glasses. It's

Havana, I said to myself. This humidity will be the death of me someday, but then we all die, after all. And full of happiness and new stories to tell, I made my way through the airport.

Outside the terminal, a group of relatives and friends leaned up against the barricades and with a mixture of joy and envy watched us come in from outside.

The first thing I did when I got home was to unpack the watch, the Giorgio, and the postcard. The jet lag, six hours' worth, kept waking me up all night. In this waking dream, Miosvatis appeared in many different guises: daughter of a mill worker, schoolteacher, taxi driver, or simply a hooker who'd opened Wolfgang's eyes to the fact that she was not just another ordinary black woman, a streetwalker like all the others.

The only thing that took my mind off my friend's sweetheart was my neglected apartment. The towels hung crooked on the towel racks, the plants had dried up, and the dust gave the place an air of faded dereliction that kept me from enjoying my happy return home. When I went to pick up the telephone, my mother informed me fearfully, "It's been broken ever since you left." I resigned myself. "Fine, now my stay in Europe will be extended, since without a telephone I'm simply not here, I am no one, one who hasn't yet arrived."

I waited patiently for my telephone to be repaired, and then made a few calls to give signs of life. Unable to hold off any longer, I headed for the barrio Colón bearing gifts like one of the Magi.

The barrio Colón isn't really the barrio Colón anymore. Now it's one more barrio of Havana, a hive of motley people sitting along the sidewalks or playing dominoes in the streets, the men shirtless and the women in plastic sandals and hair curlers. Just another barrio with a few glowing embers of its ancient and celebrated fame—an old red-light district come down in the world, where idleness spreads like an oil slick, or something even more viscous. The Revolution rooted out prostitution but not the Cuban habit of living one's most intimate life, without shame, in the middle of the street.

It wasn't easy to park my car because a number of chairs had to be moved and a couple of sharply dressed young women had to be asked to get out of the way so that I could get close to the curb. They laughed and took their time climbing up onto the sidewalk, convinced that I was insolently robbing them of their space. The barrio reeked of rotten cabbages and cheap cologne, a peculiar stench that one soon gets used to. Neither of the girls was Miosvatis. I knew it without even asking.

Miosvatis was something else again. I didn't ask after her, because that would have aroused curiosity. I simply knocked on the door of the address I had, and a thickset woman with hair dyed with *bijol* opened the door. To her, I did mention the name of my friend's darling.

She answered me with an evil smile. "She lives on the top floor," she said, "but she's not there, she went out with a boyfriend. But come in, come in. In this barrio everybody wants to know your business; gossip spreads like weeds here. Look, they're already watching us."

The old woman invited me into her ground-floor apartment—the ceiling peeling, and the floor a carpet of silent cats and dogs. "Don't your dogs bark?"

"No, that's the way they are, I've got them trained." She ignored them as if they weren't there.

Against the light, I was able to make out a tinted photograph of the old woman in her youth, pretty and with her lips accentuated by an imprudent use of lipstick that dated the image to the mid-fifties—an era of thick features and lurid colors. She said something softly that I couldn't hear because she feared eavesdroppers. She talked a lot, eager to take advantage of a stranger's ear, and of course she wanted to know what I was doing there. I explained that I wasn't sure of Miosvatis's apartment number. And she looked up wide-eyed, but not so much surprised as complicit. "You're bringing her something? That little package is for her? You're Spanish?"

"No, ma'am, I'm Cuban..."

"Ah, Cuban! But you live outside."

"No, ma'am, I live here and I've come to bring a present for your neighbor."

"Good enough, but she's not here—I told you she went out with a friend. But not a guy from here, from this barrio, no. Me, it's the first time I've seen him. He's mulatto, lighter-skinned, a lot lighter-skinned than her."

The woman's opaque eyes searched mine. Staring back at them, I realized the irises were ringed with a halo of white, and that her eyelashes were white as well. As I did not speak, she told me, "Miosvatis is always going off into the streets and leaves the kids up there with her younger sister. They can't stand me. They call me a witch when it's them who're witches because I go to the Catholic church and I don't think they've ever set foot even in a chapel. But that's life. Look, nobody's up there because the window that faces my courtyard is closed, unless the sister's asleep and the girls are running around in the street. If you want, I'll hold on to something for you. The little package, that's for Miosvatis? Don't worry, you can leave it with me, but with a receipt from the president of the CDR because I don't want to be responsible. They don't deserve the favor. They throw filth down at me. I'm sorry to have to tell you this, but yessir, just to annoy me, they throw down wads of Miosvatis's daughters' shit out the window, and I've reported them to the police, but nothing, they won't even listen to me. But come on through here—would you like some water? You could suffocate in this heat. Where'd you say you were from? Oh, yes, Cuba, but you live on the outside! Well, however you want, either you leave the little package with me and I call the president of the CDR or you come back another day, make up your mind."

A statuette of the Virgin of la Caridad del Cobre, her robe stained with grease and her sparse hair also colored by the dust of *bijol*, was on a shelf high up on the wall. The floor in this room was uneven and seemed almost like an ancient artifact, made up of filthy tiles, shabby and broken.

The old woman was about to say something when an ear-splitting scream came from up above. "It's her, she was there all the time, but they hide to spy on people— and I only do them favors. It's on account of me that those baby girls drink condensed milk." A second scream, this time a little less sharp, as if the screamer knew she'd been heard down in the first-floor apartment, where I was now sitting in a wicker armchair with a broken seat. The old woman pointed at me and said, "Go up, go on up, it's four flights, you'll know which one is theirs."

"I'm Yalaine," said the woman who answered the door. She was a beautiful black woman, compact, a sculpture composed of solid volumes. "It's a pleasure, come in, make yourself at home. Pardon that I haven't dressed the girls—it's the heat, it puts us right to sleep. I heard you talking to that old gossip and I said to myself, 'That's a message for me from Manuel.' Right?"

"No, *compañera*, it's for Miosvatis."

"Ah, for my sister! You can leave it with me—don't worry, that way you won't have to come back. My sister went out on an errand about an hour ago, but she won't be back till late. It's from Gunther?"

"No, no, it's from Juanito."

"Ah, Juanito, yeah, yeah, my sister's fiancé. Thanks!"

Yalaine shut the twins in the other room, and between the girls' screams and my own uneasiness in that slum I don't remember the moment when I handed her the perfume, the postcard, and the watch.

"Miosvatis has been waiting to hear from Juanito for days," she said. "He wants to marry her, but my sister's not sure because of the two kids and her and she just got a little job... it's not easy, you know? But you're not German."

"No, no, I'm Cuban and a great friend of Juanito's. I saw him over there, and he gave me this for your sister. He talked a lot about her."

Yalaine offered me coffee. "Juanito bought these cups because he likes to drink Cuban coffee in fine cups. He's sure got white hands, and delicate. He's a man who's very..."

Miosvatis and Yalaine's apartment could have been a set for a vernacular piece at the Teatro Martí. To one side, near the window that opened onto a tiny balcony, was a pair of vases with wax flowers covered in soot. On the other side, a broken clock that had stopped at ten sat next to a statue of Saint Barbara with black ovals embroidered on her cloak and the tip of her nose chipped off.

The smell of rotten cabbage was now mixed with a sweet and penetrating French perfume to which I had an allergic reaction that was impossible to hide. "Excuse me," Yalaine said, "I'm going to put this stuff for my sister under lock and key because if I don't, the girls will finish it in no time—they grab everything, but everything. And for my sister what comes from Juanito is sacred. Would you like some more coffee?"

"No, thanks."

Yalaine came out again dressed in brilliant blue satin, with earrings she'd got from the diplomats' store brushing against her Baulé princess shoulders. She looked at me with suspicion, but also with appreciation. She'd have liked me to stay longer. She apologized for the disorder and the dust that covered everything.

"With these girls, there's never time for anything. And my sister and I are alone here. Our mother died and we're all the family we've got." I didn't look at her in any way indiscreetly. I just wanted to get up and leave. Then she asked, "Did Juanito say he was going to marry my sister?"

"No, he didn't say."

"I'm asking because I'm not going to get stuck with the girls. Imagine! She's going to have to take them."

"They're very pretty—they look like you."

"Yeah, but they're not mine. It's on account of my sister and me, we look alike."

I started to sneeze, I don't know if it was the dust or the cloying supersweet perfume. I said good-bye thinking of Wolfgang in that Zurich pastry shop, under those orange umbrellas in that dry and elegant autumn in the city of Giacometti.

As I went down the stairs, the odor of rotting cabbage got stronger, now mixed with cat piss. Dirty black stains splotched the marble stairs of what might once have been a bright and flamboyant house of prostitution. The cat woman had her door open, but she made no move to say good-bye to me. Maybe she was afraid I'd been indiscreet and told Yalaine something of what we'd talked about. I looked in and saw empty indifference.

Coming out into the high afternoon sun, with my shirt sticking to my skin, I saw a group of men around my car. I shot a quick glance at the tires, the rearview mirror, the windshield wipers, and opened the door, feigning confidence in this barrio and its people. I didn't start the car right away; I even looked up. Yalaine was waving good-bye and I realized from this distance that her front teeth had an even wider gap than I'd noticed. Who was the lovelier, Yalaine or Miosvatis? Perhaps I'll never know.

The engine turned over, and I was about to step on the accelerator when two girls approached the car window. Curious, and with assumed familiarity, they asked in unison, "You're a friend of Juanito's?" I smiled and stepped on the gas. At that hour, the Malecón was almost deserted. Only a tourist couple in Bermuda shorts, and a sad and sickly dog, like Giacometti's, were silhouetted against the landscape.

A LOVE STORY ACCORDING TO CYRANO PRUFROCK

By Lourdes Casal
Translation by Zoë Anglesey

Introduction: Where is it said that should you wish to write a novel, begin by making love to Beatrice on the banks of the Hudson.

This is absolutely absurd. But in the middle of this overwhelming depression something makes me think that I could get into writing a really sexy novel, even if you won't be able to read it; your Spanish is so poor, you can hardly understand this Castilian cocktail that has become my way of speaking after so many years of exile and the sundry conversations with so many different people. You'll either experience my writing as the purity of speechlessness (or at least fidelity to Havana Spanish) or feel as if I'm navigating through multiple tongues, all literal descendants of the grand Miguel—not our beloved radio host Miguel Villalobos, but the other: Cervantes, whose language cannot be swallowed in tidbits.

Here, facing the iridescent Hudson, there's an aroma of mint and a faint sun that stirs up memories deeply embedded under the skin. You're gone and I remember my face between your breasts, the sun, and that it's been twelve years since I've gone swimming. I remember you playing in the water, and the transparent Caribbean at Guanabo, its particular blueness, the sandy bottom, mother-of-pearl pebbles and water washing over my eyes. I loved being alone on the beach and floating along the coastline the way I loved being afloat in the vast sea between your arms.

I told you life is an excuse to write. I liked coming up with such statements because you'd laugh so openly: *épater les bourgeois, fasciner les petites*. When you laughed, the air seemed cleaner.

I recall the scent of your skin, tanned by a sun much warmer than this one. "I'd forgotten sweat smells differently when you sweat from strenuous exercise," you said. I smiled. "Let's go!" you shouted. "To the great outdoors!" We laughed. The smell of mint—I go crazy with the thought of mint on the banks of the Hudson. And just because there was no mint on the banks of the Hudson, I said, "The water is polluted and the fish is no good." No mint and a Dominican Cibaeño on the banks of the Hudson.

Joyce, what shit. Once I swore that if I ever write again, I would never amuse myself like the Cuban literati, as Benito says, with the apologia to the ass. But yours makes me vacillate in my thinking. It makes me feel deranged, speechless. With you reclining on this rocky ledge just made for you, with the Hudson in the background, and although just paces from me, you, too, could well be fifteen hundred miles from here. Damn. I would like to write a happy story, but this fucking nostalgia drains me, the shit of just existing, being in this state of depression. I get bored with myself. I should have had the courage to fuck you last night.

Digression: In Cain's defense or the singing of liturgical songs on *La Rampa*.

I discuss *Three Trapped Tigers* with a poet, wondering whether or not people will think of Havana that way, what people will think about Cubans after reading the novel, with no money, so many poor, a people without dialects, that life is just one big party? What if Cabrera Infante was a sorehead?

And I think, what shit. If you haven't lived it, you should think twice before mouthing off. My generation schemed just as much on that boardwalk, as under a hail of bullets. On those few blocks we learned the science of good and evil. That's where Estrella, Elena, and Lupe sang songs and where we discovered "feeling" and scotch and sex and daybreak after too many drinks and everything else between the beach and *La Rampa*, and from *La Rampa* to the Plaza, where we ate Chinese. And Guillermo may have been a sorehead, but he lived it up totally—in *Three Trapped Tigers*—the most all-encompassing testimonial to Havana's nightlife and those desperate years just before the Revolution. That was my *Before the Revolution*, Bertolucci, so different from yours, even though some of us would also pursue the white whale, while others just became corrupted.

The demonstration with banners and bodies squeezed together winds down the hill past the intersection of Twenty-third Street. I got on a bus going in the opposite direction. Going toward Infanta, fleeing from everything, the last thing I saw were Fabian's eyes suprised and accusing as he handed out flyers. Through the window, he threw a bunch at my face. Fabian with his thick glasses and blue eyes wide open—I wouldn't see them again until that photo in Bohemia. Shortly after, they closed forever.

Years later, photos of the martyrs were published. I'd known Fabian since '52 up until the fiftieth anniversary, when we met every Sunday at the free university. After the rallies in March, we began to meet every week at the radio station CMQ in order to plan our protest, to toss out provocative questions, to make certain we weren't living in a dream, to test the limits of our freedom. Then one day, some strangers took over the theater and jumped us, swinging clubs and pumping rubber bullets. I remember Fabian's bloodied head. And running down *La Rampa* toward the sea with Gabriela, hysterical, clinging to my arm, I understood fully for the first time that the dictatorship had begun.

The boardwalk and the small club where we went, hungering to see everything that was to be seen, with an incessant desire to talk, and yes, why not, to show ourselves off, all the guys and transvestites, and the girls and lesbabes (to use Cain's lingo). The boardwalk and the corner newsstand where we could imagine ourselves in some capital of the world, escaping into a European mirage—salvation through anything "cultured" and snobbish, and only paces from the Malecón and from death. The boardwalk and the cinema where we saw *Hiroshima, Mon Amour* and where we all became part of the new wave of the Revolution without understanding much about ours or anyone else's. Plainly, we were confused and amazed by it all.

During those Havana nights on the boardwalk, trotting behind you, for the first time I saw the world through your eyes—dazzling tigress, irremediably sad—loping through the weeping wheat fields of Havana nights, sidestepping the nets, winding through fishes and foxes and black birds—all manner of creatures and all sorts of saints made strange—and the fantastic flora, purslane on the walls of St. Michel. Loping around the Fosca, and up and down the stairs of the funeral home.

Yes, dear poet. The tigers were not three but thousands, hanging out on the sharp rocks of the jetty where we grew up too fast because there was no time to lose. We knew deep down that these were times of giving birth to ourselves. We sang "A Little Gate of Light," read Hesse, and made the revolution. We made love, and yes, all of this transpired within the matrix of those interminable Havana nights. Paradise was the boardwalk and Cain its prophet and evangelist. Amen.

Chapter I: Beatrice found with a little help from my friends, from Johnny Weissmuller to Jean Luc Godard.

I have followed you through all the corners of this city, eyes dazed by the lights from the illusory paradise that crowns the cliffs on the opposite side of the Hudson. I have followed you, pen in hand, from the doorway of the *New Yorker* to Frini's, pursued your elusive figure down Broadway, then just before arriving at Lincoln Center, when I could hardly drag myself another step, I saw your triumphant entrance into Rizzoli's. And I know that I have followed you many other times, and in many other cities, yes, including, Havana. Someday in honor of your memory and your prophet, I will make a pilgrimage along the boardwalk; but for now, I get by making ablutions and belting out "Delirium" with my face turned toward Radio Central every night at nine, when the cannon booms and the soap goes on the air.

I was not looking to fall in love. Even if I had been, I certainly wouldn't have chosen you. You're such an unlikely heroine for a love story. Although things seemed securely under control, I was wandering aimlessly between frustration and frustration, looking for someone to trust.

I was on the prowl, a lion on the streets of New York, among sharks and more sharks, with a little telltale thread of love precariously caught in my mustache, my hair parted in the middle from hairline to nape, I held a peach half eaten. I found you submerged in indescribable improbabilities. You were swimming in a sea of seaweed and Portuguese men-of-war. (Oh, translation of translations, and all translation!) You were seated on a bench and I asked if I could join you. You were crossing the street and I offered you my arm. You were going to step into a puddle wearing Japanese sandals, when I threw down my poncho. We were in the public library looking for the same book by Stekel; I let you check it out. On the subway, a group of insurance agents and jerks in public relations were giving you the lookover, so I gave you my seat. You were walking along Eighth Street, your cigarette unlit, and I offered you a light. On the corner of Broadway and 155th, some Indian, knife in mouth and hatchet in hand, was threatening you, when I plucked his feathers and scalped him.

I Tarzan, you Jane, I yelled, standing next to a humongous nanny in a Central Park made fertile by the fecund creations of Niki de Sant Phälle. I shouted Tamangani and scared off Holden Caulfield's ducks. Me John, you Yoko, I muttered sweetly before offering you a ten-speed Peugeot.

I found you in a forest inhabited by cannibals. First I wanted to explore your teeth—your eye teeth seemed to be of normal size and, fortunately, your vagina didn't have any. Your body, unpampered but still promising, concealed its arcane voluptuousness under overalls. She has occult treasures, noted the expert. The alter ego answered, they don't look particularly tempting. You should get to know her, really know her, said the expert, and don't forget the biblical sense of knowing.

It was then that I sat down next to you to deliver my very serious discourse on the destiny of the decade, about what had happened to us in the sixties; how the dreams of reason had created monsters (check it out, girl, everything ended for us with President Nixon). All the gallant men with charisma (I gave you a poster of Malcolm X) were devoured by the consumer society that gluts on everything. I presented you with a rare LP auto-graphed by Marcuse that I got on sale at the Marboro. Peter, Paul, and Mary separated, and the Beatles broke up. Erosion takes everything. But we consoled ourselves with marijuana and listened to Janis Joplin. Suddenly, the seventies—so full of life, like your armpits—offered us hope . Presto! On the seventh day God saw what he had created. He caught a whiff of a woman and decided the earth was good.

Chapter 2: Héloïse and Abélard play chess, Delilah curls Samson's hair into little ringlets, while various other obscenities occur.

Sweet Sundays in the small room on Peña Pobre, our walks along the narrow streets, entertaining ourselves by tapping out rhythms on the old paving stones, riding bicycles on Avenida del Puerto, peregrinations through all of Havana's bookstores, perhaps looking for *El Lobo Estepario—The Wolf from the Hills*—but in that old Madrid edition, or *Cantos de Maldoror* in any edition.

We did crazy things back then because we were in love. We visited the Ponce Room in the Museum of Bellas Artes for thirty days straight, bought Brahms's Double Concerto (yes, the version by Heifetz and Piatigorsky), on innumerable 45s because they didn't have LPs where we were in old Havana and we didn't want to waste time going by Radio Central, because you had to be home at six and we had only one hour for ourselves.

One full year passed before I kissed you. I made love to each of your breasts for hours at a time, certainly for as long a time as the pyramids have contemplated us. Under the coconut trees, I read Andrew Marvell to you: "My love, let me count the ways I love you—no more no less than the million plus years that the Almendares

River has poured itself into the bay." But then, I was struck mute; just at that moment on the bank in front of us, I noticed some old man masturbating. You were having fun watching him, and Andrew Marvell as well as the Almendares metaphor were merely going in one ear and coming out the other.

Chapter 3: The villain appears here—a wolf in a lamb's coat—and he offers Beatrice little sugar cubes.

"Real love, you can never forget it or leave it," you said when Alejandro the Great stepped into my life, blocking the view with his impressive bulk, and stamped my old green jacket into the ground with his fake cowboy boots.

"He's as beautiful from the back as from the front," I said remembering Fernandel's favorite saying.

"We are all German Jews," said Alejandro, who could repeat such things with impunity. All his clichés were out of sync with time and place and completely irrelevant. Alejandro could, however, commit any disorderly act, like calling out "Cohn Bendit" in the middle of an S&M bar on Manhattan's east side, without having to pay any consequences.

I knew that I had lost you, Beatrice, maybe forever, when I saw you wiping his forehead with your favorite maxi skirt. I knew, when you slammed the door in my face, that I had been through all of this before. When you pushed the door right up against my nose and I knew you were sleeping with him, I suddenly remembered that I had experienced this before: me alone in a cab from a joint in St. John to the Sierra Club because you had left in the car with him (Alejandro, Jimmy, or Abel). Without knowing exactly what I was after, without the faintest notion of what to do after entering the cabaret and confirming that you were there. (What bad taste! It all seems like a scene from "Guantanamera," a cheap soap opera, or a page out of a dirty novel.)

Also before: I, walking along G toward Línea to see you. I arrived just as you were leaving arm in arm with Jimmy. You were wearing your school uniform, your breasts pressed tight beneath a white blouse.

Then later: taking you to the door of your apartment, after drinking for hours and walking up and down the streets of Manhattan, after frenzied kisses and lighting a fire under the skin, I left you knowing full well you'd not be sleeping alone.

And now the door's right up to my nose, as you silently send me to hell. I imagine you licking Alejandro's boots while he holds a branding iron to your ass that indelibly marks you as one of his.

Epilogue: *Consumatum est.*

Slowly, I walk to every single place that was ours. I ponder the final moments, and nostalgia wells up inside me. I know that I'll meet you again, Beatrice, my Sweetness, always slipping between my legs. The next time it will be in Madrid, and I'm sure I'll be daring enough to go down on you at the feet of Cybele. But meanwhile I'm all alone because of you and fretfully so. I recall that the Hudson, exactly in the middle, exactly under the George Washington Bridge, is 300 feet deep, and I remember that over the past twelve years, I've not gone swimming, and the memory of you—bittersweet and deep green—is like the stones at the bottom of the river. Then I think I could have made you happy if I'd dared to eat that peach or, like now, dare to jump and end it all and finally look eye-to-eye and face to face at that savage god, the one with the immense mouth.

BLIND MADNESS

Miguelina Ponte Landa
Translated by Chris Brandt

A newsboy was hawking papers by the bus stop. The insolent afternoon fell upon the stones of the park; the beggars had all gathered. The cockroaches were telling each other of the latest dangers.

The men were fighting in the mountains; in the city, wine and cognac spread their circle of stench. Women were working as waitresses and there was still talk whether that was a suitable job or not. Fleeing those voices and the malicious murmurs, I went into my other hiding place and stayed there quiet, my head between my knees. Too quiet, so when my father came looking for me, he had to take his eyes out and put them on the table.

"Where's my little girl?" he practically shouted, shaking, and me like a piece of cardboard, like a bottle top, I started swaying and bumping against his shouts.

But my father was like that and I wasn't in my right

mind either, because I was seven, and when you're seven, you don't think, you just want to die.

For sure, I missed Mama, and my brothers, and I ended up going crazy.

The radio came on early. Its tinny music scratched around in the corners of the room and brought the crickets out from hiding. I was carrying my little spear because it was Three Kings' Day, and my brother had his revolver.

"Kill Mama!" I told him, and he started jumping up and down like a dog with ticks.

"'Kill mama!' Look at her, she doesn't know anything. Can't you tell it's Daddy, it's Daddy?"

And no sooner had he said it than he spit in my face. Well, what else could happen, Daddy was already dead, what could we do! Mama had brought him back dragging him by one arm all the way down the street, because Mama was strong and had a huge voice, while he... just wanted to live.

Afterward they stripped off his clothes...

And the others came down from the Sierra. But I'd already gone crazy.

What else did that man want? Besides, Daddy was blind, like the beggars in the church; what did my eyes matter, full of sharp cinders as they were?

And the radio around there kept giving out the news: "Batista's fled, Batista's fled..."

And my heart opened up and flew off with the butterflies from the courtyard. It went up so high, so high, to reach it again, I had to throw myself on Daddy's legs swarming with flies and see the baby spiders opening up an enormous hole in his belly.

"What's the matter, Daddy, tell me! What's the matter?"

"Nothing, baby, nothing. But no sooner do you close your eyes than the bugs come and eat you up."

I hid in his arms, covered with dirt as he was, and I carried him down to the sea so he could sleep easy among the fishes. I left him out there on the waves where a gigantic whale came and swallowed him and went off dancing, and I stood there scratching my head—what else could I do but start looking for my heart again? I went on for a great distance, so far that my knees buckled and my feet swelled up, and one day with hardly any warning an eagle brought it back: brought my heart back all pecked and bitten.

"Poor Mama," I said to myself, and somebody shouted down the street, "Poor Mama." I screamed, and somebody told me from the street, "That's all there is. Hold on to it." And I kept on going with my eyes full of pins, I couldn't explain it to anyone again.

When the clocks struck eight in the morning, I went to mass with Oriesa. Oriesa—poor woman! I remained kneeling in the pew, convinced that no one existed outside of Daddy and his death. Father Angel came to believe it, too, and at nine we left on the bus. I wore a dark dress, and Mama, where was she? Nobody knew, nobody, poor woman!

Five years went by and Daddy came back. He was walking slowly and covered with mud. I kissed his hands and buried him again, but when I lay down to sleep at night, the sound of his loud breathing kept me awake.

"Daddy, are you breathing, are you breathing?" And

the windows flew open and everyone fled the house. I heard Mama's voice saying:

"Leave him in peace, can't you see we are alone?"

But I knew she was a liar and what she wanted was to separate Daddy and me. She was jealous of him, who only wanted to live in spite of everything.

"Go to the hospital, the hospital!" She pointed it out to him, but she was crazy, poor woman. He kept saying no, and hanging on to the sheets, to the bed, to the floor. The black dog in the courtyard started whining all night long, but he stayed planted there, growing his roots into the grass.

"Why to the hospital, Mama? Nobody wants to go to the hospital, sick people die there in heaps, and everyone around you is wounded. Leave him there in his dark room with his brown socks. Bring him some water. He's so skinny, he looks like a baby sparrow. Trace him on my hand, Mama, I want someone to know him after me.

And my sister came with her greedy eyes. Everybody sang in their tiny voices:

Yesterday they took him away,
he had big ears and lemon lips ...

But I knew that was a lie, it was a lie.

One afternoon when I was nine, I met him in the street.

"Daddy!" I shouted, and stood there waiting for him with my mouth hanging open. He came over to pick me up; I couldn't go to him since I'd become a drop of water on the sidewalk. Mama was right next to us in her white dress. He gave me a little blue chicken. I wanted to put it under my pillow, but it would have broken. I told Daddy to keep it for me (nobody loved him, poor man), and like a little boy all proud of his first big job, he kept the blue chicken for me in his casket.

"Daddy, Daddy! Where's the little blue chicken?" I asked him the other day.

"In my house, baby, in the good-bye house."

"Why did you take it there?"

"Because... Bah! It was a naughty little hen, it was painted; when it grew bigger, white feathers came out from under the blue paint!"

"White, Daddy?"

"White, baby, like lies."

"Why, Daddy?"

"Because that's the way it is, my baby girl, everyone deceives us, everyone, don't you see? That's why I wanted to take her there, where everything recovers its true form."

"And you, Daddy, you?"

"You'll see. In time... "

"Go on, Daddy?"

"How do I know? That's your business, so how should I know? How can I answer you?"

And he grabbed his eyes, put them in, and left, without waiting for me to reach out to him, and despite the speed with which I ran after him.

"Mama! Mama! What letters spell *live*?"

"What a question! Don't you remember, girl?"

"Yes, Mama, yes... "

And I turned away. I moved off slowly, knowing that it was I, myself. I was carrying a book tightly under my arm and an album full of strange figures... "My brothers are there," I thought. "Mama too." I was, I was. That's how I learned it, and when I got to the corner, I waited for the light and crossed the street. The bus came. I got on. The conductor smiled at me—he was a friendly old man who made jokes with the driver—but I had no hope of anything. I looked out the window at the street. I knew Daddy wouldn't be coming home this summer.

LITTLE POISONS

Sonia Rivera Valdés
Translated by Alan West-Duran

How could I know I would react this way? It had been a long while since I had stopped loving him.

Of course, it was I who left the son of a bitch. He never would have left me. Of the two I was the more mature, understanding, serene, the sucker and the asshole.

That's why it felt like a jug of cold water was being poured over me when I saw on his desk the photos of that young thing he hooked up with the year after we broke up. I was upset. Yes, it was twelve months from the day—and after five years of therapy to free myself from my codependency—since I had told him we were done for good. He didn't believe me. He thought it was just another one of our fights, maybe a temporary separation like before, but I was sure this was final. I said it over and over again to the point of bursting: don't unload your neurosis on me; don't get pissed with me, making me always the guilty one until proven innocent. Say I had a problem at work, what a hassle if I told him about it! And if I can't talk to him, what's the point in having a companion? Always, his first question was what had I done to get into trouble? Me, the most easygoing person in the entire company. For seven consecutive years I've won the company's Public Relations prize.

When I moved into the tiny bedroom, he had to accept my decision. Then, as he had done a thousand times before, he accused me of having provoked the fight to break up. It wasn't that way. What happened was that little by little I had been curing myself of my addiction to him. And when I heard him making jokes about some private memories of my childhood—that I had shared with no one except him—with two couples friends of ours, I thought, He's blasting holes right through our relationship. You know, relationships get colds, they develop allergies, sometimes pneumonia, and, well, according to the disease, they are cured or not. He, with his ragged, warped sense of humor, killed ours off at point-blank range. There was no cure.

In reality, I had been trying to leave him for years, and finally I did it. Aside from therapy—from which I don't want to take anything away—I was helped immensely by a Patricia Evans book, *The Verbally Abusive Relationship: How to Recognize It and How to Respond.* By chance, I found it at Barnes & Noble while looking for a book on bereavement, to console a colleague at work who had lost her husband. So, I found this book described the dynamic of abuse in our relationship and the personality structures that exacerbate it. I'm going to be honest with you; at that moment I was still feeling sorry for *him*. Imagine how sick I was! I always felt sorry for him. That was the problem. And it's a problem that all women suffer from this addiction. The husband does whatever he feels like, and as soon as he suffers, or says he is suffering—God knows if it's true or not—your heart is crushed and you go back to the same old pattern. Living with that demon is difficult, says Patricia Evans, even for the person who has it inside. All I know is that for me it was hell. That last time I told him it was over, I knew it was for real.

As days and months went by, I began feeling proud of myself, strong, free from his subjugation and my neurosis, even when his romance with the young woman began and he told me about it. In our fifteen years of marriage he would tell me everything, even about his sexual escapades—if he couldn't share them with me, who would he share them with? Besides, that way no one could come running to me spreading rumors. In the end, he couldn't live without me: his wife, friend, lover, and mother. Can you believe that I listened to these stories and even felt proud of the trust he had in me? Anyway, since I never saw any proof of his romances and my life was boring, I even came to be entertained by the stories. Besides, his schedule never changed; he left the house in the morning and he always came back for dinner. Now I am wondering if he was making it all up. He was such a strange guy.

When he told me he was in love and mentioned her name, Fermina—something he'd never done before—I figured this meant he would not be coming back to me, and I felt good for the moment. But thinking it over, well, everything has a limit, and leaving photos of her naked where I could see them seemed a bit much to me; he was doing it to torment me. Even with this, had he left home quickly, nothing would have happened. But months came and went and I saw no signs he was moving out. Photos continued to pile up on the desk, and then the love notes appeared. Ridiculous and poorly written, they bugged the shit out of me. One would understand his wanting to stay on in the apartment if he didn't have any money and couldn't find another place. But he always had real good jobs, not only because he had a Ph.D. in chemistry, but also because he was a poison specialist. Simply, it was really hard for him to make decisions. I was always the one who managed the practical aspects of our marriage.

Yes, I tell you, he was strange. Only his poisons entertained him. He would go on for days about each new one he studied. Then, on a trip to South America, he discovered that the tiny pistil of a certain flower contained a chemical so potent that two of them could annihilate a two-hundred-pound man without leaving a trace. Its effect on the human organism was similar to getting food poisoning from eating shellfish. He truly became obsessed. He bought a small expensive crystal perfume bottle and put some pistils in it, and kept it at the bottom of a drawer among his socks. I was the only one who knew where they were, and that's because I saw him putting them away, not because he told me. Tell me he wasn't crazy. He never wanted to reveal his discovery, and it could have made him rich.

It was a difficult situation for me. Since I was always the understanding one, I felt ridiculous telling him how much the ostentatious display of his relationship with the young woman bothered me. I didn't want him to interpret it as jealousy.

Things got worse. When we separated, we decided to
sell the apartment, which belonged to both of us. Of
course, the transaction required time and lots of effort,
and as I've already told you, he was interested only in his
poisons. It was all going to fall into my lap, I knew it. I
insinuated that living under the same roof would feel
uncomfortable. He—he made more money than me—
could rent a small apartment temporarily, I suggested.
He refused. It was too much work to look for a place now
and then to have to look for something more permanent
later; he said I should move instead. If I hadn't taken
charge, things would never have changed, such was his
inertia. His relationship with the young woman hadn't
made a difference. Apparently, he felt satisfied with the
life he was leading, seeing her from time to time, eating
with her, and sleeping in the room next to mine. I
needed to sell the place fast so that I could buy another
with my half of the proceeds.

Everything was a mess. From the papers on his desk I
found out that he was paying for the studio apartment
where she now lived. He could have lived there; but for
six months he didn't show the slightest inclination to do
so. As time passed, my obsession grew. Instead of coming
home from work to enjoy the tranquillity that I now feel,
I would dedicate myself to looking at the photos and
reading the letters on the desk. I scoured the drawers,
searching for scraps of paper, receipts, movie or theater
tickets. I bought a book written by a couple who had been
photographic analysts for the CIA and studied it carefully.
I took a course on handwriting analysis at the New York
Open Center, and bought a high-powered magnifying
glass to look at the photos. I was no longer content with

just reading the letters that he left opened. I started going to my job at a quarter to nine so that I could leave work fifteen minutes earlier and give myself time when I got home to check the daily mail carefully. Meticulously, I opened any suspicious-looking letter, examined it with the magnifying glass if necessary, and sealed it again.

There was a hell of a battle raging within me, and no longer with him. While the clearer part of my mind led me to speak to Iris, my lawyer friend, so that I could finally get a divorce—she got in touch with the realtors to sell the apartment—my dark side would rummage through the corners of the house and in his clothes looking for things with which to torture myself.

Two weeks before Raúl died, Fermina started to call him on the phone—something she had not done before. In a tired voice, unexpected in a person in her twenties, she would leave messages on the machine asking him why he hadn't gone by the studio the previous evening; she had made him empanadas—his favorite food—and had sat waiting for him. That if she had upset him in some way, offended him without meaning to, to please forgive her. Please, please. Several times that first week and every single night during the second week, it was the same old song and dance. And he lost no sleep over this. Don't ask me why, I don't know.

At the end of the second week, Fermina had begun to call past midnight. I was close to sleep when I would hear Raúl enter the apartment and head directly to the answering machine to hear the teary message of the night, taped an hour before. This went on for three nights. He would enter and go to the machine without even stopping to take off his jacket and tie.

Suddenly, my heart gave a jump and I sat up in bed. I realized that not showing up for dinner with her, leaving her stranded with his favorite meal after probably having asked her to prepare it, not speaking to her for days, all these were signs of torture. This, together with his extreme interest in listening to his victim plead daily over the phone, all added up to his love for her. Terrified, I opened my eyes; he had stopped loving me. No wonder the previous weekend he'd taken the books on poisons off the living-room bookshelf and put them in a little pile on the bedroom floor; he was ready to take them away. He was leaving. I couldn't sleep. I saw the sun come up and the first little bird land on the feeder by the window. The thought gnawed at me. He was giving that other woman what had been mine for fifteen years: a twisted affection tangled with rage; it was the most legitimate thing he could give when he was able to give something from the bottom of his soul. That's what I felt—confessing it sears my soul—and it was the reason for everything that came afterward. How was it possible that another woman could be so important to him that he would do to her what he was only capable of doing to me? Me. I was an extension of him, indivisible from him, the person he hurt as if he were hurting himself.

Believe me, that was my saddest night. That jealousy was a thousand times worse than the one I felt knowing he shared kisses and caresses; it had been years since the bond that held us together was not love but fright. And look, you don't know me, but I'm the calmest person in the world, abnormally calm, says a girlfriend of mine.

The next day I got up and, as always, made coffee for myself. I went to his bedroom—he had just woken—and offered him some. He looked at me perplexed, because I never took coffee to him in bed, and he took it. When he went into the bathroom, I opened the closet and my suspicions were confirmed. Almost all the hangers were empty, and on the floor against the wall was an open suitcase filled with shirts and pants meticulously folded. I waited to hear the shower go on, opened the drawer halfway, grabbed the little bottle of perfume, uncorked it delicately and deposited into my palms the five tiny pistils it contained. Two little poisonous filaments would kill a 200-pound man, I remember Raúl saying to me. Since he weighed around a 155, I put three in the coffee, to be on the safe side. They dissolved with the first teaspoonful of sugar. I put a second in; he liked his coffee real sweet.

Raúl was a great chemist, that's for sure. Shellfish food poisoning was the diagnostic. Since he had not eaten at home for a while, I had no way of knowing what could have produced the effect. I wasn't up on his eating habits. No inkling of suspicion. When the body was taken from the house, my relief bordered on happiness. I couldn't believe it, but I felt liberated. As my grandmother would have said: dead dogs don't bite.

But wouldn't you know it? There I was at my calmest in the funeral home that night, listening with resignation to the condolences offered by work colleagues and the wailing of the family, who brought chamomile teas to calm their nerves, and who worried that I couldn't cry, when I see a young girl with short hair and slightly slanted eyes come through the door. Immediately I know it's Raúl's girlfriend. Her presence put me in a rage, rabid even, because in the end, as so often happens with me, I was angry at myself. Why should I care if she was there? Actually, rather than it bothering me that she wanted to see him one last time, it should have been worse for her that I was there mourning him. I really had nothing going with him for the last year and a half, well, not physically anyway. But emotionally, yes. The proof of that being what I was forced to do to him. I felt the urge to shove her out of the place, toss her out on her ass! But in my delicate situation, even though no one knew it, I couldn't allow myself to act out of character. Everyone knew me as Miss Politeness, and the last thing I needed was to let on that I was jealous. I swallowed, looked at the floor, and acted as if I hadn't noticed her presence. But what do you think she did? She came right to me crying with her hair all in a mess.

"Ay, señora, ay, señora," she repeated.

I looked at her. Her eyes weren't as slanted as I thought when I first saw her at the door. She could barely open them, they were so swollen from crying. I felt sorry for her, I couldn't help it. Kneeling in front of me, she lay her head on my lap and began her lament.

"Can you imagine my misfortune, señora?"

She had arrived from Guatemala less than a year ago without papers and had found a job as a live-in domestic. When the lady of the house learned about Raúl, she lost her job because she was out too many nights. Raúl rented her a studio apartment, but he never stayed over.

That much I knew.

She never did understand him. Such a fine gentleman, so tender and, all of a sudden, during the last month he stopped talking to her; days would go by without her knowing what was happening. He wouldn't

go over to eat, and all she was trying to do was find ways
to please him.

I felt like recommending Patricia Evans to her, but I
was sure she didn't speak English.

—"Then, he disappeared for a week, señora, until
this morning when a friend at work telephoned to tell
me he had died of shellfish poisoning. It wasn't my fault,
señora, he had not eaten with me for a week," she kept
repeating.

I asked myself, Where had he spent those nights?

—"And now, what am I going to do? Where will I
live? I don't make enough money housecleaning to pay
my own rent. I would have been better off staying in my
country and being killed by the army or the rebels. What
difference does it make? Where am I going to live now?"
She repeated this last phrase, wailing, almost choking.

—"With me, if you like," I offered.

She stopped crying.

—"Would the señora do that for me?"

—"Yes," I said, nodding my head. "The apartment is
large and Raúl's room is empty."

Were Raúl alive, I would have had only half the
money from the sale of the place, I thought without
saying a word. Now it's all mine.

Soon, I acquired the reputation of a saint. Shortly
after the funeral, I helped her move. That was three
years ago, and Fermina is still with me. She is intelli-
gent, clean, hardworking, and grateful. From the very
first moment she reminded me of myself when I was
her age. I found a school for her where she could learn
English, and helped her enroll at the university. I put
her in touch with Iris, my lawyer friend, and she

arranged for her to get her residency. In reality, we
have both helped each other out. When I started to
empty Raúl's room for Fermina, I realized how lonely I
would have been for him had this girl not been sharing
the house with me.

For two years all was perfect. And then things got
screwed up. Fermina fell in love. When she introduced
him to me, immediately I realized she had chosen Raúl's
exact likeness just by the way he treated her. After getting to know him better, much to my horror my hunch
has been confirmed. This guy is going to beat her, if he
hasn't done so already. The insults have grown astro-
nomically in the year they have been going out. Fermina
already reads English, and I've given her all my books on
the topic—I have an entire library in the apartment,
enough to get me a Ph.D.—but she doesn't read them.
It's horrible. For three weeks now she's kept me awake at
night. I see myself in her. I know what awaits her: years
of putting up with a lot of shit before she realizes what's
happening, and then more years before she can extricate
herself from this mess, if she can—no one can be sure of
that. And if she does manage to get out of it, only God
knows how. I've learned that from experience.

Right now there's nothing to be done. What I tell her
about myself she doesn't relate to. She thinks I'm exag-
gerating, that her situation is different. Everything will
improve with time. The strength of her love will make it
work. Poor thing, I know the pattern only too well. He
does whatever he wants, then he returns and they patch
things up without his having to explain a thing. He says
he doesn't know why he did it, he couldn't help it, let
bygones be bygones, that he's hopeless. She forgives him

and it's off to a clean start. Poor thing. That's no life, and it won't change for years; who knows if she will be able to get out of it someday?

I've become obsessed and that's why I've come over to see you, not because I feel bad about what happened to her three years ago but because I want to see if after this talk my compulsion to settle this situation once and for all will go away. Alice Miller says that if an adult is tempted to commit incest with a child and speaks with a therapist about it, he won't end up doing it. I know you are not a therapist, and it's never crossed my mind to commit incest, but I'd like to see if this talk can exorcise my intentions.

This is what's going on. This morning I open up the little perfume bottle where Raúl kept his pistils and I see that there are two left.

No, that's not what I'm thinking. Listen, getting rid of this guy is not going to solve the problem. Sure, it would mean one less son of a bitch on the planet, but the world is full of them. The real problem is that women put up with them. It's Fermina who is breaking my heart. I know her. If this guy disappears, she will go out and find another one to abuse her. Do you think it's worth living like this, at best for a bunch of years, at worst all your life? If she marries and starts having kids, given how docile she is, forget it. It's all over. Or possibly, one of these guys will beat her to death. Or shoot her. Or stab her.

Anyway, this dingbat that she has snared weighs about 190 pounds, and there's only two pistils left; I'm not going to risk blowing it, because then they will initiate a full investigation. On the other hand, Fermina barely weighs 105. Too bad. She is so pretty.

CURRICULUM CUBENSE

(from *From Cuba With A Song*)

Severo Sarduy
Translated by Suzanne Jill Levine

CURRICULUM CUBENSE

Feathers, yes, lovely brimstone feathers, heads of marble carried down a river of feathers, feathers on her head, a feather, hummingbird, and raspberry hat in fact, from which Help's smooth orange nylon hair stretches to the ground, braided with pink ribbons and little bells; from her hat the albino locks cascade down the sides of her face, then hips, down her zebra-skin boots to the pavement. And Help, in stripes, an Indian bird behind falling rain.

"I can't go on!"—she shrieks, and carves a hole in the bread crumbs.

"Drop dead!"—Mercy speaking—"Yeah, drop dead, put up with it, kill yourself, go tell the president, go tell the gods, shove it, split into two like an orange, drown in beer, in franks and sauerkraut, fuck yourself. Turn to dust, to ashes. That's what you wanted."

Help pushes aside her locks. She peeps out, Baroque:

"I will be ashes, but meaningful ashes.
"I will be dust, but dust in love."

MERCY: *Tu me casses les cothurnes! (en français dans le*
texte). Shut up. I can't go on either. Wipe away that
tear. A little modesty, please. And poise. Chin up. Take
your compact.

The small mirror is signaling. It directs the sun
toward the glass skyscraper. On the balcony of the twen-
tieth floor a girl comes out with another mirror in her
hand. She hops up and down and moves it around in
search of the call.

"Look at yourself. Your tears have made a furrow in
the first five layers of your makeup. Make sure they don't
reach your skin. Of course for that you'd need a drill.
You've lost the asparagus cream. The underlying strawberry is mixing with the lawyer of Max Factor's baby
pineapple. You're graph-papered. Vasarelic. Let's sing:

"the ever-absent, ever absent
"gives us evil as a present."

Help, almost singing:
"Yes, that's him. The riddle of riddles. The sixty-four-
thousand-dollar question, the definition of being. Our
cupboard's empty. No ham for Tom. No cheese for Jerry.
This is how it stands: we stayed behind and the gods
went away, they took the boat, they left in trucks, they
crossed the border, they shat on the Pyrenees. They've all
gone. This is how it stands: we went away and the gods

stayed behind. Sitting. Hiding, taking a nap, happy-go-lucky, dancing the "Ma Teodora," The First Cuban Song, the repetitive *son*, swinging in midair, like strung-up corpses."

"Shut up. That's what you wanted."

"No. I didn't want this. I asked for life, all of it, with the rattles and the tambourines. I asked for my daily bread and sausage. No go. They sent me the hairless old woman, the plucked, bald, shaven, lonely bitch of death."

"One of your cheeks is showing. It's like the face of the moon: full of craters."

"Rat. Rogue. Frog. May the Being swallow you. Inhale you. May your air-conditioning break down. May a hole open all around you. May the Lacanian fault suck you under. May you be absorbed, not seen because unnoticed."

"That's it. I'm leaving. I mean it now. No matter how. They're throwing me out. I'm cornered, and with my lance I strike right and left, to and fro, like a Japanese warrior fighting an invisible enemy."

Help moves her head. Golden fringes against the windowpane. Woolen locks. Windmill wings.

"Go away. Inessential. Leave the House. Yes, house with capitals. The *Domus Dei.*" And she nods the way.

MERCY IN THE DOMUS DEI:

But how could you not be confused? There were thousands. Thousands of little feet. Little worm-eaten hands. Such screeching. Tin plates and spoons. They'd come out looking green and charge against the waves. Siren, and they'd appear. Screeching, and they'd disappear. At the same time. A woman would go to each window. And at each, shake a black tablecloth. The front of the building would disappear behind a curtain of bread crumbs. River of feathers.

"Good morning. I've been phoning and nobody answers."
   "Ah," the maid says.
   "May I come in?"
   "Won't do you any good. She's not in."
   "What? After all the time. All the waiting. All the bootlicking and backslapping. I've gone down on my knees in waiting rooms, bounced between the sheets of every minister, bribed doormen."
   "Sorry, no."

The maid opens the door wide, as if she were opening her legs, her transparent little box, to the being *par excellence*. A light erupts from inside: the light reflected from the bald pate of the Great Bald Madame. Mercy contracts all over, turns white, like squid in boiling water.
   "Now do you see?"—the acolyte utters hoarsely—"She's conspicuous by her absence."
   By the time Mercy's on the elevator, poor thing, she's screaming at the top of her lungs. A crying little frog face. She mixes up her buttons, bumps against a black man, catches her finger in the door. And so she reaches the ground floor: moaning, bishop purple, cowering in a corner of the aluminum box, surrounded by plucked chickens on all sides, alone with them except for a block of crushed ice and a shopping bag of bitter oranges in one corner.
   You ought to hear the cute words the midget doorman saves for lady visitors! He comes out from

under his scarlet cap and exhausts the synonyms. With Mercy it's a different story; frozen and all as she is, she kicks him at the first flattery, ties him to the stool with his own belt, presses the button to the roof-garden, and launches the echo chamber.

There are mirrors in the hall, and, although threadbare, Fate just can't stand herself; she pulls out her hog's bristle brush, her orange, diamond-studded eye shadow, the false beauty mark that she places painstakingly on the right corner of her lips so that it rises with each smile; lastly she pulls out her Yoruba necklaces, and when she steps out on the street, she is something else. To the point where Help, waiting for her with coupon in hand—good for two mango milk shakes at the Milk Bar on the corner—jumps with joy upon seeing her and waves a handkerchief: She thinks Mercy was received.

"No, I wasn't."

When they turn, slender and symmetrical, toward the building, the windows are already dark. There is no noise. The bread crumbs have bleached the treetops, the black lawn.

"It's like snow!"

SELF-SERVICE

"My, we're metaphysical, we must be hungry! Let's go to the Self-Service!"

No sooner said than done. They're off on tiptoes, sucking in their tummies, slipping among the shells of rusty cars—their silky hair flows through tin scraps—stumbling, jumping over flattened and spokeless bicycle wheels, over handlebars, moss-covered horns, headlights stuffed with paper, aluminum circles with red bars. Yellow

deities. Flavian birds. Stags. They walk among glass, gir-
dled by rain, crowned with frozen orchids from Palm
Beach, clean among the dregs, clear-cut as mushrooms
upon horse dung, fragrant among the debris of diesel
motors.

Following the scaffolds of a construction site—in the
foundations, puddles of green water—they walk along
singing *Ich bin von Kopf bis Fuss auf Liebe eingestellt*,
opening their hungry little fish mouths into heartshapes,
tightrope-walking on a steel bar.

And behind them, thousands of paper balloons
simultaneously light up within squares. Cones upon a
red tapestry. And over the buildings, the milky wake of
the subway streaks the night. Intermittent blue rhombi.

And off they go, the Flower Girls, the Ever-Present,
cross another scaffold, another avenue. There they go,
under the three-leaf clover of the highways watched by
helicopters. Echo tunnels. There, by the escalators, by
the rails, where all the trolleys are, a second before the
go signal. How speedy!

One potato, two potato, one by one they pick up the
potatoes under the table, crouching among feet; she
crawls along the gallery of legs, behind a rolling tomato,
the paper cup, the bowl of grated beets—little purple
strands on somebody's shoe.

People jump over her. Down there, on all fours,
entangled in her own wig, soup-soaked Help has fallen
with her plate among open tangerines (a spiked heel per-
forates her jellied egg).

She picks it all up—dirty home-fried potatoes—
looking up from side to side like a frightened squirrel.

She puts on her green glasses. Covers the other half of her face with bangs.

"I want to disappear!"—and she's no longer a squirrel, but a mole: she rolls herself into a ball, and hides her head.

Mercy is now seated, but not eating. She's looking at the food and sobbing rhythmically. She boohoos and blows her nose with a Kleenex. When Help arrives empty-handed—she threw her plate into the garbage can—she shakes her by the shoulders.

"It's nothing," she says.

"It's nothing," she answers.

And they laugh again.

Now both are seated, calm and collected, in front of a celluloid picture window. Not one stain, not one hair out of place, not one drop of tomato sauce on their cheeks. Motionless, their heads, a few inches apart, coincide with the crossing of the diagonal lines in the landscape—blue domes punctured with windows, an airfield: Drones and twin engines are taking off—pale hands on their chests. They don't move an inch, but it's useless: Everybody's looking at them. They feel on trial.

"Mocking eyes give us the once-over."

"Fingers point at us, put asterisks on us."

Then Help puts her finger to her right temple, jumps up, shaking her mane like a feather duster, clinking her little bells; the girl's all music.

"I have an idea."

She opens a crocodile-skin box that hangs from her shoulders like a canteen on a thin silver chain, and, counting them, she takes out fifty color photographs. She throws away two that have yellowed, hands Mercy a

close-up in black and white, and goes to the end of the
dining room with the other forty-seven. From there she
starts handing them out, table by table. With each photograph she smiles, combs her hair, introduces herself
to the addressee with a bow, and doubles his surprise
with a detailed description of the picture. Mercy follows
her a few steps behind, adding adverbs to the adjectives,
curtsies to the bows, cooling the air with an ostrich-
feather fan, spraying it with balms. At Help's signal,
Mercy gives each a little Caridad del Cobre medallion
and a piece of candy.

The first picture is already faded. Help, with her face
painted yellow, is in a guayabera shirt and cap, drinking
coffee in front of a cardboard tower, or a Mardi Gras
float, or a mausoleum lettered in Arabic.

"Here I am in front of the blue mosque of
Constantinople, even though you can't see the four tur-
rets. The suit is Empress Ming's, that's why I have that
dragon-painted teacup in one hand and this single-flow-
ered long-stem in the other. As you see, my eyes are
elongated by means of black lines that, in profile, if it
weren't for my ears, would turn into little fishes."

"You forgot to say that these sniveling, bare-assed
little boys who are playing mandolins, mouths agape
before the lens, are your interpreters."

"My followers. Look at this one. Here I am among
the Cauvean or Cadivean Indians, reading Franz Boas
with a tape recorder. What the native is handing me is a
mask whose general lines correspond to the map of the
city. I look good, don't I?"

And thus, she hands out all the pictures. Except one.
She keeps the passport-size, six-by-eight, in which she is

face-front, looking slightly to one side, not really serious, in short, her spitting image.

"I don't think we left a bad impression."

"Maybe. But let's go before they change their minds."

"Wait. I forgot my scythe."

Note: The Self-Service is on the ground floor of a Bakelite octahedron. Walls of Coca-Cola bottles support a ceiling decorated by a Fall of Icarus in pale pink and gold. From the corners four spotlights move sinusoidally along the walls and sometimes stop on bowls of grated carrots, jellied eggs, or red beets in almond sauce that are embedded in wicker nooks between the bottles. At each sweep of the light a xylophone arpeggio ascends or descends in the scale according to the altitude of the light beam, and stops on a note when the beam stops on a plate. Since the red beets in almond sauce are practically at ceiling level, the corresponding note is a shriek that turns hoarse when the focus descends in the sinusoid.

The delicacies, like the plates that contain them, are made of plastic.

A NEW VERSION OF THE FACTS:
FATE AND THE GENERAL

If she entangled him in her champagne locks, if he pricked her with the open brooch of one of his medals, if the cherry tart fell on the Carmelite khaki of his uniform, if he scratched her with a gold braid, if both got entangled, if they held their tongues out of courtesy, if they insulted each other, if the creamed asparagus remained among the decorations of honor, if the Pyrrhic victor invoked the patron saint of artillerymen, the invincible goddess Changó, if she retorted by calling upon the queen of the river and the sky, her antidote and talisman: we will never know.

Let's make a note, then, on how it stands at this moment: facing the dessert department, among synovial trays and trembling like a burned butterfly, Help has entangled her hairs... No: her hairs are tangled in the aluminum forest that armors a skinny general of the fleet.

There they are—two plumed serpents—cheek to cheek, stuck to one another, their trays stuck together too. Struggling Siamese twins. Bacardí bat, ink spot, double animal, open oyster, a body with its reflection; that's Help and the General.

There they stay, touching at their vertices, extremes meeting. Like a rattlesnake that finds a jiggling, appetizing little mouthful for itself, a pyramidal cupcake that it downs in one gulp, letting loose the scream then, because it's just downed its own tail, and thus disappears and returns to Bald Nothingness.

"But why doesn't the General simply take off his coat?"

Listen to the question that Mercy, and only Mercy, asks.

I: My dear, can't you see that if the General takes off his hardwares, he would be like Lacan's woodpecker without his feathers? Like a goat who takes off his black stripes to create a Vasarely with them?

MERCY: I just want Help out of this mess, that's all.

I: She'll get out. She'll go home well-mannered, conceited, chaste.

MERCY: Listen to that! Three adjectives in one breath! It wasn't like that in my day. What today's literature is coming to...

I: Yes, dearie, three adjectives in a row, but well put. So shut your mouth and swallow.

MERCY: Digressions are not my line, so to the point: what's happened to my friend?

Nothing really, just that this cosmogony-in-the-making simply attracted, sucked in the world. As a magnet in a river does to fishhooks, or as a vacuum cleaner in a chicken coop to feathers, so did the binomial Help-General suck in all that was around, and naturally, a black girl and Chinese chick: thus completing the *curriculum cubense.*

As always, the fourth element, that is, the Unnamable Baldy, was already present. It was stuck on to the third, which is always hero-worshipped for its strength; well, then, the two that were missing came running. They arrived, twin stones, fish of identical eyes, to get caught in the hair and medals, to entangle themselves in Help's Conception of the Universe:

1. an Oriental, in white rice-powder makeup, prima donna of the Shanghai District Opera;

2. a round-assed, big-titted black girl, very semicircular, very double-breasted, snuggly squeezed into a bright red weave, her hair freshly ironed like a river of creeping vines.

So that, seen from above, in an imaginary mirror that we can place on top of the Self-Service counter, for example (and that is probably there, to see if someone is taking the silverware or hiding, as he passes a chocolate cookie in his pocket), the group is a giant four-leaf clover, or a four-headed animal facing the four cardinal points, or a Yoruba sign of the four roads:

the white of the wig and the coat,

the China doll of the lottery and the mouth cat cabala,

the Wilfredo Lamesque black girl,

and the last—who was the first:

the red-headed fraud, the Waxen Woman, the Keep-Your-Fingers-Crossed Loner. We come upon them, the four parts of which the wise stud of Heidelberg intones.

MERCY: Yeah, the one who put the lid on the box.

They're all yours now. Four different beings and four who are one. Already they are breaking loose, already they're looking at each other. How cute!

SKIN DEEP

Antonio Benítez Rojo
Translated by Mark McCaffrey

Máximo suspects there is something strange in the house and he checks for it every day. But, as he has each night of this hot winter, he sets the air conditioner at eight and fails to notice Mariana. It is peculiar to watch Máximo brave the equipment in the study (especially the stereo). Abandoning the vast triviality of his usual gestures, he applies himself to the different controls quite seriously, as if mending stockings. Tonight I considered his question about which records I am going to play, and to satisfy his black ears from my side of the door, I replaced the Gerry Mulligan with a Benny Moré. Puffed up by this nod to his services, he walked out smiling beneath the gray frame, smiling a bit savagely, and leaving me alone with Mariana. Mariana in the study, well hidden behind the curtain with orange dots like eyes.

When I met her (four years ago), the musicians were getting set to play, and though she didn't know

"Tenderly," she sang *"Tu, mi rosa azul"* with a modest, indeed a very professional, quality. I realized that night that it was she who was at the bottom of my fight with Laurita. It hit me after the spotlights had bathed her in a sticky chartreuse and the bartender murmured her name to me. It hit me after she walked off in her arrogant sort of way—behind the musicians, up to the red stage—and I sat there looking at another shot of whiskey and thinking what an idiot Laurita is as I stirred the crushed ice. Those were days of bearded *comandantes* on the front pages and wild gun battles, Mariana—and how we loved each other.

"I'm in love with a black woman," I told Laurita over the phone a week later. It was true, and she was trying to cope with it.

It was true, Mariana. And now I can hear the songs, the ones we liked so well; and you, nude and saying nothing to me, behind that hallucinatory curtain with the orange eyes that kept you hidden from Máximo.

It was after I lost the jewelry store, sometime in between staying and leaving, that I placed all my bets on her card—the queen of hearts; Mariana, reigning supreme from the stage, welded to the microphone, the baited hook complete with barflies.

We made love on Mondays, talked things over from Tuesday to Sunday amid the rise and fall of feelings and the endless greetings of her friends. We would sit in a corner of the bar drinking, our heads close together and under the tipping of glasses divulge to each other in mysterious tones the small details of our lives. Or we would reveal hasty half-truths so as to get to know each other better. I was an inspired liar, accusing myself of promiscuity while seeking an admission of the same from her in regard to the before-she-knew-me times. A useless ploy, I might add, with such sensitive matters at issue: the uncertainty of a dense silence or her unbroken smile. My obsession for knowing the identities of lovers she had had in other times drove me to direct methods of questioning her, and more than once I crushed my cigarette on her brown arm, so unnerving was her inscrutable reserve.

But you would walk away from me, Mariana. After a silent spell and with the tears running down your face, you would say you had to touch up your makeup or fix your wig, and off you would go to the ladies room, dignified, your dress wrapping your buttocks into a tight, fleshy fold.

And so she would elude me, never really opening up, but coiled up on herself like those Mulligan lines playing inside the record player. Then the long looks while the fingers turned the ashtray in circles—a black paste, almost like molasses, under reconciling curls of smoke—and suddenly the need for an incidental, definitely an incidental, kind of music. "Sorry, I ran into Martica in the powder room and..."

Sometimes, without any leading questions from me, she would volunteer some quick and disconcerting bit of information. "I've never been involved with anyone of my own color." And she was serious, and half surprised, as though the voice coming out of her were there to please me, so that I would know that no one like Máximo had possessed her. And I was grateful and clung to her all the more tightly, forgetting her rigid hair and the puzzling odor of her underarms during fornication. And that is how we got through the first year, with firing squads and undiscussed sabotages for a background. It was a time when a person stiffened up and took an aspirin before opening the newspaper.

We listened to a lot of records, usually jazz. We liked the West Coast sound, with its arch tones and ineffable harmonies: Chico sweeping in behind the hum of a string bass; Kessell in "Indian Summer," or Laurindo accompanying Shank on a concert guitar. "Why Do I Love You?", a tune on one of Brubeck's Columbia albums, was one of our songs. We played it every day, after she quit singing and came to live with me. And sometimes at night, when we were in a playful mood, we would ask each other, "Why do I love you?" An appropriate question.

April brought with it the Playa Girón revolt, which caught us by surprise. Máximo fell under the spell of the old lady from the lower floors and, giving up half his nights' sleep, started on as a watchman at the front gate of our building. He carried himself like a centurion, interrogating startled passers-by and feeling pretty full of himself with his faceless Defense Committee ID card. Máximo was impossible. I'd come home from my own doings to find him reading Marx's *Kapital* or thumbing through faded pamphlets that he would acquire in bulk, with a stamp collector's zeal. We lived very frugally. Mariana helped Máximo with the household chores, especially the cooking. On weekends she would masterfully season our allotted portions, thereby easing, in quality at least, the squeeze of rationing.

Oh, Mariana, how I miss your cooking, those boldly sprinkled spices, your perfect fried dishes, your inimitable sauces. And now I am subjected to Máximo, who poisons everything with all the virtuosity of a Renaissance groom, stuffing me with hastily prepared legumes and plantains. And you, standing there in your panties free of all malice—the evocation of an endless, individual sin—hidden anywhere, the savoring of your charms almost within reach of Máximo.

With our meetings on the fringes of her past now forgotten, Mariana one day indulged in a whim that grew into an incident—an almost- forgettable thing that, like a tiny needle prick in a tattoo, forever marked us with contrary signs.

"What a beautiful day! Why don't we go to the beach?" she said, letting her hair down as she stood before the window. "We haven't gone once yet and it's almost the end of October."

"It's always summer in Cuba," I said sententiously from the bed, without really knowing why. I may have been afraid to meet her idea head-on, I may have been waxing meteorological, I may not have had the nerve to explain the embarrassment of the color difference: we would be nearly nude among all those people in broad daylight.

"You used to say you loved the beach."

"I went now and then, usually in winter. Anyway, it was at the Biltmore, which is a public beach now. Either that or the scholarship students use it."

"Some beach. Once I sang there and some drunks threw bottles at us and the musicians threw them back. They almost didn't pay us and I tore my dress. And to think that you might have been there."

I denied participation in any such event and, taking

my copy of Proust from the night table, told her emphatically:

"I would rather read. I'm not going to the beach because I don't like being around all those people. Is that clear?"

"Oh, it's clear. Just like it's clear that you don't like to feel surrounded by black people," she said. Her breasts trembled like rich custard pudding, so violent were her words. She drew near the bed.

"Hah!" I exclaimed.

"Or maybe you don't like to be seen with me?"

"Mariana, you know I have left everything for you. You know I love you above all else."

"Are you sure?"

"Of course."

"Very sure?"

"Yes."

"Then why don't you marry me? Why does it bother you to talk with me or go into restaurants with me?"

And so the darts flew. She kept coming back to the same thing, again and again and hardly shedding a tear.

The crisis began to bud in October. It started slowly, like a poppy flower well out of season. And then, all of a sudden, the ultimatum: red petals quick to fall under the brush of every insignificant gesture, under the ambiguous breath of assumptions. And Mariana blithely carrying on, her life a shuffle of everyday frets and cares. She was oblivious to consequences and traded patriotic palaver with Máximo while relentlessly reviling the Pax Americana.

Almost at the zero hour, amid news flashes and sudden alerts, Máximo gathered his war gear and asked me for fifteen pesos to buy himself some boots. I fronted him the money, hoping they would find him a trench somewhere and he would stop pestering Mariana with his revolutionary song and dance. He had been working on her with it since the previous winter. Then, before he left, while he was filling his knapsack and she was helping him, I caught him bad-mouthing me, telling her to get away from me, to leave me at that very moment and with everything up in the air.

How about that Máximo! Give them an inch and they'll take a foot, as my mother so wisely used to say. And to think that you fell for all that, Mariana, with the war drums beating. You just couldn't wait to see if things would calm down. It's hard to believe, Mariana. How untrue you turned out to be after four years! How could you believe him? If I went out and got a passport, it was only as a precaution, one well worth taking, I might add. Then, the way you said good-bye (without making breakfast and me still in bed). "I'm leaving," you said in a quiet, a simpler way than usual, as though announcing the title of a song. And I am lying there rubbing my eyes, still groggy, wondering if I have heard right. "I am leaving," you said again, standing next to the night table in a cabaret dress, your wig tipped slightly over your right ear and the smell of napthalene overpowering your perfume. Then the doorbell, the indecipherable gleam of your last look, your steps crossing the room and the sound of the suitcases dragging along with you, the distant indecipherable calls of the driver, again the doorbell. Your "good-bye" came through under the door.

Caught unawares, I smiled vaguely from the gray blinds, having nothing to say but a useless "I'm sorry."

What else could I do? Anyhow, I found out yesterday that you are singing again, and that you are going to marry a black man, a television announcer.

But what's the use of talking about it? A fox knows its own hole, and you're no exception. And to top it all off, your ingratitude in making off even with the pictures. If it weren't for the Polaroid of you in the nude that I took one afternoon at siesta, there would have been nothing left of you here. Thank heavens I was thinking ahead. And now I listen to the records we used to enjoy, and you behind that curtain, stuck up there to the lining by a straight pin.

Mariana, Mariana, what a sad day I have had. And Máximo ignoring me, listening from behind doors and following me around the house to see if I will destroy anything. He is hoping I'll go so that he can have it all. What can I do about it now? This is the last night. Tomorrow I take the plane... it shouldn't make any difference to me... and yet... but no, to hell with hesitation... before I go, I'll burn your Polaroid thighs, your untouchable breasts. Then I will let the wind have the remains, pack my bags, and close the door for the last time. I will descend the stairs with grave and stately steps. When I get beyond the gate, I will turn and take a long look at the house—Máximo will be gesturing from the front balcony. And I will walk pensively away, the memory of your skin burning slowly and evenly, like the finest Havana cigar.

THE CHARM

Pablo Armando Fernández

Translated by Alan West

$\int$uddenly, the wind grew harsher announcing a storm and a dense cloud of sandlike dust strained its way through the windows and doors. The bartender hurried to close them. The bar, an old wooden house deteriorated in part by the constant lashing of the elements, was in itself gloomy, and the lack of natural light made it more lugubrious.

Seated at one of the tables, the man took off his glasses and rubbed his eyes with the back of his hands. For a moment he felt himself buried in the dust. He hardly noticed when another man, much older, arrived at the table unscrewing a bottle of rum, which he planted next to the empty glass.

There had been few customers. They would come for a drink and would abandon the premises as soon as they downed their booze. He had arrived looking for a phone, which he didn't find, and for a drink to quench his thirst.

On the detour, a sign with the name of the town Vega de la Morena made him change his route. He had been on the road for many hours, and the car started having trouble when he had entered that area of canefields and mangrove swamps. The monotony of the landscape—on the one side the endless canefields, on the other, the coast—had induced a certain fatigue. The sea air blew with ever-increasing force. That and the exhaustion made him decide to come into the town. He stood up to shake off the dust, when he felt the other man's hand threatening him to sit down again. He adjusted his eyeglasses in order to look at him head-on. The intruder, in turn, had been observing him at moments slyly, at other instances with decided impertinence.

The man's look provoked a certain unease. He wanted to get up, abandon the premises, and go on his way, but something hidden in those eyes and that voice bid him to remain. He spoke slowly, demanding attention, as if what he were to tell him or what was being told were already extremely important. Extremely important to him.

Listen here. My granny, a black Lucumí woman married to a Spaniard, was a midwife. I would accompany her to the countryside on horseback or in a carriage when she went to pick up the women about to give birth. She used to say she didn't like to be alone out in the woods where dark spirits were waiting to take hold of the flesh of newborns. She would drive away the dark spirits; she didn't want any evil soul to enter the tiny body of such a biddy creature, for him to first open his eyes on this earth so filled with evil, that's what she would say. A woman with powers, she knew how to pick the spirits that would help the children she brought into the world: my three aunts had married Spanish men from Vizcaya, successful businessmen with public prestige. One of them, Leonela, from the day of her wedding, went to live in Camagüey, my granny's favorite city. When I was born, I was born with a spirit, with a virtue, as the saying goes around here, and my granny said to me, "This spirit that you were born with is a womanizer." Truth be told, instead of my making women fall in love with me, it was the women who would make me fall in love with them. You know when a woman is in love; without her saying a word you know it; you know by the looks, the gestures, by the way she remains silent... She told me, "Look, son, you were born with a spirit that is lucky with women."

Sure, all my life I've been very reserved in my own matters, but the truth, the real truth, is that I've never lacked women in my life. I don't want to sound vain, but I've always had them lining up. And not just dark women, also white women. The white ones would just give themselves over to me. My guardian angel, according to my granny, is the Virgin of la Caridad del Cobre; this has been borne out in all places and circumstances. And the Virgin of la Caridad is inclined to fall in love. White women would choose me because my spirit, the one that was born with me, is Galician. The truth, the real truth, is that white women were easy to get. Dark women were more slippery, more leery. And it's not because I tried to be white, like my Spanish grandfather; in my town everyone knew my Lucumí grandmother. I was more attracted to the dark ones, because of my guardian angel, the Virgin of la Caridad, a dark woman with good hair and fine features like mine, but with pure blood.

204 ⮜ Dream with No Name

It's blood that rules: it says to you here I go and
there's nothing you can do about it. I have always been
very reserved and somewhat timid, but nevertheless it
was clear I appealed to white women. You don't know
what that's like, you can't imagine it: men without any
luck with women. I've met many such men. I knew a
white guy who had a ring made to order. Any woman
who laid eyes on that ring was bewitched. Then he had to
deal with the very devil to get them off of him. I don't
know what you think of these matters, but white gals
wouldn't leave me in peace. It was them, you know,
above all them, and all on account of that spirit my
granny let into my body when I was born.

You can't imagine how many things that spirit has
got me into since I started to shoot up and grow.
Somewhere around here in a trunk with things from
another time, there should be a photograph of those
years, if the termites haven't eaten them up. Even if it
sounds ugly to say it, I was a good-looking man then. I
don't think that in our town, or in any other for miles
and miles, there was another man who could rival my
looks—strong and skilled, and with that Spanish look
from my grandfather, who left lots of offspring all over
the place. You could recognize all of them even if they
didn't carry the surname Ocejo. My granny, who was
aware of everything, would look at me for hours without
saying a word, refusing to make comment. It is as if she
were not looking at me but instead the other one, the
spirit in me. I could almost assure you that what I saw
in her eyes was a hard look, a little bit of pain, of jealousy, that instead of seeing me she was seeing my
grandfather in his youth.

My granny was black and tiny, just so. She barely reached my waist. Beautiful face. Her eyes, two beads blacker and more brilliant than her skin. When I stared at her, I could see—I don't know if I can explain it—another world, another life. I didn't like to look at her straight in the eyes. Her eyes obligated you to see, see, and see that other world of dead souls. And it is as if she were trying to tell me something, something she never did tell me, not even before she died, and I was there at her bedside, looking at her, searching in her eyes for those things she preferred to take with her to the grave. But that day, not the day she died, but instead the day in which she stopped seeing me as a child and began to look at me in another way, I, who up until then had only noticed women of my own race, saw in the depth of her pupils other women. And they were all white.

Well, that bit about feeling and thinking in my body for the dark women of my race I know it now, because the truth the real truth is that for black people I wasn't black, nor was I white for white folks. But I can't say I was a mulatto either. For mulattos, no matter how light they are, and no matter how good their hair, and how fine their features, something that isn't the color of skin or the shade of the gums, something that I couldn't exactly say what it was, always gave them away. It's a matter of blood. Blood that isn't pure doesn't flow in the same way. Mine was like my Lucumí grandmother. My Spanish grandfather furnished the outer part, what people see, he put it into my father first, and later in me. If you think about it closely, as I have thought about it every day of my life, there's no reason for me to be as I am. When I was born, my Spanish grandfather had

already died; the saying that I look like him as two drops
of water do, that's something I've never believed. My
aunts, the ones married to the men from Vizcaya, never
tired of telling me this. So much so, that since I was a
boy, and, of course, in front of the family, they would call
me Ocejito or Lito, just like they called my Spanish
grandfather. In my very town, where there were many
whites, very few were as white as I was. As I grew up surrounded by my grannie and my aunts, women who spent
their lives telling me how handsome I was and how
much the ladies were going to like me when I grew, I
started forming an idea in my head about what a man
had to be like so that he could be attractive to women. To
be honest, not all of those ideas I had came to be. Some,
I found out later, were a lifelong mistake. But the truth,
the real truth, is that I really didn't need what I learned
from the women in my family. I'm speaking about my
granny and my aunts. I was the only man among them.
One day my father—and this we found out almost a year
later—left on a boat. We never saw him again. At home
we only spoke of him when we received letters and
money. As soon as the letters and money stopped, he was
never spoken of again. What he was like, I don't know.
My mother died giving birth. May God and the memory
of my dead granny forgive me, but many times I felt my
Lucumí grandmother...—I don't know if I should say this
to you; when you start getting old, you think that not
everything that races through your head should be
blurted out; anyway, here goes—my grandmother, she
was happy with the death of my mother. I have the blood
of my granny, of her direct ancestors, and that,
according to her, was enough to make my body grow.

Inside of you are the desires, illusions, ambition, and the steadfastness to bring them about. One's true race is in the blood. With it you inherit defects and virtues. A pure blood, complete, makes a person upright, without duplicity. Look, it's not the bones, that is what people who don't know what they're talking about say; it's the blood that sustains you, keeps you from losing your nerve, it's what keeps the eyes steady, makes you alert to danger and docile enough in order to understand. The blood of my Lucumí grandmother was whole: blood for a real people.

The women of my house, of my family, my aunts married to the men from Vizcaya, were women of solid character. I wouldn't want to offend anyone, even less these real women. There are some things that I don't even like to hear in my dreams, that's why I never say them, but the truth, the real truth—and by this I don't want to raise any false testimony—it's that they would spy on me—I hope you understand this well—on each one of the impulses that my body took in order to grow, until the day they all got together and agreed that I was completely formed. It is as if each had put in her little part to finish a work of which all of them could feel proud. I don't want to be too modest because that would be pure hypocrisy, a lie, a cheap deceit of people without conviction, but I must confess that I'll still mess with anyone, even with the cleverest of the lot. They were hardworking women, and spared no effort. I can assure you that just as they bustled about doing fine needlepoint or a dessert, in the same way and with the same patience and hope, they crafted, like bees in the queen's hive, the sweetness that other women were going to enjoy.

What the heck! the silly things women say and do when one is male and a boy; like asking who your thing is for, touching one's privates, they being sure you'll respond as they've taught you to, that it is for the girls. "Who are the little balls for? Who is the pee-pee for?" It makes you want to split a gut laughing when I think of those titillating remarks.

What these women wanted in the house was a man through and through, and I can assure you that I didn't disappoint them; not even in things, because of my way of being, that would alter my moods. From them I learned that a man is born and made to be served by women, and to adorn them, to make them look better. I was, as I've already said, a man of few words; with my aunts I spoke little; I would distract them with my mere presence; they couldn't complain about that. Being in the house all the time I was clean, dressed in smartly pressed clothes; you could look at the tips of my shoes as if they were a mirror; my face was practically bathed in cologne, and my chest, underarms, and privates were fragrant with the finest talcum powder.

So they taught me from a tender age to show off, to strut my stuff in front of them. My aunt Leonela would have cried to the heavens if she would have found me dirty or sweaty. I would take real extra care to enter the house through the front door after my crazy forays on horseback. I always ate everything, heavy food, strongly flavored, prepared by the hands of those women expert in making stews and fritters. My aunt Encarnación despised little men. She was a full-statured woman and she liked to have to lift her head to look at a man. Majesty in a woman, she'd say, crowns a man. My aunt Leonela was a whimsical, capricious person. She enjoyed watching me with my head uncovered, during the hottest part of the day, to see my hair shining like a bolt of lightning. My aunt Augustina was of pure character, how to say it, a pure soul; a being with her own source of light, the kind that gives a man a sense of security. The three of them spent the years of my childhood and early adolescence fussing, plastering, smoothing over, adorning, polishing me. All this without me being aware of it. They were convinced that a man who was tied down was not a man but a puppet. And I lived, as they say, without any fetters, like the wind. Have you ever thought of that? Anything that's not the wind has something hemming it in, on one side or another.

But I would like to talk to you about those days, of those times when I started to get into trouble chasing skirts, as they say, and... the things that would happen to me! I've always been a quiet kind of guy. I don't like dandyish men, either on the dance floor or in a fight. I wasn't a troublemaker either. If they came after me, well, sure, they were certainly going to find me: I never dodged any commitment or responsibility. I hold my liquor well: half a dozen bottles wouldn't even make my head spin once. I have no memory of indigestion from stuffing my face. My aunt Encarnación thought that men have to be fed well, without affectation. It was like raising studs. The times I heard her say, "When he becomes a man, he's going to drive women crazy." My poor aunt: who was almost driven crazy was me, by all these women.

As a boy, I was very taken with horses. I would get great pleasure in galloping on the open savanna, with my shirt pressed hard against my chest. What? Your shirt inflates on your back when you race! Riding horseback was a passion in my blood that I couldn't control. One time I fell in love with the colt born to one of the Thoroughbred mares of Don Eulalio Mayor. I started to go around his land stoking the illusion of having the animal to myself. At first, the old man was happy to see me haunting it. He even let me break it in. What a full-blooded, spirited colt! It almost negotiated a sympathy, a friendship between Don Eulalio and me... until the morning he tried to ride it, and it resisted. Grasping the reins, Don Eulalio said to me, "I don't want to see you around this ranch until Kingdom come. And as far as this one is concerned"—pointing to the colt—"there will be time for him to learn that he was born to serve me." He turned his back and started walking, the animal trailing him. My blood helped hold me in check, respecting his age, but I had the feeling things were not finished between us. Something rushing through my veins was foreboding another opportunity. I didn't want to think about it because I didn't want the rancor to seep into my blood.

I couldn't stop at home. I would pace from one place to another wanting to forget everything: the colt, Don Eulalio, the humiliation. I was about seventeen, but ever since I was fifteen, I have been the man I am now, a lanky soul of bone and hard muscle. My granny, pretending to be unworried, would watch me come and go, until that day I've told you about, when she stared at me. I was standing right in the middle of the door, and, she, about to leave for the eleven o'clock mass, looked at me from the parlor and, without taking her eyes off me, walked by brushing me with her shawl and said, "Come, I want you to accompany me to see your true mother, the Virgin of la Caridad del Cobre." Since it was all the same to me, I took her arm and we walked a few blocks. While crossing the park I felt another pair of eyes looking at me the way my grandmother had. I felt them, but I didn't turn to see whose they were. In the church we sat in one of the pews next to the altar. I said all those prayers with those eyes fixed to my nape, piercing me, but I didn't want to look, I didn't want to see. When mass ended, we stood up, and as I turned, I saw her: mature, but of firm flesh, well-kept figure and bust line, pink cheeks, dry lips. They moistened when we passed by, and she reverentially greeted my grandmother. I had never seen her before. It surprised my granny that I didn't know her, and that I was disinterested in what the two were talking about. In an instant the woman said, "We never see your grandchild around the house. My husband has a great affection for him. The colt that Enamorada gave birth to has both of them up in the clouds with joy." And turning to me, "My daughters and I wouldn't go out to the porch when you would go around the ranch riding Gallardo. What a shame you never got closer! You never thought of coming closer?" A certain complicity in the smile that shined in my grandmother's eyes, and that was secretly acknowledged by the other lady, put me on guard, but I didn't want to give it too much importance.

My granny had a great reputation as a midwife, and as a woman of spiritual power and authority, although she claimed to be off the mark when it dealt with family problems; then she would turn to my *comadre*, her soul sister, the black woman Fundora. Granny was respected not only because of her wisdom but because she knew where she belonged, which to her meant putting others in the place where they belonged: she at home with the kids, and when she married them off to the men from Vizcaya, then alone with me. My granny would dash to attend someone about to give birth, someone who was sick, but she would carry on little conversation, and with white folks even less. "They have their ideas, their science, and I have mine. If I can help them out with something, I do it in goodwill, but poking into their business or lives, forget it." This she would say sitting in her rocker, with needle, thread, and thimble, doing her sewing. Her hands were always occupied with something.

If there's something that still amazes me, it is that encounter. I tell things how they happened, each one at its own moment. As she got into her carriage, the woman stuck out her head and, once again, I felt her eyes now fixed on mine. I've already told you that until that afternoon, when I thought of women, it was always black women. Something sang in my blood, a happiness with a feeling that made my body feel sweet, easy, with a desire for giving. A dark woman feels the same thing, believe me. I know from experience. The first woman who took her clothes off for me was a black woman from Platanillo. I followed her in the street, with her consent. She didn't have to look back to know I was following her; she walked with the gait of someone waiting, of someone who knows she won't be walking alone. When our steps matched up, her mouth was a smile the size of the sky, and it opened up my heart. I can assure you my blood and hers knew it, too, even though that was the first time I hooked up with a woman. I still remember her. And I remember her because for a man the essential thing is that he be the one that seeks out and finds. The times we were together, and they were many, I always felt that same happiness in my blood. That *morena* was mine because I wanted her to be mine. My aunts knew nothing about this, nor did my granny, at least I think they didn't. Those last inches of growth, when my bones became hard as steel and my muscles turned agile, came about when I found this black woman. A portentous woman, better than all the joys found in life. This woman affirmed the flesh of my body and taught me things. No, I'll never forget her. Not even with my passion for horses and my crazy riding throughout the savanna, which would leave me exhausted.

From these encounters—with Don Eulalio first and then the woman in the church—it was as if some evil had entered me between the skin and bone. I started to feel frail, impatient, distrustful. I wanted to flee from the eyes of my granny, from the eyes of that woman following me. That summer was ferocious, with a draft that split even the rocks. The heat would stick to your breathing; it produced a kind of thirst that singed every pore.

One afternoon I found the woman in my own house. I knew her name was Fulvia and that she had been married only a few years to Don Eulalio. I knew the daughters, fully grown, were not hers. What she came to see my granny about is not something I felt I needed to be suspicious of. I know they spoke in a low voice. I haven't told you why, but my flesh started to feel weak. Look, since I had stopped seeing that dark woman from

Platanillo, and not only at night, at any hour of the day, it was as if my temperament as a man had come out on its own. I never laid eyes on another woman. And yet, it seemed like I had a dame on top of me all the time. Just like that, as blood seeps from a wound, or breathing through the nose, the seed of life would ooze out of me. And that woman entering and leaving my house, all dolled up as if she were going to a party, each time appearing more beautiful, offering herself, provocative, generous. My granny watched my every move, until one day, and all because I refused to drink a punch scented with cinnamon and soursop leaves, she said to me, "Tomorrow you're going to see Fundora, the black woman." She said energetically, "If you don't go, I'll go. You don't have to tell her what's wrong with you."

The black woman Fundora was in the garden, sitting on a stool leaning against the window of her room. She had a white kerchief wrapped around her head, and her sandals, very white, were loose, made into slippers to shuffle around the house. "I know what you're coming for," she said. We entered. "Drink this bit of coffee and sit down, be calm." She looked for an empty firewater bottle and she was washing it out with soap, grains of corn, and hot water. Later she went out to the well. She brought a bucket of water and went out again, and when she came back she had some herbs she had washed, and she plucked the leaves from the stems. She put them to boil. Again, she offered me coffee. I thanked her, rejecting the offer, but she put the catch basin in my hands. It was an order. A thick, strong coffee, bitter as hell. Then she strained the concoction through a white cloth and filled the bottle. She told me to put it out in the cool of the

night and that every morning I should drink a little of
the brew before drinking coffee. She also told me that
there are women who don't like to eat from where other
women have eaten. "Your granny knows what she has to
do and she'll be in charge of you drinking from that
bottle. Give her a kiss." All of this seemed to me like old
women's foolishness, but I went to please my granny so
that they would leave me in peace. Of course, you didn't
know her. Anything that got into her head, would get
done in a jiffy. "Whatever is left for tomorrow will remain
undone."

By the time the moon changed phases, I had recu-
perated. I started to feel full of life. But my blood wasn't
singing, I had lost that kind of joy evoked in me by only
thinking of that *morena* from Platanillo. Don Eulalio's
wife began visiting more frequently. She always found
some pretext to linger with my grandmother. Even
though her eyes shone more brightly and her lips
became fleshier, I took little notice of her since I was so
immersed in my own world, that you can be sure of.
There are people with two sides to them, people who
don't need to pretend, because they make lies a kind of
persuasive truth. People who believe in their own deceit.
Don Eulalio's wife was just that sort of person. That
afternoon the heat was like a block of cement. There was
no god capable of producing the slightest puff of wind.
One would blow air to relieve oneself of the heat and the
lips would burn. The night before, my granny had
received an urgent message from Leonela, who was suffering from ailments which the doctors assured us they
could find no explanation for. She spent all night
insisting I accompany her to Camagüey. Much to her

chagrin—she didn't want to leave me alone in the house—Grandmother left. We would keep the house shut, since my grandmother was in the habit of saying that shadows produced dampness and moisture coolness. There was a knock on the back door; I was barefoot and shirtless. I ran to get dressed. This made the person knocking more impatient. I feared it was someone with news of my granny or aunt Leonela. Unless there was bad news, no one would knock with so much desperation. The door faced a little stretch that only stray cats and dogs passed through. Behind that was the thicket, which we called the Monte del Isleño. Who could be knocking from there? Only a friend of the family, someone who knew the thicket, the alleyway, and the back door that led to the backyard. I opened. Don Eulalio's wife was at the door.

Looking suffocated and pale, I didn't react until she herself insinuated with a gesture that I let her in. In the corridor adjacent to the patio, she asked about granny. I told her she was away for the whole day. She sat in a rocker drying her forehead very delicately. Her hands trembled. I wanted to open the shutters, but she forbade me to do so with a gesture. I offered her a glass of water. She hesitated. I asked her if she felt ill. She said no, shaking her head. When she spoke, it was to tell me that she didn't think it was right to be alone with me. I paid no attention to this; I supposed she wanted to rest and, in order that she feel at home, I told her I would go to the patio, where from time to time I entertained myself polishing a saddle. She stopped me with a gesture. My presence comforted her. I noticed she was still trembling; I've never figured out when she calmed down. "It's hot," she

said, and placing the tip of one shoe on the heel of the
other, and then repeating the same move with her shoe-
less foot, she showed her bare feet. They were small and
thin. Her silk stockings made them look more pink. She
told me not to worry, that she would soon depart: it wasn't
right if it were known that we two were there alone. She
looked all around, waiting to make sure that no one else
was home. The slightest noise would upset her. When she
stood up, it looked as though she were going to faint. I ran
to hold her upright. She leaned her body on mine and was
crying. In my arms she seemed weak and tiny. Crying, she
told me no, that I shouldn't do that to her, that she didn't
want that, but her hands were bustling under my shirt,
and her mouth, salty from tears, rubbed against mine,
saying that I didn't have eyes for her, that I only thought
about the *morena* Andrea. This disconcerted me. My passion for Andrea was a secret, just like everything that happens between a real man and a true woman. I don't know
when I lifted her in my arms and took her to my deceased
mother's bed. She hid her face in my chest, saying that I
didn't want her, that I shouldn't do this to her, but she
wasn't wearing her bodice; still crying beneath my body, I
felt her nails in my back. I couldn't see her eyes, but I felt
on my neck the moistness of her tears. Obstinate, she
repeated the same thing, no, no, no, but her body intertwined with mine, she crying all the time. Just like that,
over and over, she wouldn't even come up for air; dug into
me, weak and tiny, trembling, scared to death, telling me I
would soon tire of her, and if that were to happen, she'd
die, she would expire calling out my name. "Don't make
me feel like I'm dead again," she would say. And she grew
calmer between sobs, immersed in that body that was not

mine because I had not sought this out, nor hers because she was surrendering it without joy, with a sick, sad blood. And I knew from that afternoon on that she was going to pursue me, find me, and that I was not going to hide from her, because her shame was also my shame.

The time my granny spent with Aunt Leonela turned out to be weeks. Twice I went to see them. Reluctant to let me go back home, they insisted I accompany them, because they needed me there. I discovered that my granny's eyes would look at me with a mixture of rancor and shame. You can believe what I'm about to tell you: it is as if that look were not directed at me. Maybe I don't know how to express myself well, but life is strange. Her eyes had changed. I was sure I had not let her down. I was still the same: quiet, polite, clean... all the things she appreciated in me.

The truth is I wasn't able to understand that sudden change in her look. I can assure you that when we walked together through town and some woman would turn and discreetly look me over, the first one to wink an eye or produce a malicious little cough was her, my grandmother. What could she reproach me for? To be brief, I must explain to you that many years later I found out that tiny woman, so sweet and affectionate, had suffered greatly with the Spaniard Ocejo; he gave her children and a good position in life, but suddenly he would escape for weeks or months, and wouldn't return until she made him a good *amarre*, a spell to tie him down. Maybe it was this. Already an old woman, she would recriminate what she thought was a natural attribute in men: having a fondness for women. Or maybe she was foreseeing what would later come to be?

During those weeks that Granny was absent, every morning, or almost every one, before or after mass, and always by the back door, Fulvia would show up at the house. We agreed to keep the door half open so that it would be easy for her to enter without calling for me. She would slink by the patio and the corridor and drop into my bed, always with a man's voraciousness that nothing could satisfy. Maybe the shame impeded her satiety. I'm not going to talk to you about those things: they should remain between the sheets, the bed, and the walls of the room. And always the same dry wailing, the same complaints: I was only interested in Andrea. If I made love to her, it was out of obligation, because she looked for me, but in my mind I was thinking of the other woman. It was a savage love, of animals battling without illusion, defeated beforehand by shame. But by the same token, this same disenchantment, this same defeat, made the encounters embody a greater ferocity and bitterness. No, son, I wouldn't want you to see this putrid blood, the spittle of lust that leaves the body slimy and dirty. I would wait for her, it's true, with rage, sometimes with indignation for making me forget those times that Andrea and I would calm ourselves with the sweetness of our blood and we would remain quiet and still, one next to the other, without the slightest unease perturbing our mood.

When Granny announced she was coming back, Fulvia seemed like she was at the point of going crazy. She said I would be happy not to see her again; that I would be able to go back to the arms of Andrea without any remorse; that she was going to die and the whole world would know why. That woman didn't know that the two of us were condemned to those afternoons and to the bed of my deceased mother; I already had the vice of her bitterness buried in my body.

It seems as though things were going to let up. The man who had been speaking stood up, went across the room in the direction of the bathroom, and disappeared. The other man thought it the right moment to pay the bill and escape. He called the waiter, snapping his fingers. A group of young men who had just entered were getting the waiter's attention. Impatient, the man clinked his glass against the empty bottle, and everyone turned to look at him. Bothered, the waiter replaced the empty bottle for a full one. Standing, he was about to initiate a discussion when the older man reappeared among them, almost ordered him to go back to his seat, and served two long drinks into the glasses.

Don't think I'm a charlatan, I heard him say serenely, I spent many years away from town, did you know that? I returned because my grandmother's eyes would have never shut without seeing me one last time, and also because I wanted to know, you understand me? what I still don't know. That bit about having been born with a spirit that is a womanizer might be true or not, but the truth, the real truth, is that they never left me alone, not even after my return, my deceased grandmother already buried, and, believe me, it was the white women who were all over me. Maybe it's not so good that I relate these matters to you, but something tells me you're in a similar type of danger right now, and maybe you're not prepared to face it.

With the return of my granny, Fulvia disappeared from my house, from church, and from the town. It was

I who sought her out, looking for her at the stable where Enamorada was, or at the ranch where Don Eulalio kept his corn and beans from the last harvest, or even in the inclement outdoors of the pastures, night after night, without finding her. With the light of day I would return home. I would fling myself on the bed and in an instant I'd jump up and go looking for her in the town, at church, in the places where I thought I might find her. I waited for night and would go back to the farm: to the stables, the ranch, circle around the house. With all of that coming and going I saw little of my grandmother, who would spend hours and hours with the black woman Fundora.

One night when Don Eulalio didn't come home, surely he was in Holguín, where he bought and sold cattle, I found Fulvia waiting for me. She dragged me to her husband's bed, or I dragged her, God knows who did what, and we filled the sheets and pillows with our hell. After that she gave me no respite; day and night she would plot her escape. She placed in my ear a kind of whistling sound, which was the echo of her mind, of her heart, an eerie signal that would make me turn my head no matter where I was. She was able to make me succumb. Fulvia has been the only woman, who, without my wanting to, has made me give in to her whims. We planned the getaway. I'll never be able to forget the look of inevitable misfortune that was so visible in my grandmother's eyes that afternoon: in them I saw the faces and bodies of other white women that awaited me like a curse.

We had agreed to meet each other in a pasture. Fulvia was going to let loose Gallardo, saddled up, after one of those rides she would take that left her breathless and made her exhausted at night as she fell into my arms, somewhere between dazed and frenetic. We were going to meet before midnight, after her stepdaughters had gone to bed. We had taken advantage of the fact that Don Eulalio was away on a longer trip, so it seemed. With a jumping motion, I got on top of Gallardo and I pulled Fulvia up by one arm, who was waiting for me at the entrance gate. Without using the spurs, as if the colt were an accomplice to our impatience, we became a piston of dust that disappeared into the night. You could no longer see the lights in the town when we came to a halt. I loosened my grip on Fulvia and wanted to quench her startledness with a kiss. That's when she turned her face. The road lay ahead, and for her to convince me that there was no turning back, she threw herself from the horse, dragging me with her as she fell. Already on the ground, she hid her face in my chest, saying between sobs that I no longer wanted her, no longer loved her, while her whole body intertwined with mine more and more and the crying wouldn't let up. We stayed like that again and again without her even coming up for air, digging in to me, weak and tiny, scared to death, telling me that I would soon tire of her and that she would die, would expire calling out my name. I felt how her body grew calmer and began surrendering itself with joy, a joy with feeling, which made my body sweet, easy, desirous to give, receive. Her mouth, her eyes, her hair, that face I had seen so much and up so close, started to transform itself in such a way that it provoked a dizziness in me: it was the faces that had turned up so surprisingly in my grandmother's eyes, and with each change I noticed, my body became harder, more agile, happier. A racket made by some roosters jolted us out of our fray. To my right, night's thickness began to bleed, I saw the sky redden. When we started to go again, I still felt the rooster's call in my blood. We left Gallardo behind near the bus stop at Minas. Fulvia, with a gesture and a smacking of her lips, ordered him back to his stable. The sky went from orange to rose-colored to mother-of-pearl. We walked slowly. Fulvia rested her small head against my shoulder and wrapped her arm around my waist, provoking a desire in me to throw her into the river, or of sinking into the earth with her, among the thick grass, to bury ourselves in the same pit. Walking, I felt her breathing become more and more serene, her embrace softer, so much so that for a moment I thought I was walking alone. Approaching the waiting room, I thought I recognized the voice of Don Eulalio. Fulvia squeezed against me. Her face showed no fear, not even surprise. We pressed up against the wall, and between the iron balustrades of the open window, I heard the station master tell another man that Don Eulalio had sold his properties and was going to Spain with his daughters, to the village his parents came from. Fulvia was so close to me that she almost disappeared: again I felt I was alone. I looked into the waiting room where the girls, dressed in black down to their ankles, with black hats and gloves, were whispering among themselves. The voice of the man resonated in my heart and mind. A few months ago, he said, Don Eulalio had buried his beloved wife. Standing, unable to move, holding Fulvia to me, I felt as if I were bleeding to death without remedy.

DREAM WITH NO NAME

Ramón Ferreira
Translated by Paul Blackburn

He woke up feeling the sun, sat up on the bench and looked at the morning. A policeman was coming toward him through the park making a noise with his stick. It was the fat policeman who had at times treated him well and one day had given him a peso. On another day he had not given him anything and had told him to beat it. Today he was coming unhurriedly clacking his stick against the ground and saying let's go. Probably he was going to give another peso. For that reason he waited for him. When he came close he looked at the ground and crossed one bare foot over the other. He put his hands between his knees and continued waiting. Let's go he heard him say and then the sound as he knocked his stick on the walk. He got up to leave. But first he looked at him. He stood unmoving and looked at him asking for a peso. That was what he wanted to ask him with the look. But the policeman did not understand him

and went back to saying let's go. He walked a few steps
and then he turned. He looked behind him and waited to
tell him I'm hungry. He looked up at his face and told
him. I'm hungry. The policeman stopped and said not
even if I were your father. And then he said let's go and
went back to knocking his stick against the walk. Of
course he wasn't his father. He knew that well enough.
His father was his uncle. Or his uncle was his father. It
was the same thing. He hit him if he didn't bring any
money and if he brought some he'd take it off him. Then
he gave him something so he could eat at the lodging
house. If he didn't bring him any money today then he
wouldn't give him any. People were not giving as they
used to. Because now he was bigger. So big that they
wanted him to go to school. Or to work. Some of them
even looked at him meanly. It was bad to go on growing
like this. Someday they wouldn't give him any more and
his uncle would hit him with a belt. That was what he
told him when he got tired of hitting him with his hand.
But if no money came in today he wouldn't go back
home. Yesterday there hadn't been any and because of
that he had stayed in the park and had had to eat leftovers
stolen from the cooks and to run off when the policeman
arrived. Some policemen treated him well and others
treated him badly. The thin policeman had threatened to
take him in. But he was not on this beat today and the fat
one treated him well. He hadn't given him money but he
treated him well. And he let him beg and let him walk
behind the tourists. The tourists were different.
Sometimes they gave you money if you just looked at
them. But if you touched them then they would not give
you anything. He knew that already. You had to pay atten-

tion when they started drinking. And not do anything until they asked for another drink. Then one could look. He leaned against the column and looked at them without begging. Sometimes they took two drinks and did not pay any attention to him. They saw him but pretended to look in the other direction. Those were the ones who gave most. At first they did not want to give and then they gave more. But today there weren't many tourists. The situation and the heat the chauffeurs said who drove rented cars. And they sat about swapping comments with the whores that things were bad. The whores were odd. Sometimes they treated him well and wanted to put their arms around him. One time one of them kissed him. And then brought him to the lodging house and told the cook to give him something to eat. The cook didn't want to and so she took money out of her wallet and began to scream at him and the cook had to give him beans and rice. The whore watched him eat and called him m'boy. But when he finished eating she told him to beat it. And now it had happened that she did not remember him. Because she didn't want to continue giving to him. They were all the same. They only gave once. It was because of that that you had to walk so much. But that was not important. It didn't bother him to walk. He liked it. Because only by walking would he be able to meet her. That woman who covered him up in his dreams. Sometimes she passed without stopping and did not notice him. Although he shouted she did not pay any attention to him. Because he didn't know what her name was. Dreaming he would set himself to find out her name in order to call her. But he could not find it. Today he hadn't dreamed with her. Nor yesterday. When he wanted to dream of her he did not dream. But when he dreamed it was easier to look for her. At the end of the dream he remembered her. Her face no because he always saw her in shadows. But when he met her he was going to recognize her. He knew it. Someday he was going to meet her. And when he met her she was going to speak to him. In the dreams she did not speak to him. She looked at him very seriously and said nothing. She only looked. And if he was cold she covered him up. But if he was hungry then she went away and if he began to cry she started to run covering her ears with her hands. For that reason he did not cry. Even if he was hungry he did not cry. And he let her come close to the bed. It was a different bed. Not like the bench in the park or the stone step of a doorway. It was a real bed like those they advertised in the display windows of the stores. Even bigger than those they advertised in the windows. Only he never had anything to cover himself with and had to wait until the woman came. If he was cold she would come and cover him. Then he would wake up. The heat of the blankets woke him up. Today it had been the sun. But in the dream it was the heat of the blankets that woke him up. It was still early. Some cafés were already open but it was still early and he had to wait. There were no tourists at that hour. And the whores had already gone to bed. In the morning it was more difficult to find a meal because in the morning people were in a bad mood and it wasn't worthwhile to begin to look from the doorway. The waiters cleaning up told him to get out and if he did not go threw water at him with a bucket. He was tired and he leaned against the wall. He had just gotten up and he was already tired. But the sun took the cold off him. The hunger no but the cold yes. He could close his eyes and think of whatever he wanted to. Except food. If he thought about food he felt sick. So he thought about the woman in the dream. And this time he saw her as though she were coming walking out of the sun. It seemed true. She came walking from the sun and he stood quietly and immediately thought of what he could do. He would make himself sleep and that would let her come. It was the first time that he had seen her awake and this time he would not let her get away. He had to speak to her. And afterward touch her. And later let her touch him. Something like the whore. But not like the whore. Who would touch him and call him m'boy. For this reason he was not going to think about wanting to eat. He went on feeling hunger and not thinking about food. Only about the woman who was coming nearer. And when she was close he would open his eyes even though the sun bothered him and he would see her face and call her by her name. Yes now. Now she was going to know him. She was going to know him as soon as the sun stopped concealing her. She was so close. She was so close that he opened his eyes wide to see her. But she was going to pass by without saying anything to him. He stretched out his hand to touch her. And he touched her. The woman yelled and gave him a hard slap. Then she gave him another and called him fresh. When a woman yells everyone starts to look. And if he did not begin to run she would call the police. He began to run. The woman stood yelling on the corner pointing with her finger. But he kept on running. He crossed the park and then the street. He dashed in by one archway and came out by another. Until he was tired and leaned against a column. Then he saw these two guys. One looked at him and took a sip of coffee. He said something and then the other one looked. He was also drinking coffee and then both of them were looking at him. He put on his begging expression and played the innocent. One looked at him again. Then the other looked. And then they both kept looking at him. He continued playing the innocent and let his head fall on one shoulder. From time to time they took pity on him and said poor little thing. And once an old woman had given him a peso seeing him like that. Afterward he had kept on doing that but no one gave him anything. But now it could happen again. While he rolled his head down on his shoulder one of the guys called to him. The one who had seen him first was the one who called him. He told him come over here. So he had to look at him. Come here he said and he came up. Sit down he told him and he sat down. One of them continued looking at him and said no he's very little. But the other told him to be quiet. You must be crazy he began to say. The other guy paid no attention to him. Then he asked him if he were hungry and he said yes. The waiter brought him coffee with cream and toasted bread with butter. And when he had finished he brought him more. The two men watched him eat saying things he did not understand. One took him by one hand and looked at it and the other said to be quiet. How do you feel he asked him. He said that he felt fine. And when he asked him what his name was he told him Raúl. And then that he lived with his uncle. And that he was not going home because he hit him if there wasn't any money. And that there hadn't been any money because things are bad. And that the tourists were not coming and were not going to come. Both of them looked at him and then they asked

him if he wanted more. He said no. Come said the other
one. He got up and they stopped. One put a hand on his
head and looked at the other as if he were going to hit
him. See how thin he is he said and placed it on his waist.
But the one shoved him by the shoulder and said that he
was no baby. Then he squeezed his shoulder and he liked
that. They left the café and walked along the sidewalk.
Where are we going he asked and they told him you'll see.
They continued walking and crossed a park. Then they
continued past the gates and reaching a doorway one of
them stopped and said it's impossible. The other called
him an imbecile and said he should get out of the way
and he moved. Upstairs one kept standing in front of him
and said you'd better think about it carefully. Then the
other one pushed him and said if he were afraid he could
leave. You're the one who's afraid said the first one and
they began to argue. Go in and don't pay any attention
said the other and he went in. Immediately they were in a
corner and continued arguing. He sat down on the bed
and waited. Finally they agreed and one came and told
him that everything was all right. And he answered that
he was not afraid. The other laughed and told him to take
off his clothes. He asked why and the other said to him to
clean you up. He helped him take off his clothes and
asked him if he never bathed. Then he led him to the
door of the bathroom and began to laugh. As he passed
him the other gave him a whack on the butt. And before
opening the door the first one gave him another.
Presently he heard them laughing together. At first the
water was cold but then he liked it. The other came and
gave him some soap. He began to look at him and said
that he didn't know. He took the soap away from him and

told him what he had to do. The first one brought him a towel and began to dry him. Then he asked if he felt all right and he said yes. Good said the first one. The thing is said the other. And the two of them were silent. Well the first one started to say. Look said the other. Leave me alone said the first one and the other withdrew. He asked him how old he was and he said he didn't know. But you're already a big boy and he said yes. Grown and blown and he said yes again. And you want to earn money and he said sure. And not see your uncle anymore and he said no. Then he went to the table and took the newspapers from on top. Everything was in disorder. There were bottles and cans and nuts. And screws. And pieces of metal. And little boxes and big boxes. And words in American. Look at this he said to him and showed him a metal tube. Then he talked about the big store where they sold mattresses. And of its doorway where he sometimes tried to sleep. He asked him if they let him sleep there and he said the guard always threw him out. That is where you 're going to put it. He asked put what. And he showed him the fuse. The other came and explained to him. Because they are lousy and won't let you sleep in the doorway. Because they won't let you go into the store. Because we're going to give you a peso, and if you do a good job another. And probably afterward we will let you live here. He looked at the bed and he liked it. It was mussed up but he liked it. And one of them liked him. And the other liked him. Now both of them liked him. They had given him something to eat and they put their hands on him all the time. But now said the first one you have to be careful. You have to carry it like this said the other and he fastened the fuse in his belt. When you get to the doorway sit down as though you were going to sleep. Stay quiet until there is no one passing. Make sure no one is passing and turn it the other way around. Then. Then one started to say something and shut up. Then said the other you get up and you go. Without worrying said the first one. Nor running said the other. And don't get nervous and look behind you. Wait said one and went to get the fuse. He gave it to him and he said that he would do it. He put it inside his belt and asked like this. Yes said the first one. Perfect said the other. Now he walked as if the window were his corner. He walked to the corner of the room with the fuse fastened in the belt. Imagine that this is the window and sit down to wait. He sat down. Now look and see that no one's coming. And he looked. Now no one is coming and you take it from the belt and you put it next to the glass. Now you turn it the other way around. Now you get up. Now you go away. Without being afraid and without looking back. And you come back here. Just like that. Come straight here. Then they came running over and the two of them embraced him. They squeezed him hard and passed their hands through his hair. Then they asked him to do it another time and he did it again. He put the fuse in his belt and started to walk again toward the corner. He sat down beside the pretend widow and put the fuse on the floor and then he turned around the other way. He got up and started walking again. He did it one time and then once more. And that took a long time. Until he got tired and said he was hungry again. The first one went out and brought in some food. Later they made a telephone call and a woman came. When he saw her come in he thought that she was the woman from the dream. He looked at her wishing that she were the woman from the dream but the woman did not look at him. She only looked at the first one. She looked at one and then she looked at him. The other guy walked out. He said he was coming but he walked out. Then the woman asked him if he couldn't carry it. But the first one said that it was impossible. He explained it to her in a low voice and the woman looked at him again. Then she came close to him and said to him baby. But she did not touch him. The person she touched was the first one. But he told her be quiet. Then she asked him to send him out and the first one said again impossible. She threw herself on the bed and lifted up her clothes and showed her legs. The first one went and pulled her dress down and she lifted it again. Then she grabbed the first one by the arm and he sat down on the bed and looked at him angrily and said he should look the other way. The woman from the dream was not like that. The woman from the dream was no whore. The woman from the dream would embrace him but she would not throw herself on the bed. Nor show her legs. And she would not whisper with another man while he was looking the other way. He wanted to know what they were doing. And if he looked from the corner of his eye he would be able to know. He was certain that it was the same thing as the thin policeman with the whore on the staircase. He had watched and seen them do things. It was because of that the thin policeman threw him out of the park. And now if they saw him looking probably they would also throw him out. And they would not give him the money. Or let him sleep in the room. But he wanted very much to look and if he turned his head a little he

could see. And he began to turn his head. Till he saw
them. But when he saw them they were already not
doing anything and she came over exhausted and gave
him a kiss on the face. Then she went into the bathroom
and began to sing. The first one ran his fingers through
his hair and came over and said to him comrade. Then
he searched through his pocket and brought out a
handful of money. He gave him some coins. But that
didn't come out to a peso. He said that they would give
him a peso later. When he did the business in the
doorway. At this point the other arrived. He came in and
said that everything was okay. He opened his shirt and
showed them the fuse which he carried attached to the
belt. He took off the belt and put it on top of the table. At
this the woman came out of the bathroom and came
over to him. She looked at one and she looked at the
other and immediately said that it was no good. She had
another face now. Not how she was when he had thought
that she was the woman from the dream and she wasn't.
Now it was possible. She looked like the woman in the
dream washed like this and without any makeup. Only
she was younger and her hair was another color. But she
looked at him with her face serious. She gazed at him
just like the woman in the dream. As though she wanted
to cover him up. And she said again that it was no good
and the two guys looked at her. Tough shit one said, you
didn't come here to screw. The other said that it was his
fault for getting women mixed up in this business. She
said I'm going to do it and went and picked up the real
fuse. Put it down said the first one and planted himself in
front of her so that she would not be able to. Then he
grabbed her by the wrist and they began to struggle.

Leave her alone said the other and see if she gets to the corner. And then he asked her if she wanted to wake up with her mouth full of ants. She said okay but it's no work for a kid. Just for that reason said one. He doesn't run any risk said the other. Then they looked at him and one asked him if he were afraid and he said no. And you know how to do it the other one said and he said yes. Then they gave him the false fuse so that she would see that he knew how. They put it in his belt and he went back again to do it. She began to tremble and then she said I can do it myself and once again wanted to pick up the real fuse. He's already good said the first one. There's no other solution said the other. She went over and turned on the light and then went to the window. They stayed there looking at the real fuse and for a while they said nothing. I would do it said the first one. But that's no good said the other. Then don't do it she said and kept looking away. Then she said again that that was bad. And that it would be better to let it go until it was possible. Then everyone was silent. The first one got up and went to where she was at the window. The other came close to him and told him to listen to what I'm saying to you. He looked at him so that he would say it. He said you're not afraid and he said no. And you're going to go straight there and he nodded yes. All right said the woman and took her purse and went to the door. What are you going to do said the first one and she did not answer. What are you going to do he asked again and she still did not answer. I'm not saying anything right now and she went out slamming the door. It was better now. The three of them were alone and it was better. They would give him the money. And if he did it well they would give him

more. Probably later they would send him to put more
fuses someplace. If people wouldn't give him money anymore because he was big now he was able to earn it. One
came and loosened his belt. He put the false fuse in it
and then he tightened it. You have to be sure he told him
and tightened it more. You're going to confuse the kid
said the other and came and took out the false fuse. Let's
go it's time he said to him. And he went to the table and
got the real fuse. When they got downstairs one went out
of the doorway. The other stayed with him fastening the
fuse with the belt. He tightened it until he said it's good.
Very straight and carefully he told him and he said okay.
The first one looked at them and motioned with his head
that they could go out. The other shoved him by the
shoulder and said let's go. Remember come back slowly
and without confusion. And without looking behind. He
said yes and went out the doorway. When he walked the
fuse pressed against his belly and after a little while
begun to hurt him. With his shirttail out no one noticed
but if he touched his belly he could feel it. He walked
more and it kept on hurting. But the store was not very
far and he wasn't going to split. No one looked at him.
And if anyone looked at him he looked in the other direction. Because now he ought not to beg. Nor amuse himself. Nor go looking for the woman from the dream. That
he would do later. When he had money he would look for
her in other places. Probably he would find her in the
stores where they wouldn't let him go in. When he had
new clothes and was clean they would let him go in. And
if he did not find her there he would look for her in some
other place. Because now he was surely going to find her.
And she would ask him where he had been keeping him-

self. Because she also was looking for him. The pain in
his belly began to make him slip and he had to stop to
overcome it. He pulled his trousers up and raised its
position. And then he went on walking. At the beginning
it did not hurt him and later yes. But there wasn't much
farther to go. And when he had crossed the street he
would go into the doorway. And now there was only half
a block to go. At that point the kids saw him. They saw
him and they began to call him. He played the dummy
and went on walking. Then they broke into a run and
caught up to him. How's it going the negro boy said and
the white boy pushed him. He defended himself with his
foot and told him to leave him alone. But they wanted to
go on playing and went back to shoving him. The fuse
hurt him in the belly button and he had to put up with
it. The little negro looked at him seriously and then he
said he was hungry. Same as me said the white boy.
We're going to rob the Polack said the negro and crossed
the doorway and sat down at the café. The white boy followed him. And he took advantage of this move to keep
walking. There was not far to go now and he couldn't
lose time. Only that now the Polack began to yell in the
café and the little negro and the white boy passed him
like a flash. And he stopped so that they would not think
that he was going to run too. And he was standing there
when the Polish woman arrived all choked up and yelling
stop. Coming up to him she stopped screaming and
looked at him. Then she grabbed him by one hand and
called thief. I wasn't there he began to say and she said
you'll see. And without letting go of his hand she began
to yell for the police. People began to stop. Some were
laughing others not. Some said let him go and others for

shame. One woman came up and said to the Polack that she had to let him loose. But the Polack paid no attention and kept yelling police. The policeman did not come. And more and more people began to gather. The woman also grabbed him by the other hand. She hauled at him and told the Polack that she had to let go. Don't mix into this said the Polack and tugged from her side. That made the fuse begin to hurt him again. Every time they pulled him this way and that it began to hurt again. He wasn't there said the woman and began to pull very hard. But the Polack did not let go and the fuse began to slip. I'm going to lodge a complaint against you for beating up a baby. And the Polack said she had not hurt him. Yes you did you hit him said the woman and I'm going to lodge a complaint against you. The Polack let go of him. Then she said in this world there's no justice and went off talking to herself. But the woman did not let go. He pulled at his hand but the woman did not let go. Come and eat something she kept on saying but he did not want to eat. He was hungry but he did not want to eat. He wanted the woman to leave him alone and the woman would not leave him alone. She grasped him more firmly and she said ungrateful and that boys of your age ought not to be out alone at this hour. Let me loose he said and she got angry. And then that she was going to take him to the station to see why he was out alone. Now he was scared. He was frightened because now the policeman was coming. She saw him too and held on tight with both hands. Then he had to bite her. As soon as she felt his teeth she let go. She gave a cry and let go. And again he had to run. To run and to run stopping the pressure of the fuse with both hands. Until he arrived at the doorway. There were still a lot of people in the doorway. It was like when the movies were out. People were walking little by little looking in the windows. And he always took advantage of that to beg. Only that now he was not able to. And there were so many people looking in the windows. It was the best hour for begging. He went up to one and began to look. Sometimes if he only looked they would give to him so he would go away. But now he had to go straight up and sit down beside the window. When he got there he met a man and a woman who were looking at the suits. Then they looked at him. The woman said poor thing and looked through her purse. Here take said the woman. But he did not move. Take it she kept on saying and he took one hand from the belt and held it out. Poor thing the woman said and the man said to him beat it. When he was alone he sat down. He leaned back against the window and the fuse began to hurt again. But he could not take it out yet. There were still people looking at the windows. Some of them went that way and some of them went this. But the fuse hurt more and he had to take it out. He lifted his shirt and got hold of it. Right away like they had shown him. And he put it between his legs. He stayed that way for a while. Leaning back against the window and letting people pass. Until no one was going by and then he could do it. He grasped it by one hand and leaned it against the wall. Then in a single motion he turned it around. He turned the fuse around the other way and he stood there. There were still people looking in the windows. But they were going off. And in that direction he began to walk. He passed the first window and then the second. Then the third and then alongside the people who were going that way. Until he arrived at the corner. When he was turning the corner he saw the other policeman. And he began to be afraid. And to tremble. And to want to run. And to get back to the room and hide. Where there would be no policemen. Or people looking. Or anyone who would say that what he had done was wrong. That was what he wanted to do. Although he knew that he ought not to be afraid or run. He was about to run when it happened. It happened that there was an explosion like the nine-o'clock cannon. And the earth shook. But it wasn't the nine-o'clock cannon because the glass of the show windows began to rain. After the explosion it began to rain slivers of glass. And someone cried out. Cried out once more and then was quiet. People began to run toward the sound of the explosion. Then he saw smoke coming out of the window and some who were running in that direction. Not him. He began to walk. Because there was something on the ground that he wanted to investigate. Something that everyone looked at. When he got to the group they would not let him see. They only said what a horror and did not let him see. And then a policeman kept striking his stick against the pavement. No one drew back until the ambulance arrived. Then everyone began to run. Except the policeman with the stick. And he could not move. Because he had seen the woman. Thrown mouth down and covered with slivers of glass. And one arm bent backward and the other did not have a hand. The blood that poured out seemed to be the other hand. The flow grew larger and ran along the ground. Until it ran so far it could not be the other hand. At that point more police arrived. They ran up to the woman and began to get the glass off from on top of her. They swept the glass off with their sticks. One caught her by the arm that had a hand and turned her over faceup. And then he saw her face. Because of that he did not understand what the policeman was saying. Nor feel the whack that another gave him. Nor the threatening signs they were all beginning to make at him with their hands. The woman's face yes he understood that. And what the wide-open eyes were saying to him. They looked at him very wide and said to him m'boy. The same as the woman from the dream. Because she had found him and did not want to lose him. Only now it was she who was cold. Because of that he tried to come close to cover her and so that they wouldn't carry her off. But another slap would not let him. Because this time he felt the pain in his face. And the pain of being pushed against the wall. And the other blow they gave him because he hadn't yet gone away. But he still kept back the urge to cry. Until he saw that they were really taking her away. And how the arm without a hand was streaking the glass with blood. Then he could cry. Because he hurt everywhere. The shoulders. The legs. The face. Where the fuse had hurt him. And then all together when the police car screeched off at top speed. It was running behind the ambulance that he began to scream. Because of everything that hurt him. And because of something that hurt him more the more he felt it waken. The woman's name. Finally he had remembered it and could call her. As long as he ran and ran behind the ambulance the name for which he had looked so long was torn from him between sobs.

THE STORYTELLER

Onelio Jorge Cardoso
Translated by Helen Lane

Once upon a time there was a man from around Mantua or Sibanicú who was named Juan Candela and was a first-rate storyteller. It was before the restriction on sugarcane harvesting, which brought together people from villages upriver and down. I remember Candela well. He was tall, with prominent bushy eyebrows, and a flat, high forehead stretching up to his dark hair. He had lively black eyes, a great gift of gab, and a head filled with rivers, mountains, and men.

When harvest time came, we would gather together in the workers' cabin, with a lantern in the middle. They all came: Soriano, Miguel, Marcelino, and others whose names I don't recall. Then as soon as Juan began to talk, a person would turn into a downright idiot just listening to him. There wasn't one bird in the forest or a single sound on the guitar that Juan couldn't pull out of his chest. Everybody fidgeted, slapped their legs to chase the mosquitoes away, but stayed anyway, their eyes riveted on Juan's face, as he used his whole body and came up with a different voice when the other characters in the story spoke. There we all sat, with credit vouchers for the general store, and our bodies doubled over from the sun that had beaten down on us all day, all ears to hear about things that might have been and never were.

But there's no denying one thing, you could never contradict Juan Candela, because he would break off his storytelling with the look of somebody who's been badly put upon, and you sat there, not saying another word, seeing how powerful a thing the man had deep down inside him. Juan would take the precise, exact word out of a sack of words all his own and tie it to the air with a gesture that held everybody spellbound and made us drowsy.

That was why he told things like this in his own words: "The Lajas River, over by Coliseo, was full of fish. One time, mind you, the waters overflowed their banks earlier in the year than usual and flooded San Miguel and all the countryside round it. First some clouds went by, just skimming the hilltop, and then came that black tide with a cold wind ahead of it that flattened the esparto grass and bent the guava trees till finally a steady rain set in. I was an itinerant peddler in those days, and had a strong pack mule, a good walker. So as soon as the waters began to form a channel and a gentle breeze began blowing across the fields, I headed for the main house and the outbuildings on the plantation. I went along making my calculations about the river—because there's nothing better for thinking than the plodding of a mule beneath the open sky. Still a bit full, I said to myself, but crossable. I had gone through higher waters than that and knew those parts so well that all I would have needed was my she-mule's eyes. So I set out in search of the river, and by afternoon I had my feet in it. Its waters were still a muddy chocolate color, but by then it was no more than half a meter over its bank. So I led the mule into the water and started crossing. Everything was going along fine. Her hoofs echoed dully on the smooth stones underfoot, but halfway across the river the poor creature slipped and fell a quarter of the way into the water. I thought of the load, of the thread, of the face powder, of everything that the water was going to ruin, so I got her firmly on her feet again. The little animal gave proof of her good lineage as usual. She shuddered, pricked up her ears in fright, and got to the other side, with no trouble, the water sweeping past her chest. But the thing is, now that I'm out of the water, I feel a heavy weight dragging on my spurs. 'What the devil's going on!' I say, and I see that I have two fish, a good pound apiece, caught on my spurs. Well, I looked at the river and said to it, 'You've got more fish in you now than you can hold.'"

And Juan wiggled the long fingers of his hand like fish crowded into a few inches of water. Then next: a look around the room as though he were pointing a knife.

Another one he told was about a wild dog he'd caught as a pup and lovingly tamed. Mariposa, Butterfly—that was what he named him—was what people call an outstanding dog. Among other things he learned to hunt deer. The only bad thing about him was how good his legs were: "like when you try to see the wind whistling through a wire fence"—Juan said—that was what it was like to see Butterfly's legs chasing after deer. That was what made him come to a bad end, for late one afternoon he went to the forest alone and the chill of the night brought back the sound of his barking scattered to the four winds.

He's picked up a scent—Juan thought, drowsing in the hammock and imagining the deer running by and the dog following close behind him with the devil in his legs. But when daylight came and early-morning chores along with it, Juan forgot about the dog. But around noon or so, above all the other noises, a terrible racket was heard from the direction of the sugarcane field, and just then the deer came flying by, heading in the direction of the sugar refinery. "You should have seen the poor thing's eyes: he'd had a rough night of it!" Juan went on sharpening his machete and thought about the dog. No time for anything. The devil take that deer! Butterfly, poor Butterfly, who'd spent the whole night running. Then Juan stuck the handle of the machete in the ground so the dog would stumble over it and he'd be able to catch it, but luck wasn't with him. That was one of the few times that Juan wasn't lucky. The deer leaped and Juan rushed at it with the machete. Then, like a bullet, a spot the color of the dog appeared. Mariposa had hit the blade of the machete, all a matter of half a second, and got sliced exactly in half.

"Ah!"—Juan said—"it's good if a dog is a good runner, and if he chases deer, better still, but that was what did my poor Mariposa in, seeing as how I hadn't yet discovered that you can glue the two halves of an animal sliced down the middle with sap from a guásima tree."

On those nights Marcelino, Miguel, or Soriano told a little about their own harvests, but nobody could bear to listen to them after Juan. None of them had that big bunch of words of his, none of them the precise movement of his hand in the air.

After that we went off to our hammocks and no more was heard except for the metallic chirp of the crickets or the exactness of the roosters in the distance.

One morning in the cane fields Marcelino unexpectedly asked me:

"Do you think there could have been so many fish?"

"Where?"

But he was looking straight ahead now, and I caught sight of Juan Candela, there at the far end of his gaze, against the light, bending over pulling up weeds.

Another morning Miguel and Soriano were talking together as they sharpened their machetes:

"I don't say it's not true; something that's running could cut itself in half on the blade of a machete."

"Butter, for instance," I broke in, and Miguel and Soriano burst out laughing. Then there was silence, and Soriano, hitting the whetstone with the flat of his machete, said:

"That man is lying!"

"That's plain to see," Miguel murmured.

And the three of us looked at each other with satisfaction. We all felt the same way. Without a word we'd made up our minds that one of us should destroy the power that Juan had inside him and that showed in his eyes.

"Well, one of these nights I'll catch him and tell him so..." Soriano declared, hitting the whetstone again, harder this time.

"That's what's needed, no doubt about it," Miguel finally said, and then each of us went on with what he was doing.

To tell the truth, we thought at the time that it was necessary to choke off that power of Juan's because it's possible to put up with a man's lie when it's the first one, with a second out of a sense of decency, but the third one sounds like a slap in the face that must be answered then and there.

That same night Juan came with his cigarette twisted at both ends and his broad forehead. Then he began telling about the war and said:

"I was just a tad then and everybody was always hungry. My uncle, a man with a good eye for pack animals that are good walkers, and my mother's sister, saved us from starving to death. Because the rebels razed the fields and there was no way of growing a single row of corn, or of keeping a pumpkin on the vine. My uncle climbed on his gold-colored pony and went off for a few days, and then came back loaded down with wonderful things, the like of which I've never again eaten. He kicked the door open, and laughing the while, poured the saddlebag out onto the floor.

"'There's enough here to feed all of you for two weeks!' he said, and everything he'd brought scattered all over the room: yams, squashes, bananas, tomatoes bigger than a wild calabash. The floor was filled with green, with red, with the color of soil turned over, I don't know what-all! My mother then began gathering everything up in her skirt and shouted to me to bring a sack to fill till it brimmed over. Ah, those days! But even at that time, I can tell you that nobody ever found such good forage as that! Where, then, did my uncle find all that blessed food?"

Juan left the question hanging in the air more or less swathed in smoke and smelling of tobacco. I made good use of the pause to take one quick look at everyone's face. Marcelino was watching, with a mosquito sucking on his temple, Soriano with his eyes glued on Juan, and Miguel and everybody else as helpless as flies.

"So when my uncle was dying," Juan went on, "he gestured for everybody to leave the room. 'You stay behind and listen.' He had sat up straight on the cot and was looking at me with glazed eyes. 'There are certain things you can't tell everyone, Juan,' he went on to say to me. 'People laugh and don't believe anything except what's right in front of their eyes, but you're not one of that kind and I need you now so that my secret doesn't go to my grave with me. Listen now: near the Zapata Swamp, at the very headwaters of the black river, there's a path, overgrown with button trees and mangroves, and it's the right one. Take it early in the morning while it's cool, because you're going to be journeying for six days, and on the last one the volcano will appear. The city is going to be between the path your mount is treading and the volcano, but don't go to the city; head instead for the countryside where there are lots of things to forage, and the Indians are kind people.'

"'What city, uncle?' I asked him. 'Mexico City, my boy, Mexico City! Where do you think I was going to get food?' and he breathed his last as he was putting that question to me."

Juan fell silent for a moment and nobody budged an

inch. Then he raised his head to look around and added, looking very pleased with himself:

"To tell you the truth, I intend to go there one of these days. I'm sure that nobody else knows the way to Mexico City."

Soriano stood up then. He straightened up, clutching at his wide sash, but Juan lifted him off his feet and held him suspended in midair. Then Soriano swallowed hard and sat down again.

The next day, after Juan took his plate to the kitchen, Soriano showed me a dirty piece of paper all folded up. It was a faded illustration showing an excursion boat and above it were the words *This many pesos round trip to Mexico City.*

"And why didn't you speak up last night?" I asked him.

"I don't know, I had something stuck here," he said, pointing to his neck.

Then we took the firebreak and each of us stayed in our assigned stretch of cane overgrown with weeds. Soriano didn't say a word all that morning. Miguel talked about the tobacco bug and how it could be exterminated, and Soriano said nothing to contradict his age-old argument that came up periodically.

Later, as we were smoking in the doorway, and the sun overhead was passing over the Italian woman's hut, Soriano exploded, kicking at the hens' drinking basin.

"Hang it all, tonight I'm going to speak up, you'll see!"

But that night was when the cane fields of the Asta plantation caught fire. Don Carlos came from the main house and ordered us to give his neighbor a hand and we all went to put the fire out. It went on burning all night and part of the next morning. Afterward we were given a day off to sleep, still reeking of smoke. Juan came down with a fever and a cough. The moment he finished eating, he would go straight to his hammock and cough for the next few hours till he was worn out. Little by little, almost without realizing it, we forgot about the whole business, because we went on telling our stories there with the lantern in the middle, though we missed Juan. We all told something; but our eyes unintentionally ended up wandering over to the empty wooden crate that he always sat on, and nobody remembered anymore that Juan's power needed to be stifled, but instead we went on talking about how the plagues, and the tobacco plague in particular, were coming to an end. But Juan recovered from his attacks of fever. He still had a cough, but that made his tales even more interesting. He held his cough back till it came time to ask a question, certain that in that way he was saving time as he waited for someone to answer. And one night he began again in earnest. He was already on his feet, waving his arms and tying his words to the air with his gesture, as he told this story:

"That was some boa, I can tell you that! A Santa María, it was. Its back marked with dark splotches, but just let me say that I had arrived in those parts without knowing what anything was except the sun and the stars.

"We were in a stretch of forest at the very foot of the Sierra Maestra. One of those forests that are a green roof stretching out for twenty leagues. The work party was beginning to tether their horses, and I found myself confronted with one of those age-old bully trees that the arms of three men together can't reach all the way around. I grab my ax and: Chop!, the first blow; Chop!, the second, when, *¡caramba!* I feel something big and cold wrap itself around my neck. Ah, comrade, you must know what it's like to be scared if you're forty years old and have been poor all your life. You no doubt know what it's like, but it was that day that I first fully realized what it's like to be scared out of my wits. What was squeezing my neck was keeping me from breathing and making my eyes leap out of their sockets. No matter how hard I dug my nails into it, it kept slithering about without my knowing what the devil it was. Then, half choked to death, half dead, I remembered my belt and my knife and by feeling around I found the sheath and little by little raised my arm that felt as heavy as a stone and finally slashed it just a few inches above my head. I fell flat on the ground and the boa's warm blood spurted out and came dripping down on me. I can tell you I almost died when I saw the critter, without a head, the blood gushing out of it like a pipe that's burst. Well, you should have seen it, it was a Santa María, and then when we stretched it out full length, we saw that it measured exactly forty yards,"

Juan fell silent, opening his two long, skinny arms. Soriano was already on his feet breathing in so as to say something, but Juan stood there staring at him. He was as thin as a rail from his fever, but his eyes were still as powerful as ever and he kept his gaze fixed on him with all his energy. But Soriano went on standing there, with enough breath now to say heaven only knows how many things. Silent nonetheless, motionless. Then I had an idea and got to my feet:

"Maybe you didn't measure it with a good yardstick, Juan," I said to him, and he gave me the same look he'd given Soriano. His prominent eyebrow ridge was hard, underneath it a spark. I withstood his gaze as long as I could, until finally he went back to looking at Soriano and said:

"Well, it's possible."

"Maybe it wasn't more than thirty!" Soriano said, almost in a shout, seeking Juan's eyes now.

"Less, maybe," Miguel laughed, and we all laughed with him. But Juan crossed his arms, raised his chin, and said calmly, his eyes sweeping over each of us:

"It was surely a full thirty."

"Come off it! Surely no longer than six!" Soriano attacked.

Then there happened what happened:

Juan took out his machete, raising it above his head and announced:

"I'll kill anybody who takes half a yard more of it away from me!"

Nobody dared budge. His eyes were ablaze and his coarse hand turned dead white as his grip on the machete tightened. So we fell silent. Then he lowered his weapon and said:

"Idiots, a bunch of ungrateful idiots!"

And he turned his back and disappeared in the darkness of the workers' cabin. The sugarcane went on growing and the weeds waging war. A battle that allowed us to go on killing time until the cane was ripe enough to harvest. The small daily wage and the credit vouchers went on too. On several nights we heard from the workers' cabin the guitar of the plantation overseer in the main house, but Juan didn't tell stories anymore. He lay in his hammock the way he had when he was suffering from fever, and we stood there in the doorway with the little we remembered and Juan's wooden crate still unoccupied.

One warm night Don Carlos came and said something about the moon and the stars. Then he ended his remarks by declaring:

"The earth is round."

"Well, it looks as flat as a board." Miguel laughed. Don Carlos let out a puff of smoke from his cigar, and as he took off for the main house, he said:

"There are many things that are as they are and yet do not appear to be so."

Nobody said anything more, but I could feel that those words distressed me, because I was beginning to understand that that was what Juan was: something that has to do with the stars, *something that is as it is even though it doesn't seem to be.*

Something surely outside of time, of the cabin and of the world. I think now that the same thing was happening to the others, because I remember that when we left, Marcelino said, not speaking to anyone in particular:

"It's necessary to believe something is nice even though it isn't."

That night I couldn't sleep the way I usually did. There was a dense, cool silence, perhaps broken by a rooster in the distance, but the hours went by without my getting a wink of sleep till dawn came. Then I heard—vaguely at first—Soriano's pleading voice alongside Juan's hammock.

"Tell stories again tonight. Do it, Juan."

"You're a bunch of unbelievers," Juan answered without bothering to lower his voice the way Soriano had, and the latter went on emphatically:

"Don't pay any attention. We know very little. We've never left here and we've never seen such things. But we're sure now that you're telling the truth."

"Why now?"

"Well, it may not having anything to do with it, but last night Don Carlos said something about the earth and about things that are as they are and don't seem to be."

"What does that have to do with me?"

"I don't know, Juan, but it has something to do with you..."

So I overheard them talking and held my breath, hoping that Juan would say yes, because he was who he was and deadened people's senses and hid the floor of beaten earth where we lived... What's more, ever since then I've been certain that even on a good floor, after supper, anywhere in the world, a person can't help but hear Juan Candela's wondrous words.

THE GREAT BARO

Virgilio Piñera
Translated by Mark Schafer

The Great Baro, the revolutionary clown, made his debut that night. And we say he debuted because until then he had never performed before any audience whatsoever. It is true, the circus owner found him in the last place you would expect to find someone clowning around—that is, at a burial. There, mourning the passage of a beloved friend, was the man whose misfortune it would be to be transformed overnight into the Great Baro.

The circus owner got it into his head that this man, drowning in tears, choked with emotion, lugubrious-looking, dressed in black, staring into the grave, was the clown he had been searching for to open his circus this season.

Of course he was mistaken. The man hadn't even gotten close to being a clown in his entire life. He was nothing but an obscure employee in a ministry. He was about fifty, with no ideas, plenty of hunger, no one who loved him, today the same as yesterday and tomorrow. Now and then a funeral. His obscure friends told him he did it well and even congratulated him on it.

As you can see, he was altogether dark and somber. From one sunrise to the next, he spent his obscure life in mourning. So what humor, what clownishness could there be in such a worm? Well, that which the boss of the circus believed he saw. Or more likely, he didn't even believe it but leaped into the arms of absurdity. In any case, what is certain is that he followed Baro all the way home, belaboring him with promises of great triumphs and great earnings.

"I know," Baro responded. "You want me to play the clown."

Deep in thought, he looked intently at the circus owner and, very politely, added:

"I have never tried to make a clown of myself, but as you insist, I'll give it a try."

And he continued deep in thought—so much so that his interlocutor, who was already rubbing his hands together, success in sight, grew alarmed. Grabbing Baro by the shoulders, he said:

"Hey! Don't assume it's going to be so hard. Besides, a great tradition exists..."

"But with my face... Do you think I'm going to be any different in the ring than I am at a funeral? I'm afraid…"

"What are you afraid of?" the circus owner interrupted. "Are you afraid of cat calls from the audience? As for that, rest assured you are the most laughable person I've seen in my many years as a clown scout. You don't know it, but

I'm telling you the truth, my friend. I have discovered you and I expect the audience to applaud my discovery."

Baro was thunderstruck; he was already opening his mouth to object. His visitor didn't give him time. In a soothing voice, he said, "We have to give you a nice clown name. Yes, right this minute. You will be called Baro, the Great Baro, the One and Only Baro, he who knocks them dead with laughter..."

"Or with sobbing," replied Baro. "It isn't an objection, but I'm afraid that my clowning around will smack of funerals..."

"Don't look at it that way, not at all," the boss protested warmly. "Don't forget that people go to the circus with the intention of laughing. Anything that takes place there, however dramatic it might be, turns into guffaws."

"Since you insist, I'll give it a try," Baro said enthusiastically. "You've practically convinced me with your theory. But tell me, what should I do?"

"Clown around! Just clown around! Nothing but clowning around!" the boss shouted in a booming voice.

One week later (enough time to publicize the act) Baro made his appearance in the circus. The boss's optimistic calculations were met, doubled, and quadrupled. At the age of 50, Baro had at last tapped his hidden powers that carried him to the pinnacle of fame and to— oh!—a tragic ending.

Baro revolutionized the whole great tradition of clowning, stood the ancient technique of the clown on its head. He went beyond, far beyond, the leaps, pirouettes, makeup, and tricks of Pierrot. Or, to be more precise, he didn't turn his nose up at such elements but communicated them to the audience so that each spectator might dress every act of his life in the costume of a clown.

His first night, the Great Baro, with an exquisite sense of graciousness, performed before the accredited diplomatic corps. Using the aforementioned devices, he received one, ten, a hundred times ambassadors who presented him with their credentials, all to the thunderous applause of a deeply moved audience.

A spectacular success. The entire diplomatic corps climbed down into the ring to congratulate him. No longer as a diplomatic corps *per se* but as diplomats clowning around. Taking the Great Baro as head of state of an imaginary country, they enacted before him the craziest presentation of credentials the art of clowning could have conceived. But things didn't stop there: they didn't regain their composure, they didn't revert to the corps's insolent pomposity, they didn't go back to exhibiting their celebrated frosty smiles or the toothy ones either, the former displayed to break diplomatic relations and the latter to sign offensive and defensive alliances. No, nothing of the sort. They left there clowning around and even now continue to lavish their clowning across the face of the earth.

At that moment there was still time to back down. For a diplomatic corps to turn into a clown corps is a serious matter, but it doesn't cross the line drawn by the logic of madness that defines the world at large. If the problem could have been restricted to that sector— essential but, when all is said and done, exclusive and exclusionary—all other sectors would have remained intact. But no, Baro had been launched; nothing could stop him now. Night after night, Baro mimicked one facet or another of the great body of society: doctors, shoemakers, cooks, teachers, pianists, priests, bakers, seamstresses—in short, all the corporations, guilds, professions, the chosen ones and the dispossessed... And since there was at least one member of those groups present at each show, what would happen is that that person would leave the circus as a clown in his line of work and, ipso facto, would win hundreds of converts, since man seeks happiness even in clowning.

And to a certain extent that populace began to live happily, by which I mean, to the extent that clowning around transcended the ridiculous and became a common good. Perhaps that is why the Great Baro began to find himself alone. For Baro, who created clowns by the dozen, could not make himself into a clown. On one of his last triumphant nights, someone from a guild that had yet to be turned into a bunch of clowns shouted out to him at the beginning of the show: "Listen, Baro! You aren't a clown. Watch out!" And that same man who had been kind or weak enough to warn him, and who by the time he left the show had been quite thoroughly turned into a clown—he belonged to the butchers' guild; this guild attended the late shows, for it took its members a long time to wash off their bloodstains—that man grabbed the Great Baro like a side of beef in his butcher shop and hung him from a hook on a streetlamp by the side of the road.

A priest who happened to be passing at that very graceless moment for the Great Baro unhooked him. He took him to a dark corner of the street and told him that he was being tempted by the devil and, worse still, that he was provoking the fury of the Almighty with such diabolic art. Baro just stood there listening. When the priest had finished his harangue, Baro repeated in clown fashion everything the man had said, such that the poor priest was turned, then and there, into a consummate clown.

That was when the new religion—three distinct persons and one true clown—made the terrible accusation against Baro that he was nothing less than the Anticlown. Could the new faith tolerate this Maker of clowns living among clowns without being a clown himself? To add to Baro's misfortune, the authorities got mixed up in the matter as well: they were not about to allow the great masses of people to be ridiculed. If you live as a clown, how can you allow someone to walk around looking serious? Or, to put it in other words: seriousness for a clown is his own clownishness; through it he realizes every act of his existence, and if someone in a state of clowns has the temerity to stand out from the great harmonic clownish whole, he ought to pay for this imbalance with his life.

Then something happened that finally pushed the proud Baro to the depths of the abyss. Seeing that there remained not a single person upon whom to practice his sublime teachings, compelled by a demon within that demanded new victims, he dared to launch a surprise attack. He would attempt nothing less than stripping the Cardinal-Clown of his clownishness and transforming him in the eyes of the people into a Cardinal ad usum. But if Baro had a gift for making clowns, he was not by the same token empowered to unmake them. Now, we don't deny that somewhere on earth there might not exist another Great Baro whose magnificent gift is to unmake clowns, but unfortunately it is not in our power to supplant Baro with his Anti-Baro. So, given that the Great Baro stood alone, he had no other recourse but to enter the temple one morning like the great pontiff.

He needed to change the Cardinal-Clown into a Cardinal-Primate *ad latere*, or simply a newly promoted Cardinal, but in any case, to change him into something serious. To do that, he took the divine solemnity of the Church to inconceivable limits. The Cardinal-Clown allowed him to do it, was sublime in his clowning, and gave the most brilliant opportunities to the Great Baro. But all in vain. He managed to copy the Cardinal brilliantly but—oh!—nothing but copy him, and we all know that the only virtue a copy has is to highlight the original. Without a doubt, Baro was lost. With redoubled clownishness, the Cardinal-Clown seized him by the ears and with a kick in that blessed place, drove him from the temple.

Several constables were waiting for him at the door. As they were carting him off to prison, he saw the President of the Council of Ministers and the Chief of the Armed Forces heading for the temple, doing cartwheels. Baro shuddered in the depth of his being: the die was cast. The cartwheels were devastating and defiant. Furthermore, their guffaws could be heard for a league in every direction; great must have been the anger of such high authorities for them to emit such booming laughter.

But if Baro could have witnessed the meeting of those three leaders, whatever glimmer of hope remained to him would surely have flown from his soul. No sooner did the Cardinal-Clown see the Chief of the Armed Forces approach than he took a gigantic leap, launched into somersaults, and let out a thunderous guffaw. Then the Chief of the Armed Forces planted his feet solidly on the ground in order to form a human pyramid. The Cardinal-Clown leaped onto his shoulders. The moment was so serious that the people gathered in the plaza expressed their circumspection in stereotypical laughter.

The deliberation between the three leaders was arduous. Amid a deathly silence, the pyramid leaned first to the right, then to the left, now forward, now backward. When they came to an agreement on some point, they would express their satisfaction with "Ohhh's," which seem to be expressions of ecstasy among clowns. The Cardinal, with mad recklessness, danced on the gleaming bald head of the President of the Council, and no matter how he adjusted his vestments, the full, ankle-length robe that he was wearing ballooned in the wind and put the precious balance of the pyramid in danger. But something worse occurred when the Chief of the Armed Forces threatened to behead the pyramid if Baro's life were not terminated by firing squad. Were he to carry out such a threat—that is, if the pyramid were reduced to the Cardinal-Clown and the President of the Council—the Great Baro would deem himself to have been saved. From his high perch, the Cardinal snorted. Shooting over and over again is such a vulgar method... As if a state of clowns needed to resort to altogether worn-out procedures. No, what he wanted for Baro was a kind of death in keeping with the ideals and tastes of a clown. That blundering soldier had to be convinced that, despite his being a clown and all, he was burdened by the old-fashioned mentality of his beloved War College. But the Cardinal had to come up with something quick: if the coarse soldier reduced the pyramid to two-thirds of itself, the Church would lose a valuable victim. For let us say once and for all that the Cardinal wanted for the Great Baro the only punishment a clown could invent, which is death produced by the spasms and convulsions of an uncoerced laughter.

Then the Cardinal remembered that the Chief of the Armed Forces was dying to touch—even just once—the Cardinal's biretta. He had asked in vain, he had even offered his yellow military cap, but the Cardinal had stood his ground. Now, seeing the gravity of the moment, he jammed it onto the Chief's head, and thereby the death of Baro by laughter alone was unanimously agreed upon.

The first difficulty had been overcome but not the second, which was so uncertain, it could very well end up saving Baro's life. It was necessary to obtain—whatever the cost—something that would make the condemned man burst with laughter. But what could it be? The old, worn-out expedient of tickling could not be applied by an innovative people, nor could the equally worn-out method of telling those funny stories that have induced apoplexy in many gentlemen. No, for the Great Baro they had to discover something capable of causing him to die laughing. And obviously it would not be a clown: a great artist never laughs at his own works. Consequently, the three leaders devoted themselves, heart and soul, to the search for that something within and beyond the borders of that country. Edicts were proclaimed promising riches and honors to the person who discovered the thing in question. Emissaries left for the outermost regions in search of it. To no avail: Baro, seated on his rickety bed with his plate of boiled cabbage by his side, remained serious, solemn.

One morning, the Cardinal-Clown, desperate after a year of fruitless attempts, appeared in Baro's cell accompanied by the Great Inquisitor. The presence of the latter made it plain they intended to torture Baro until he revealed his great secret: that thing capable of making him die laughing.

Out-and-out failure: Baro went through the rack, the boot, the wheel, and the branding irons... The Cardinal, hysterical in the face of such a steadfast soul, slapped him. The Great Baro replied that after those tortures, such superfluous slaps were excessive. And he added that, seeing as how nothing would compel him to declare the thing capable of making him die of laughter, he begged therefore to be left alone with his customary ration of boiled cabbage.

But imagine the surprise of the jailer (he is currently ninety years old and his hair is still standing on end) when upon entering the cell with the plate of boiled cabbage, he saw the Great Baro doubled up with laughter. What in the world! It hadn't been half an hour since the Cardinal left the cell, slamming the door and swearing by all the clowns in heaven that Baro was going to pay for this. And now that same Baro was doubled up with laughter! What had happened? He looked around him, searching for the thing that had finally managed to make the condemned man split his sides laughing. But there was nothing there at all, absolutely nothing, good God, that might constitute a novelty in the jailer's eyes. Then he approached to a prudent distance (he was afraid that this sudden laughter might bite him like a dog) and asked Baro if something had happened. But Baro resembled the gurgling of an open faucet. Suddenly the Great

Baro sat up and, expanding his chest as if lacking air, opened his mouth as wide as he could; it was clear he wanted to say something, but all he accomplished was to allow the laughter to come gushing out.

The jailer left like a bat out of hell to get the Warden. Within a few minutes the latter appeared in the cell armed with pencil and paper to take down the condemned man's statement. He was hoping that with such diligence he would get a promotion or a reward in cold, hard cash. Nothing he did was of any use: the Great Baro didn't utter a single word. His laughter prevented even the slightest articulation.

The whole city was informed of the event. People ran madly toward the circus: there in the ring, the scene of his triumphant performances, was the Great Baro illuminated by powerful spotlights, sitting on a bench. As the circus was packed to the gills, as the official boxes brimmed with the highest members of the ruling class, as the diplomatic corps graced the spectacle with its presence, it seemed as if it were the very same night of the Great Baro's debut. But—oh!—though it seemed so, it was not. Only a single laugh poured bubbling out like an uncontainable hemorrhage, like an unstanchable wound, a laugh that was like a summary of all the laughter produced in that circus during the memorable performances of the celebrated artist.

Regarding that laugh, a living enigma, we shall say that a thousand conjectures were made and the most absurd fables were spun. No one, from the highest authorities led by the Cardinal-Clown to the meekest domestic, had the faintest idea what was causing such laughter. For if no one had succeeded in discovering the thing that it was anticipated would cause the Great Baro to die of laughter, then why was he laughing himself uncontrollably into annihilation?

This enigma was clarified (at least to the satisfaction of the authorities and the people) with the explanation the Specialist in Laughter of that great people offered. After examining Baro's laughter over the course of several minutes, the Specialist emphatically declared that it was a mocking, cynical laugh and, even more significantly, anticlown. Thus, the Great Baro would die from the laughter awakened in his being by the impotent attempt of an entire people struggling to find the very thing that would make him die of laughter.

Be that as it may, Baro died, his sides split with laughter, a week to the day after having revealed his cheerful affliction. The Cardinal-Clown automatically declared him a saint, and a statue of him was enthroned with great pomp in the cathedral. But that is not where the story of the Great Baro ends, as one might suppose. After a few years had passed in quick succession, with no prior announcement the Great Anti-Baro made his appearance in the city. Overnight that whole cheerful populace was unclowned. The very Cardinal, whom we already know but who now has nothing clownish about him, ordered the statue of the Great Baro to be smashed to bits.

Those fragments, which grow fewer and fewer by the day as children amuse themselves pelting one another with them, patiently await the time when another Great Baro converts that land of solemn and respectable people into clowns so that they may once again take their rightful place amidst the peace of the cathedral.

JOURNEY BACK TO THE SOURCE

Alejo Carpentier
Translated by Frances Partridge

I.

"What d'you want, pop?"

Again and again came the question, from high up on the scaffolding. But the old man made no reply. He moved from one place to another, prying into corners and uttering a lengthy monologue of incomprehensible remarks. The tiles had already been taken down and now covered the dead flower beds with their mosaic of baked clay. Overhead, blocks of masonry were being loosened with picks and sent rolling down wooden gutters in an avalanche of lime and plaster. And through the crenellations that were one by one indenting the walls, were appearing—denuded of their privacy—oval or square ceilings, cornices, garlands, dentils, astragals, and paper hanging from the walls like old skins being shed by a snake.

Witnessing the demolition, a Ceres with a broken nose and discolored peplum, her headdress of corn veined with black, stood in the backyard above her fountain of crumbling grotesques. Visited by shafts of sunlight piercing the shadows, the gray fish in the basin yawned in the warm weed-covered water, watching with round eyes the black silhouettes of the workmen against the brilliance of the sky as they diminished the centuries-old height of the house. The old man had sat down at the foot of the statue, resting his chin on his stick. He watched buckets filled with precious fragments ascending and descending. Muted sounds from the street could be heard, while overhead, against a basic rhythm of steel on stone, the pulleys screeched unpleasantly in chorus, like harsh-voiced birds.

The clock struck five. The cornices and entablatures were depopulated. Nothing was left behind but stepladders, ready for tomorrow's onslaught. The air grew cooler, now that it was unburdened of sweat, oaths, creaking ropes, axles crying out for the oil can, and the slapping of hands on greasy torsos. Dusk had settled earlier on the dismantled house. The shadows had folded over it just at that moment when the now-fallen upper balustrade used to enrich the facade by capturing the sun's last beams. Ceres tightened her lips. For the first time the rooms would sleep unshuttered, gazing onto a landscape of rubble.

Contradicting their natural propensities, several capitals lay in the grass, their acanthus leaves asserting their vegetable status. A creeper stretched adventurous tendrils toward an Ionic scroll, attracted by its air of kinship. When night fell, the house was closer to the ground. Upstairs, the frame of a doorstill stood erect, slabs of darkness suspended from its dislocated hinges.

II.

Then the old Negro, who had not stirred, began making strange movements with his stick, whirling it around above a graveyard of paving stones.

The white-and-black marble squares flew to the floors and covered them. Stones leaped up and unerringly filled the gaps in the walls. The nail-studded walnut doors fitted themselves into their frames, while the screws rapidly twisted back into the holes in the hinges. In the dead flower beds, the fragments of tile were lifted by the thrust of growing flowers and joined together, raising a sonorous whirlwind of clay, to fall like rain on the framework of the roof. The house grew, once more assuming its normal proportions, modestly clothed. Ceres became less gray. There were more fish in the fountain. And the gurgling water summoned forgotten begonias back to life.

The old man inserted a key into the lock of the front door and began to open the windows. His heels made a hollow sound. When he lighted the lamps, a yellow tremor ran over the oil paint of the family portraits, and people dressed in black talked softly in all the corridors, to the rhythm of spoons stirring cups of chocolate.

Don Marcial, Marqués de Capellanías, lay on his deathbed, his breast blazing with decorations, while four tapers with long beards of melted wax kept guard over him.

III.

The candles lengthened slowly, gradually guttering less and less. When they had reached full size, the nun extin-

guished them and took away the light. The wicks
whitened, throwing off red sparks. The house emptied
itself of visitors, and their carriages drove away in the
darkness. Don Marcial fingered an invisible keyboard and
opened his eyes.

The confused heaps of rafters gradually went back
into place. Medicine bottles, tassels from brocades, the
scapular beside the bed, daguerreotypes, and iron palm
leaves from the grill emerged from the mists. When the
doctor shook his head with an expression of professional
gloom, the invalid felt better. He slept for several hours
and awoke under the black beetle-browed gaze of Father
Anastasio. What had begun as a candid, detailed confes-
sion of his many sins grew gradually more reticent,
painful, and full of evasions. After all, what right had the
Carmelite to interfere in his life?

Suddenly Don Marcial found himself thrown into the
middle of the room. Relieved of the pressure on his tem-
ples, he stood up with surprising agility. The naked
woman who had been stretching herself on the brocade
coverlet began to look for her petticoats and bodices, and
soon afterward disappeared in a rustle of silk and a waft
of perfume. In the closed carriage downstairs an enve-
lope full of gold coins was lying on the brass-studded
seat.

Don Marcial was not feeling well. When he straightened his cravat before the pier glass, he saw that his face
was congested. He went downstairs to his study, where
lawyers—attorneys and their clerks—were waiting for
him to arrange for the sale of the house by auction. All
his efforts had been in vain. His property would go to the
highest bidder, to the rhythm of a hammer striking the

table. He bowed, and they left him alone. He thought how mysterious were written words: those black threads weaving and unweaving, and covering large sheets of paper with a filigree of estimates; weaving and unweaving contracts, oaths, agreements, evidence, declarations, names, titles, dates, lands, trees, and stones; a tangled skein of threads, drawn from the inkpot to ensnare the legs of any man who took a path disapproved of by the Law; a noose around his neck to stifle free speech at its first dreaded sound. He had been betrayed by his signature; it had handed him over to the nets and labyrinths of documents. Thus constricted, the man of flesh and blood had become a man of paper.

It was dawn. The dining-room clock had just struck six in the evening.

IV.

The months of mourning passed under the shadow of ever-increasing remorse. At first the idea of bringing a woman to his room had seemed quite reasonable. But little by little the desire excited by a new body gave way to increasing scruples, which ended as self-torment. One night, Don Marcial beat himself with a strap till the blood came, only to experience even more intense desire, though it was of short duration.

It was at this time that the Marquesa returned one afternoon from a drive along the banks of the Almendares. The manes of the horses harnessed to her carriage were damp only with their own sweat. Yet they spent the rest of the day kicking the wooden walls of their stable as if maddened by the stillness of the low-hanging clouds.

At dusk, a jar full of water broke in the Marquesa's bathroom. Then the May rains came and overflowed the lake. And the old Negress who unhappily was a maroon and kept pigeons under her bed wandered through the patio, muttering to herself, "Never trust rivers, my girl; never trust anything green and flowing!" Not a day passed without water making its presence felt. But in the end that presence amounted to no more than a cup spilled over a Paris dress after the anniversary ball given by the Governor of the Colony.

Many relatives reappeared. Many friends came back again. The chandeliers in the great drawing room glittered with brilliant lights. The cracks in the facade were closing up, one by one. The piano became a clavichord. The palm trees lost some of their rings. The creepers let go of the upper cornice. The dark circles around Ceres' eyes disappeared, and the capitals of the columns looked as if they had been freshly carved. Marcial was more ardent now, and often passed whole afternoons embracing the Marquesa. Crow's-feet, frowns, and double chins vanished, and flesh grew firm again. One day the smell of fresh paint filled the house.

V.

Their embarrassment was real. Each night the leaves of the screens opened a little farther, and skirts fell to the floor in obscurer corners of the room, revealing yet more barriers of lace. At last the Marquesa blew out the lamps. Only Marcial's voice was heard in the darkness.

They left for the sugar plantation in a long procession of carriages—sorrel hindquarters, silver bits, and varnished leather gleamed in the sunshine. But among the pasqueflowers empurpling the arcades leading up to the house, they realized that they scarcely knew each other. Marcial gave permission for a performance of native dancers and drummers, by way of entertainment during those days impregnated with the smells of eau de cologne, of baths spiced with benzoin, of unloosened hair and sheets taken from closets and unfolded to let a bunch of vetiver drop onto the tiled floor. The steam of cane juice and the sound of the angelus mingled on the breeze. The vultures flew low, heralding a sparse shower, whose first large echoing drops were absorbed by tiles so dry that they gave off a diapason like copper.

After a dawn prolonged by an inexpert embrace, they returned together to the city with their misunderstandings settled and the wound healed. The Marquesa changed her traveling dress for a wedding gown and the married pair went to church according to custom, to regain their freedom. Relations and friends received their presents back again, and they all set off for home with jingling brass and a display of splendid trappings. Marcial went on visiting María de las Mercedes for a while, until the day when the rings were taken to the goldsmiths to have their inscriptions removed. For Marcial, a new life was beginning. In the house with the high grilles, an Italian Venus was set up in place of the Ceres, and the grotesques in the fountain were thrown into almost imperceptibly sharper relief because the lamps were still glowing when dawn colored the sky.

VI.

One night, after drinking heavily and being sickened by the stale tobacco smoke left behind by his friends,

Marcial had the strange sensation that all the clocks in the house where striking five, then half past four, then four, then half past three... It was as if he had become dimly aware of other possibilities. Just as, when exhausted by sleeplessness, one may believe that one could walk on the ceiling, with the floor for a ceiling and the furniture firmly fixed between the beams. It was only a fleeting impression, and did not leave the smallest trace on his mind, for he was not much given to meditation at the time.

And a splendid evening party was given in the music room on the day he achieved minority. He was delighted to know that his signature was no longer legally valid, and that worm-eaten registers and documents would now vanish from his world. He had reached the point at which courts of justice were no longer to be feared, because his bodily existence was ignored by the law. After getting tipsy on noble wines, the young people took down from the wall a guitar inlaid with mother-of-pearl, a psaltery, and a serpent. Someone wound up the clock that played the *ranz-des-vaches* and the "Ballad of the Scottish Lakes." Someone else blew on a hunting horn that had been lying curled in copper sleep on the crimson felt lining of the showcase, beside a transverse flute brought from Arangüez. Marcial, who was boldly making love to Señora de Campoflorido, joined in the cacophony, and tried to pick out the tune of "Trípili-Trápala" on the piano, to a discordant accompaniment in the bass.

They all trooped upstairs to the attic, remembering that the liveries and clothes of the Capellanías family had been stored away under its peeling beams. On shelves frosted with camphor lay court dresses, an ambassador's sword, several padded military jackets, the vestment of a dignitary of the Church, and some long cassocks with damask buttons and damp stains among their folds. The dark shadows of the attic were dappled with the colors of amaranthine ribbons, yellow crinolines, faded tunics, and velvet flowers. A picaresque blacksmith's costume and hair net trimmed with tassels, once made for a carnival masquerade, was greeted with applause. Señora de Campoflorido swathed her powdered shoulders in a shawl the color of a Creole's skin, once worn by a certain ancestress on an evening of important family decisions in hopes of reviving the sleeping ardor of some rich trustee of a convent of Clares.

As soon as they were dressed up, the young people went back to the music room. Marcial, who was wearing an alderman's hat, struck the floor three times with a stick and announced that they would begin with a waltz, a dance that mothers thought terribly improper for young ladies because they had to allow themselves to be taken round the waist, with a man's hand resting on the busts of the stays they had all had made according to the latest model in the *Jardin des Modes*. The doorways were blocked by maid-servants, stableboys, and waiters, who had come from remote outbuildings and stifling basements to enjoy the boisterous fun. Afterward they played blindman's buff and hide-and-seek. Hidden behind a Chinese screen with Señora de Campoflorido, Marcial planted a kiss on her neck, and received in return a scented handkerchief whose Brussels lace still retained the sweet warmth of her low-necked bodice.

And when the girls left in the fading light of dusk, to return to castles and towers silhouetted in dark gray against the sea, the young men went to the dance hall, where alluring mulattas in heavy bracelets were strutting about without ever losing their high-heeled shoes, even in the frenzy of the guaracha. And as it was carnival time, the members of the Arara Chapter Three Eyes Band were raising thunder on their drums behind the wall in a patio planted with pomegranate trees. Climbing onto tables and stools, Marcial and his friends applauded the gracefulness of a Negress with graying hair, who had recovered her beauty and almost become desirable as she danced, looking over her shoulder with an expression of proud disdain.

VII.

The visits of Don Abundio, the family notary and executor, were more frequent now. He used to sit gravely down beside Marcial's bed, and let his acana-wood cane drop to the floor so as to wake him up in good time. Opening his eyes, Marcial saw an alpaca frock coat covered with dandruff, its sleeves shiny from collecting securities and rents. All that was left in the end was an adequate pension, calculated to put a stop to all wild extravagance. It was at this time that Marcial wanted to enter the Royal Seminary of San Carlos.

After doing only moderately well in his examinations, he attended courses of lectures, but understood less and less of his master's explanations. The world of his ideas was gradually growing emptier. What had once been a general assembly of peplums, doublets, ruffs, and periwigs, of heretics and debaters, now looked as lifeless as a museum of wax figures. Marcial contented himself with a scholastic analysis of the systems, and accepted everything he found in a book as the truth. The words *Lion, Ostrich, Whale, Jaguar* were printed under the copper-plate engravings in his natural history book. Just as *Aristotle, St. Thomas, Bacon,* and *Descartes* headed pages black with boring, close-printed accounts of different interpretations of the universe. Bit by bit, Marcial stopped trying to learn these things, and felt relieved of a heavy burden. His mind grew gay and lively, understanding things in a purely instinctive way. Why think about the prism, when the clear winter light brought out all the details in the fortresses guarding the port? An apple falling from a tree tempted one to bite it—that was all. A foot in a bathtub was merely a foot in a bathtub. The day he left the seminary, he forgot all about his books. A gnome was back in the category of goblins; a specter a synonym for a phantom; and an octopus an animal armed with spines.

More than once he had hurried off with a troubled heart to visit the women who whispered behind blue doors under the town walls. The memory of one of them, who wore embroidered slippers and a sprig of sweet basil behind her ear, pursued him on hot evenings like a toothache. But one day his confessor's anger and threats reduced him to terrified tears. He threw himself for the last time between those infernal sheets, and then forever renounced his detours through unfrequented streets and that last-minute faintheartedness that sent him home in a rage, turning his back on a certain crack in the pavement—the signal, when he was walking with head bent, that he must turn and enter the perfumed threshold.

Now he was undergoing a spiritual crisis, peopled by religious images, Easter lambs, china doves, Virgins in heavenly blue cloaks, gold paper stars, the three Magi, angels with wings like swans, the Ass, the Ox, and a terrible St. Denis, who appeared to him in his dreams with broad shoulders, walking hesitantly as if looking for something he had lost; when he blundered into the bed, Marcial would start awake and reach for his rosary of silver beads. The lampwicks, in their bowls of oil, cast a sad light on the holy images as their colors returned to them.

VIII.

The furniture was growing taller. It was becoming more difficult for him to rest his arms on the dining table. The fronts of the cupboards with their carved cornices were getting broader. The Moors on the staircase stretched their torsos upward, bringing their torches closer to the banisters on the landing. Armchairs were deeper, and rocking chairs tended to fall over backward. It was no longer necessary to bend one's knees when lying at the bottom of the bath with its marble rings.

One morning when he was reading a licentious book, Marcial suddenly felt a desire to play with the lead soldiers lying asleep in their wooden boxes. He put the book back in its hiding place under the washbasin, and opened a drawer sealed with cobwebs. His schoolroom table was too small to hold such a large army. So Marcial sat on the floor and set out his grenadiers in rows of eight. Next came the officers on horseback, surrounding the flag sergeant; and behind, the artillery with their cannons. Bringing up the rear were fifes and kettledrums escorted by drummers. The mortars were fitted with a spring, so that one could shoot glass marbles to a distance of more than a yard.

Bang!... Bang!... Bang!

Down fell horses, down fell standard-bearers, down fell drummers. Eligio the Negro had to call him three times before he could be persuaded to go to wash his hands and descend to the dining room.

After that day, Marcial made a habit of sitting on the tiled floor. When he realized the advantages of this position, he was surprised that he had not thought of it before. Grown-up people had a passion for velvet cushions, which made them sweat too much. Some of them smelled like a notary—like Don Abundio—because they had not discovered how cool it was to lie stretched on a marble floor at all seasons of the year. Only from the floor could all the angles and perspectives of a room be grasped properly. There were beautiful grains in the wood, mysterious insect paths, and shadowy corners that could not be seen from a man's height. When it rained, Marcial hid himself under the clavichord. Every clap of thunder made the sound box vibrate, and set all the notes to singing. Shafts of lightning fell from the sky, creating a vault of cascading arpeggios—the organ, the wind in the pines, and the crickets' mandolin.

IX.

That morning they locked him in his room. He heard whispering all over the house, and the luncheon they brought him was too delicious for a weekday. There were six pastries from the confectioner's in the Alameda—whereas even on Sundays after mass he was only allowed two. He amused himself by looking at the engravings in a travel book, until an increasing buzz of sound coming under the door made him look out between the blinds.

Some men dressed all in black were arriving, bearing a brass-handled coffin. He was on the verge of tears, but at this moment Melchor the groom appeared in his room, his boots echoing on the floor and his teeth flashing in a smile. They began to play chess. Melchor was a knight. He was the king. Using the tiles on the floor as a chess-board, he moved from one square to the next, while Melchor had to jump one forward and two sideways, or vice versa. The game went on until after dusk, when the fire brigade went by.

When he got up, he went to kiss his father's hand as he lay ill in bed. The Marqués was feeling better, and talked to his son in his usual serious and edifying manner. His "Yes, father" and "No, father" were fitted between the beads of a rosary of questions, like the responses of an acolyte during mass. Marcial respected the Marqués, but for reasons that no one could possibly have guessed. He respected him because he was tall, because when he went out to a ball, his breast glittered with decorations; because he envied the saber and gold braid he wore as an officer in the militia; because, at Christmastime, on a bet, he had eaten a whole turkey stuffed with almonds and raisins; because he had once seized one of the mulattas who were sweeping out the rotunda and carried her in his arms to his room—no doubt intending to whip her. Hidden behind a curtain, Marcial watched her come out soon afterward, in tears and with her dress unfastened, and he was pleased that she had been punished, as she was the one who always emptied the jam pots before putting them back in the cupboard.

His father was a terrible and magnanimous being, and it was his duty to love him more than anyone except God.

To Marcial he was more godlike even than God because his gifts were tangible, everyday ones. But he preferred the God in heaven because he was less of a nuisance.

X.

When the furniture had grown a little taller still, and Marcial knew better than anyone what was under the beds, cupboards, and cabinets, he had a great secret, which he kept to himself: life had no charms except when Melchor the groom was with him. Not God, nor his father, nor the golden bishop in the Corpus Christi procession was as important as Melchor.

Melchor had come from a very long distance away. He was descended from conquered princes. In his kingdom there were elephants, hippopotamuses, tigers, and giraffes, and men did not sit working, like Don Abundio, in dark rooms full of papers. They lived by outdoing the animals in cunning. One of them had pulled the great crocodile out of the blue lake after first skewering him on a pike concealed inside the closely packed bodies of twelve roast geese. Melchor knew songs that were easy to learn because the words had no meaning and were constantly repeated. He stole sweetmeats from the kitchens; at night he used to escape through the stable door; and once he threw stones at the police before disappearing into the darkness of the Calle de la Amargura.

On wet days he used to put his boots to dry beside the kitchen stove. Marcial wished he had feet big enough to fill boots like those. His right-hand boot was called Calambín; the left one Calambán. This man who could tame unbroken horses by simply seizing their lips between two fingers, this fine gentleman in velvet and spurs who wore such tall hats, also understood about the coolness of marble floors in summer, and used to hide fruits or a cake, snatched from trays destined for the drawing room, behind the furniture. Marcial and Melchor shared a secret store of sweets and almonds, which they saluted with "*Urí, urí, urá*" and shouts of conspiratorial laughter. They had both explored the house from top to bottom, and were the only ones who knew that beneath the stables there was a small cellarfull of Dutch bottles, or that in an unused loft over the maids' rooms was a broken glass case containing twelve dusty butterflies that were losing their wings.

XI.

When Marcial got into the habit of breaking things, he forgot Melchor and made friends with the dogs. There were several in the house. The large one with stripes like a tiger; the basset trailing its teats on the ground; the greyhound that had grown too old to play; the poodle that was chased by the others at certain times and had to be shut up by the maids.

Marcial liked Canelo best because he carried off shoes from the bedrooms and dug up the rose trees in the patio. Always black with coal dust or covered with red earth, he devoured the dinners of all the other dogs, whined without cause, and hid stolen bones under the fountain. And now and again he would suck dry a new-laid egg and send the hen flying with a sharp blow from his muzzle. Everyone kicked Canelo. But when they took him away, Marcial made himself ill with grief. And the dog returned in triumph, wagging his tail, from somewhere beyond the poorhouse where he had been abandoned, and regained his place in the house, which the other dogs, for all their skill in hunting, or vigilance when keeping guard, could never fill.

Canelo and Marcial used to urinate side by side. Sometimes they chose the Persian carpet in the drawing room, spreading dark, cloudlike shapes over its pile. This usually cost them a thrashing. But thrashings were less painful than grown-up people realized. On the other hand, they gave a splendid excuse for setting up a concerted howling and arousing the pity of the neighbors. When the cross-eyed woman from the top rooms called his father a "brute," Marcial looked at Canelo with smiling eyes. They shed a few more tears so as to be given a biscuit, and afterward all was forgotten. They both used to eat earth, roll on the ground, drink out of the goldfish basin, and take refuge in the scented shade under the sweet-basil bushes. During the hottest hours of the day quite a crowd filled the moist flower beds. There would be the gray goose with her pouch hanging between her bandy legs; the old rooster with his naked rump; the little lizard who kept saying *"Urí, urá"* and shooting a pink ribbon out of his throat; the melancholy snake, born in a town where there were no females; and the mouse that blocked its hole with a turtle's egg. One day someone pointed out the dog to Marcial.

"Bow-wow," Marcial said.

He was talking his own language. He had attained the ultimate liberty. He was beginning to want to reach with his hands things that were out of reach.

XII.

Hunger, thirst, heat, pain, cold. Hardly had Marcial reduced his field of perception to these essential realities when he renounced the light that accompanied them. He did not know his own name. The unpleasantness of the christening over, he had no desire for smells, sounds, or even sights. His hands caressed delectable forms. He was a purely sensory and tactile being. The universe penetrated him through his pores. Then he shut his eyes— they saw nothing but nebulous giants—and entered a warm, damp body full of shadows: a dying body. Clothed in this body's substance, he slipped toward life.

But now time passed more quickly, rarefying the final hours. The minutes sounded like cards slipping from beneath a dealer's thumb.

Birds returned to their eggs in a whirlwind of feathers. Fish congealed into roe, leaving a snowfall of scales at the bottom of their pond. The palm trees folded their fronds and disappeared into the earth like shut fans. Stems were reabsorbing their leaves, and the earth reclaimed everything that was its own. Thunder rumbled through the arcades. Hairs began growing from antelope-skin gloves. Woolen blankets were unraveling and turning into the fleece of sheep in distant pastures. Cupboards, cabinets, beds, crucifixes, tables, and blinds disappeared into the darkness in search of their ancient roots beneath the forest trees. Everything that had been fastened with nails was disintegrating. A brigantine, anchored no one knew where, sped back to Italy carrying the marble from the floors and fountain. Suits of armor, ironwork, keys, copper cooking pots, the horses' bits from the stables, were melting and forming a swelling river of metal running into the earth through roofless channels. Everything was undergoing metamorphosis and being restored to its original state. Clay returned to clay, leaving a desert where the house had once stood.

XIII.

When the workmen came back at dawn to go on with the demolition of the house, they found their task completed. Someone had carried off the statue of Ceres and sold it to an antique dealer the previous evening. After complaining to their trade union, the men went and sat on the benches in the municipal park. Then one of them remembered some vague story about a Marquesa de Capellanías who had been drowned one evening in May among the arum lilies in the Almendares. But no one paid any attention to his story because the sun was traveling from east to west, and the hours growing on the right-hand side of the clock must be spun out in idleness—for they are the ones that inevitably lead to death.

CREDITS

"An Unexpected Interlude Between Two Characters" (*"Intromisión abrupta de esos dos personajes"*) by Jacqueline Herranz Brooks. Published here in English for the first time by permission of the author. English translation © 1999 by Seven Stories Press.

"13th Parallel South" (*"Sur: latitud 13"*) by Angel Santiesteban Prats. Published here in English for the first time in book form by permission of the author. English translation © 1999 by Seven Stories Press.

"The Waiting Room" (*"Lista de espera"*) by Arturo Arango. Originally published in Spanish in *Concurso de cuento Carlos Castro Saavedra*, Medellín, Colombia, 1994. Published here in English for the first time by permission of the author. English translation © 1999 by Seven Stories Press.

"Ten Years Later" (*"Diez años después"*) by Marilyn Bobes. Published here in English for the first time in book form by permission of the author. English translation © 1999 by Seven Stories Press.

"The Hunter" (*"El Cazador"*) by Leonardo Padura Fuentes. Published here in English for the first time in book form by permission of the author. English translation © 1999 by Seven Stories Press.

"Curriculum Cubense," from *From Cuba With a Song* (*De dónde son los cantantes*) by Severo Sarduy. Originally published in English by Sun & Moon Press, 1994. English translation © by Suzanne Jill Levine. Published here by permission of Sun & Moon Press and Suzanne Jill Levine.

"Skin Deep" by Antonio Benítez Rojo. Originally published in English in *The Magic Dog and Other Stories*, Ediciones del Norte, 1990. Published here by permission of the author and Ediciones del Norte. English translation © 1990 by Ediciones del Norte.

"The Charm" (*"El talismán"*) by Pablo Armando Fernández. Published here in English for the first time by permission of the author. English translation © 1999 by Seven Stories Press.

"Dream With No Name" (*"Un sueño sin nombre"*) by Ramón Ferreira. Originally published in English in *Prize Stories from Latin America*, Doubleday, 1960, and in *The Gravedigger & Other Stories*, Waterfront Press, 1986. Published here by permission of the publisher. English translation © 1986 by Paul Blackburn.

"The Storyteller" (*"El cuentero"*) by Onelio Jorge Cardoso. Published here in English for the first time by permission of the author's family. English translation © 1999 by Seven Stories Press.

"The Great Baro" (*"El gran Baro"*) by Virgilio Piñera. Published here by permission of the author's family. This is its first appearance in book form in English. English translation © 1998 by Mark Schafer.

"Journey Back to the Source" (*"Viaje a la semilla"*) by Alejo Carpentier. Originally published in English in *Latin American Short Stories*, Fawcett, 1974. Published here by permission of the author's family. English translation © by the estate of Frances Partridge.

AUTHORS' AND TRANSLATORS' BIOGRAPHIES

AUTHORS

Short-story writer **ARTURO ARANGO** was born in Manzanillo, Cuba in 1955. His work includes "Salir al mundo" (1981); "La vida es una semana" (1983), which won the UNEAC award; "La Habana elegante" (1995); and "Lista de espera," which won First Prize at the Carlos Castro Saavedra contest in Medellín, Colombia in 1994. He was editor of the magazine *Casa de las Américas*.

REINALDO ARENAS was born in Holguín, Cuba, in 1943. He studied Agricultural Accounting, and later Literature, at the University of Havana, but didn't graduate. He worked at the José Martí National Library and contributed to several publications. His first and second novels, *Celestino antes del alba* (Singing from the Well) and *El mundo alucinante* (The Ill-Fated Peregrinations of Fray Servando) received first mentions in the UNEAC and Villaverde contests in 1965 and 1966 respectively. Arenas left Cuba in 1980, and died in New York in 1990. His work has been translated into many languages. Other works include the novels *Farewell to the Sea, The Palace of the White Skunks, Old Rosa: a Novel in Two Stories*, and *The Doorman*, several books of poetry (including *El Central: A Cuban Sugar Mill*), short stories, plays, and essays. His best known work is his posthumously-published memoir, *Before Night Falls*, considered by *The New York Times Book Review*, and others, to be one of the best books published that year (1993) in the United States.

MIGUEL BARNET was born in Havana, Cuba in 1940. He studied advertising and social sciences at the Universidad de la Habána, but never graduated. In 1960 he took ethnology and folklore classes. From 1961 to 1966 he taught folklore at the Escuela de Arte. His work has been published in various newspapers in Cuba and abroad. He was editor of the magazine *Unión*. He received a Mention from Casa de las Américas for his book of poems *La sagrada familia*. His book *Biografía de un cimarrón* has been translated into many languages and inspired the opera *Cimarrón* by the German composer Hans Werner Henzel. He is known for his invaluable contribution to the testimonial novel, and his research in the field of "Afro-Cuban" culture. Other works by Barnet include the novels *Canción de Rachel* (1969) and *Gallego* (1983), both winners of Cuba's Crítica Award.

ANTONIO BENÍTEZ ROJO was born in Havana, Cuba in 1931. He studied at the Universidad de la Habána and at the American University in Washington. An accomplished short story writer screenplay writer and critic, he has written four collections of short stories: *Tute de reyes* (1964), which won the Casa de las Américas award; *El escudo de hojas secas* (1969), which won the UNEAC short story award; *La tierra y el cielo* (1978); and *Heróica* (1976). His novels include *Los inquilinos* (1977) and *El mar de lentejas* (1979). His work has been translated into seven languages. He has edited over ten anthologies, and many critical articles dealing with Caribbean culture. Before leaving Cuba in 1980, he was editor of *Casa de las Américas*, director of the Casa del Teatro in Havana from 1966 to 1967, and editor-in-chief of Cuba Internacional from 1968 to 1969. He lives in Massachusetts, where he is professor of Latin American literature at Amherst College.

MARILYN BOBES, a short-story writer, poet and journalist was born in Havana, Cuba in 1955. She studied history at the Universidad de la Habána, and later worked as a journalist at the Latin American agency Prensa Latina, and for the magazine *Revolución y Cultura*. In 1979 she received the David Award for Poetry for her book *La aguja en el pajar*. As a narrator she has received an Edmundo Valdés award, Mexico, 1993, and second place in the III Concurso Hispanoamericano del Cuento Magda Portal, Perú, 1994. She has also written *Hallar el modo* (poetry), 1989, and *Alguien tiene que llorar*, a book of short stories that won the Casa de las Américas prize in 1995.

ONELIO JORGE CARDOSO was born in Villa Clara, Cuba in 1914. He is considered one of the great story writers not only in his native Cuba, but throughout Latin America. His work is rich with Cuban mores, magic, and the customs and traditions of rural Cuba. Born into a poor family, he finished high school but was unable to attend college. In 1936 he received an award for short stories from the magazine *Social*. During Batista's rule, Cardoso worked as a teacher, developed photographs, was a traveling salesman, and suffered the economic hardship that is described in his stories. After 1959, he worked at the Consejo Nacional de Cultura, UNEAC, and the Cuban Embassy in Perú. Among the awards he received during his lifetime is the Premio Nacional Hernandez Cata in 1945, for his short story "Los carboneros." His collections of short stories include: *Taita diga Ud. cómo* (1945), *El cuentero* (1958), *El caballo de coral* (1960), *Cuentos Completos* (1962), *Gente de pueblo* (1962), *La otra muerte del gato* (1964), *Iba caminando* (1965), *Abrir y cerrar los ojos* (1968), and *El hilo y la cuerda* (1974). His stories have been translated into several languages. He wrote the screenplay for the film *Cumbite*, directed by Tomás Gutierrez Alea. Cardoso died in Havana in 1986.

ALEJO CARPENTIER, born in Havana, Cuba in 1904 to a Russian mother and a French father, was a leading Cuban novelist of his generation and a major influence on Latin American literature. He studied at the Universidad de la Habána before becoming a journalist. In 1928 he fled to France to escape imprisonment for his opposition to the regime of Leonardo Machado. There he became a frequent contributor to the journal *Révolution surréaliste*, but later rejected Surrealism. In 1933 he wrote the documentary novel *¡Ecué-Yamba-O!*, an account of Afro-Cuban life and culture. In 1949, after returning to Cuba, Carpentier wrote *El reino de este mundo* (*Kingdom of this World*), an evocation of the life of early 19th century Haitian leader, Henri Christophe.

His masterpiece is considered to be *Los pasos perdidos* (*The Lost Steps*), published in 1953, which defines the coexistence of primeval myths and the superimposed Spanish civilization. Other works include: *Guerra del tiempo* (*War of Time*), 1958; *El siglo de las luces* (*Explosion in the Cathedral*), 1962; *Tientas y diferencias* (*Tendencies and Differences*), 1964, essays on cultural and literary themes; *El recurso del mundo* (*Reasons of State*), 1974 dealing with Machado's regime; the novel *Concierto barroco* (*Baroque Concert*), 1974; and *La musica en Cuba*, a history of Cuban music. He died in Paris in 1980.

LOURDES CASAL was born in 1938 in Havana, Cuba. A prominent intellectual and revolutionary figure, she was part of a community of Cubans residing abroad. While professor of psychology at Rutgers University, she helped promote the Brigada Antonio Maceo. In 1974 she founded the literary magazine *Areito*. She cowrote *Contra viento y marea*, which won a special award from Casa de las Américas in 1978. Gravely ill, she returned to Havana and died in 1981.

PABLO ARMANDO FERNÁNDEZ was born in Las Tunas, Cuba in 1930. He lived in the United States from 1943 to 1959, where he attended Columbia University. He returned to Cuba in 1959 and worked as assistant editor of *Lunes de Revolución* until 1961. From 1961 to 1962 he worked for the magazine *Casa de las Américas*. He became Cultural Attaché of the Cuban Embassy in Great Britain from 1962 to 1965. In 1963 he received a Mention from Casa de las Américas for his book of poetry, *Libro de los héroes,* and in 1968 he was awarded the Casa de las Américas prize for the novel *Los niños se despiden*. He was also secretary of the Pen Club de Cuba. In 1996 he received the Premio Nacional de Literatura for his oeuvre, including the poetry collections *Salterío y lamentaciones* (1953), *Toda la poesía* (1961), *Un sitio permanente* (1969),which also won Second Place Adonis Prize, Madrid, *El sueño y la razón* (1988), *Ronda de encantamiento* (1990), and the novels *El vientre del pez* (1989) and *Otro golpe de dados (1993)*. A book of short stories, *El talismán y otras evocaciones,* was awarded Cuba's Premio de la Crítica 1994. He lives in Havana.

RAMÓN FERREIRA was born in 1923 in Galicia, Spain and came with his family to Cuba when he was eight years old. He is the author of *Tiburón y otros cuentos* which won Cuba's Premio Nacional de Cuentos in 1952. In 1959, "Sueño sin nombre" won the Life en Español contest. *Los malos olores del mundo,* a second collection of short stories, was published in 1970. His plays, *Dónde está la luz* (1952), *Un color para este miedo* (1954), *El mar de cada dia* (1957), and *El hombre inmaculado* (1958) have been staged in Madrid, New York, and Mexico City. *Maritza* is his latest novel. Ferreira lives in Puerto Rico.

JACQUELINE HERRANZ BROOKS was born in Havana, Cuba in 1968. She graduated from the Escuela Provincial de Fotografía in 1990 and is a member of the Asociación Hermanos Saíz. She is the author of *Yo fui a la guerra,* a play, and several books of poetry: *A quien dar mi maldad con humildad, Corrección del paisaje, El calificador de turno, El dragón se enrolla, Cuestiones metaclínicas,* and *Liquid Days.*

MIGUEL MEJIDES was born in the province of Camaguey, Cuba in 1950. In 1977 he received the David Award for Short Stories for "Tiempo de hombre." His book of short stories, *El jardín de las flores silvestres,* won the UNEAC award in 1982, and that same year his novel *La habitación terrestre* was published. In 1994, he won Mexico's Juan Rulfo International Contest for his story "Rumba Palace."

CARLOS OLIVARES BARÓ was born in Cuba in 1950. He studied Hispanic literature and is a professor of semiotics and linguistics at the Universidad del Nuevo Mundo in Mexico. His literary critiques and reviews of popular Cuban music have appeared in various newspapers, including *La Jornada, Ovaciones, Novedades,* and *Reforma. La* *orfandad del esplendor* is the first novel of a trilogy in which Baró relates—through the eyes of a child, an adolescent, and an adult—the miseries and travails of a Cuban family.

LEONARDO PADURA FUENTES was born in Havana, Cuba in 1955. Short-story writer, journalist, and literary critic, he received the 13 de Marzo award in 1985 for the essay, "Colón, Carpentier, la mano, el arpa y la sombra." He has also written the novels *Fiebre de caballos* (1988) and *Vientos de cuaresma* (1984), which won the UNEAC award in 1993. His novel *Mascaras* won the Café Gijón Award in 1996 in Spain. His work has appeared in many publications. He is a member of the editorial board of the magazine *La Gaceta de Cuba*, a division of the UNEAC, published in Havana.

VIRGILIO PIÑERA was born in Cardenas, Cuba in 1912. Along with Carpentier and Lezama Lima, he is considered one of the greatest Cuban writers. In 1940 he graduated from the Universidad de la Habána with a degree in philosophy and literature. He was the founding editor of the magazine *Poeta* in 1942. Later he collaborated with the group that founded the review *Orígenes*. In 1950 he moved to Argentina where he was to reside 14 years, working at the Cuban Consulate, as proofreader, and later as a translator for Argos Publishing House. His stories were admired by Jorge Luis Borges and Jose Bianco. In 1955 he co-founded the magazine *Ciclón* with José Rodriguez Feo (a cofounder of *Orígenes* with José Lezama Lima). Although his play *Dos viejos pánicos* received the Casa de las Américas Award in 1968, Piñera led a life of poverty and was relatively unknown when he died in Havana in 1979. Throughout Latin America he is now considered an important playwright, short-story writer, poet, and essayist. His work includes the novels *La carne de Rene* (1952) and *Pequeñas Maniobras* (1963), as well as the poetry collections *Las furias* (1941) and *La vida eterna* (1969). *Dos viejos pánicos* and *Una caja de zapatos vacia* are among his plays. His work has been translated into many languages.

MIGUELINA PONTE LANDA was born in Havana, Cuba in 1938. She studied journalism briefly and moved on to concentrate on Cuban,

Latin American, and North American literature in *Casas de las Américas*. Her short stories and poetry have appeared in *Islas, Signos,* and *Gaceta de Cuba*. Her work was greatly admired and supported by Reinaldo Arenas.

SONIA RIVERA-VALDÉS was born in Cuba in 1937 and now lives in New York where she is a writer, literary and film critic, and professor of Spanish language and literature at York College. For the past 20 years, she has been an avid promoter of cultural exchange between the United States, Cuba, and Latin America. She is cofounder of the Jiribilla Cuban Culture Association, collaborates with the Tertulia de Escritoras Dominicanas in New York, and is a member of the Board of Directors of the Center for Puerto Rican Studies. Her articles and short stories have been published in anthologies and literary magazines in the U.S. and abroad. In 1997 she received the Casa de las Américas literary prize for her book of short stories *Las historias prohibidas de Marta Veneranda,* making her only the second Cuban-American to receive the prize.

ANGEL SANTIESTEBAN PRATS was born in Havana, Cuba in 1966. He graduated in 1989 with a degree in film directing. That same year he received the Premio Nacional de Talleres Literarios for his short stories, and in 1995 won the UNEAC award. His short stories have been published in magazines and in several anthologies in Cuba and abroad. He has been a finalist three times in the Casa de las Américas contest.

SEVERO SARDUY was born in Cuba in 1937. He studied at the Universidad de la Habána and, with Guillermo Cabrera Infante, was one of the few writers involved in the fight against Batista. He became publisher of *Lunes de revolución,* the official publication of the 26th of July Movement. In 1960 he left for Paris. There, he became editor of the Latin American collection of *Editions du Seuil,* and became involved with the Tel Quel group. He introduced, among others, Garcia Marquez's *One Hundred Years of Solitude* to the French, and he himself published several works including *Escrito sobre un cuerpo (Written on a Body), Maitreya, Colibrí, La simu-*

lación, Overdose, and *Daiquirí,* a book of poems that uses Baroque prosody to describe gay sex in explicit terms. *De dónde son los cantantes* was Sarduy's first truly experimental work, in which he explores the disparate elements at work in Latin American culture. Sarduy died of AIDS in Paris in 1993.

TRANSLATORS

ZOË ANGLESEY is a poet, editor, reviewer, and translator. Recently her translations have appeared in *Boricuas: Influential Puerto Rican Writings* (One World/Ballantine, 1995) and the liner notes for Chucho Valdés's "Bela Bela en la Habána" (Blue Note, 1998). She edited the bilingual anthologies *Ixok Amar.Go: Central American Women's Poetry* and *Stone on Stone / Piedra Sobre Piedra: Poetry by Women of Diverse Heritages* (New York: One World/Ballantine, 1999). Her reviews of books and jazz have appeared in *The Village Voice, Down Beat, Jazziz, Bomb, The Multi Cultural Review,* and *LS*. Anglesey's next book of poems is titled *Eco*.

PAUL BLACKBURN was born in Saint Albans, Vermont on November 24, 1926. He influenced contemporary literature through his poetry, translations, and the encouragement and patronage he offered to other poets. During his college years Blackburn first came under the influence of Ezra Pound and came into contact with such poets as Robert Creeley, Charles Olson, Cid Corman, and Jonathan Williams. Eventually Blackburn became associated with a group called the Black Mountain Poets. While living in New York from 1950 to 1954 his literary friends became interested in his translations, and he became well known for his work on the Troubadors and on contemporary South American writers, particularly Julio Cortázar. He was central in organizing readings of work from the Beats, the New York School, the Deep Image Poets, and the Black Mountain Poets. Clayton Eshleman has said of Blackburn, "Many, not just a few, but many poets alive today are beholden to him for a basic artistic kindness, for readings, yes, and for advice, but more humanly for a kind of comradeship that very few poets are willing to give."

Blackburn authored 19 books of poetry, including *The Dissolving Fabric* (1955), *Brooklyn Manhattan Transit: A Bouquet For Flatbush* (1960), *The Nets* (1961), *16 Sloppy Haiku And A Lyric For Robert Reardon* (1966), *Sing Song* (1966), *The Journals: Blue Mounds Entries* (1971), and *Early Selected Y Mas: Poems 1949-1966* (1972). He died in 1971.

CHRIS BRANDT is a writer, translator, and teacher who lives in New York City. His poems and essays have been published in magazines, journals, and anthologies in Spain and the U.S., including *Lateral, Barcelona; El signo del gorrión, Valladolid; Phati'tude, Appearances, Crimes Of The Beats, The Unbearables,* the upcoming *Mr. Knife Miss Fork* (Sun & Moon Press); and *Modern Language Notes.* His translation of Carmen Valle's *Entre la vigilia y el sueño de las fieras/Wild Animals Between Waking and Dreaming* (Instituto de Cultura Puertoriqueño in 1996), and a translation of selected works of Joaquín Pasos (with Yolanda Blanco) is forthcoming from Hard Press in late 1998.

JAMES GRAHAM has translated Ricardo Feierstein, Severo Granados, Roque Dalton, and others. He lives in New York. He is the publisher and editor of *Machete,* a bilingual literary magazine.

DOLORES M. KOCH was born in Havana, Cuba. She has translatated Reinaldo Arenas's memoir, *Before Night Falls,* as well as his novel, *The Doorman,* and a number of his short stories for *The Penguin Book of International Gay Writing, Index on Censorship,* and *Grand Street.* She has also translated Emilie Schindler's *Where Light and Shadow Meet,* Alina Fernández's *Not in My Father's House: Memoirs of Fidel Castro's Daughter,* and Laura Restrepo's *The Angel of Galilea,* both in 1998.

HELEN LANE has translated 85 books into English from Spanish, Portuguese, French, and Italian. Among them have been works by Octavio Paz, Juan Goytisolo, Mario Vargas Llosa, Ernesto Sabato, Augusto Roa Bastos, Nelida Piñon, André Breton, Marguerite Duras, Claude Simon, and Curzio Malaparte. Among the translation prizes she has won are two National Book Awards, two PEN Awards, the UCLA Alumni Achievement Award, and the PEN-Kolovakos Lifetime

Achievement Award. For 25 years a resident of southwest France, cultural winds have recently carried her to the American southwest, where she now lives in Albuquerque, New Mexico.

SUZANNE JILL LEVINE is professor of Latin American and comparative literature at the University of California, Santa Barbara. Her book *The Subversive Scribe: Translating Latin American Fiction* deals extensively with the works of Guillermo Cabrera Infante and Severo Sarduy. She is currently completing *Naked Tango: The Life and Fictions of Manuel Puig*, to be published by Farrar, Straus & Giroux (and Faber & Faber in England).

CLARA MARÍN is a Mexican writer living in New York. Her first literary translations appear in this anthology.

HARRY MORALES's work has appeared in *Pequod, Fiction, Confrontation, Quaterly West, Chicago Review, TriQuaterly, The Literary Review,* and *The Oxford Book of Latin American Essays* (Oxford University Press). Presently he is working on *Prospero's Mirror: A Translator's Portfolio of Latin American Short Fiction* (Curbstone Press) and has recently completed a translation of Mario Benedetti's award-winning novel, *La tregua.*

MARK MCCAFFREY's translations include "First Balcony" and "The Magic Dog," included in *The Magic Dog and Other Stories* by Antonio Benítez Rojo (Ediciones del Norte). He lives in New Hampshire.

FRANCES PARTRIDGE has translated several Latin American writers including Alejo Carpentier's work for *Latin American Short Stories* (Fawcett, 1974).

MARK SCHAFER is a translator, visual artist, and poet who lives in the Boston area. He has translated a wide range of authors in a variety of genres, including Alberto Ruy Sánchez and Virgilio Piñera (novels), Jesús Gardea and Juan Bosch (short stories), Gloria Gervitz and Antonio José Ponte (poems), and José Lezama Lima and Eduardo Galeano (essays). His next projects include a translation of Belén

Gopegui's novel *La escala de los mapas* and a collage installation in the store window of a travel agency in Somerville, Massachusetts as part of the Windows Art Project.

ALAN WEST-DÚRAN was born in Cuba in 1953 and raised in Puerto Rico. He is the author of two children's books; a book of poems, *Dar nombres a la lluvia/Finding Voices in the Rain*, which won the Latino Literature Prize for Poetry (1996); and a book of essays, *Tropics of History: Cuba Imagined* (1997). He worked on the CD-ROM "Caribbean Literature: 1492-1900." He has translated Luis Rafael Sanchez, Rosario Ferré, and Dulce Maria Loynaz, and recently translated Cristina Garcia's *The Agüero Sisters* into Spanish, and Alejo Carpentier's *La música en Cuba* (1998).

ABOUT THE EDITORS

JUANA PONCE DE LEÓN, a writer, literary critic, and editor, was the founder of Cronopios Books in Amherst, Massachusetts. She was a project officer for Fifty Communities Awards Program for Friends of United Nations, and co-editor of *Creating Common Unity*. She is editor of *LS*, the literary supplement for the *Advocate Weekly Newspapers*. She has written extensively on Latin American and Hispanic literature. Her articles have appeared in many publications including *The New York Times Book Review*, *The Washington Post Book World*, *The Village Voice Literary Supplement*, *Latina*, *Hispanic*, *Publishers Weekly*, and *Sí*. Presently she is working on *Arabists*, an anthology of Latin American writers and on her first novel.

ESTEBAN RÍOS RIVERA is a poet and a member of the Union of Younger Writers of Cuba. His work has been published in several literary journals in Cuba, and he is extensively involved in theater work there. He lives in Havana.